LIARS IN LOVE

Ian Bull

Intersection Productions, Inc.

Studio City, California

Ian Bull/Intersection Productions, Inc.
4307 Vantage Avenue
Studio City, CA 91604
www.intersectionproductions.com

Publisher's Note: This is a work of fiction. Names, characters, places, and incidents are a product of the author's imagination. Locales and public names are sometimes used for atmospheric purposes. Any resemblance to actual people, living or dead, or to businesses, companies, events, institutions, or locales is completely coincidental.

Cover Design by Alexios Saskalidis

Liars in Love/ Ian Bull. -- 1st ed.
ISBN 978-1-948873-09-3

Ian Bull is the pen name of Donald Ian Bull. He has also written *Facing Reality (A Love Story),* and is the author of *The Quintana Adventures*, a series of thriller novels which includes *The Picture Kills,* and *Six Passengers, Five Parachutes.* The third book in the trilogy, *The Danger Game,* will be out soon.

You can also find his nonfiction and all his downloads at:

Ianbullauthor.com

Please write a review of this book! If I can get 100 reviews I can promote my writing and reach more readers!

Email me and I will show you how:

Ianbullauthor@gmail.com

To San Francisco, my first home, which lives within me.

I've labored long and hard for bread,
For honor, and for riches,
But on my corns too long you've tread,
You fine-haired sons of bitches.

— Black Bart, 1877

Liars in Love takes place in 1980. It is a time before the Internet, smartphones, email, texting, Google searches, social media, and dating websites.

It is a time of coin-operated payphones and electric typewriters. People write letters and read newspapers. Cash is still king, and any information about you is on actual paper and kept in filing cabinets. Businesses, the government, and police departments are just learning to use computers. Cell phones are rare, expensive, and as big as bricks. Instead, people wear pagers on their belts like *Star Trek* communicators. That is considered advanced technology.

It was a better time in some ways, and worse in others.

In 1980, the art of conversation is not yet dead. Talking is how you become friends and convince people to fall in love with you. Being a charming talker and a lovable listener can give you an advantage over the next loser.

In 1980, it is also harder to find out the truth about someone, and much easier to keep secrets. You can make up stories about yourself without getting caught.

This story is about two such people.

They lie, and they love, and it works for them...for a little while.

CHAPTER ONE

S am gets off the Muni bus at the corner of Ortega and 28th Avenue and walks past the green, yellow, pink, and purple houses, then stops at one painted burnt orange, with a black wrought iron balcony and red geraniums on the sill. Sam stares at the house, exhales, and darts up the cement stairs and rings the bell and knocks on the door, but no one answers. He walks down the steps and stares up at the dark windows.

The front window on the neighboring purple house opens and a grey-haired woman in a bright Hawaiian housecoat sticks her head out the window. She has a black patch on her left eye. "They moved away a long time ago," she says, shaking her head.

"Mrs. Wilkenson, it's me, Sam Webb!" He touches his chest as proof.

She spits at him. "I know who you are, you hoodlum."

"I'm looking for Rose, do you know where she went?"

"Are you deaf? I said they moved away!"

"If you know where she is, please tell her I stopped by. It's important."

"She and her boy are better off without you, you prison scum. Don't you dare try to get back to together with her!"

"I'm not, ma'am! We have some unfinished business is all."

"I don't believe you! You're a fake Casanova and you'll ruin her life!"

"I'll come back when I'm settled and give you my phone number. That way she can reach me herself. Okay?"

Mrs. Wilkenson shuts the window. Sam backs away and stares at both houses, a big man in a wrinkled blue suit that's a size too small.

The wind blows again, fluttering his suit and pant legs. He flips up his jacket collar and heads back towards the bus stop.

Who is this sorry sap, and how did he get here? Sad though he seems, Sam is doing better than he was 24 hours ago when he was still a convict in the San Quentin Federal Penitentiary.

Before we learn about more about Rose and Sam's great dilemma, let's go back one day.

In 1980, San Quentin prison is already one hundred and thirty years old, and its medieval turrets make it feel even older, like some knight is going to shoot arrows at you from the castle walls. Every few years they drench it with yellow paint, but that just makes the soot from the air pollution more visible. They paint the inside walls of the massive five-tier cell block seafoam green, and the cell bars white, but bored prisoners pick at the peeling paint on the bars until the salty, moist air from San Francisco Bay rusts the exposed iron pale orange. The paint job is a cover-up, but the truth comes through: it's a prison.

The red lines on the floor are the only honest color that tells the truth about where you are, because they command where you must walk and stand.

The ceaseless noise inside the cell block reminds you of the truth as well, along with the smell of clogged toilets mixed with cold salty air. A six-foot-tall man can touch both moist walls across the width of his cell, and walk its length in three steps.

But the biggest reality check is the bubbling tension between people: between white and black, between black and brown, and between guard and prisoner. It's always simmering, until it boils over into violence.

This is where Samuel Webb finishes his sentence for commercial burglary, a week after his thirty-second birthday. He stands six feet tall, with broad shoulders and the thick brown hair and blue eyes of the black Irish. He has a sly grin that curls up on one side of his mouth as he tilts his head at you, a look he perfected in his prison cell mirror. He also has a scar on the left cheek of his smooth baby face. It almost makes him look tough, and he tells people that a Cuban cut him with a broken glass in a bar fight, a bullshit move that enraged Sam so much that he knocked him out with one punch. That's a lie, however; he got the scar as a kid when he fell off his bike and landed on a Coke bottle, but the lie about the Cuban is a better story.

Sam is good at inventing stories about himself, because they help him endure the mistakes he's made. To survive his two-year stint for burglary, he couldn't see himself as just another failure in a loud, cold and wet prison. Instead, Sam imagined himself to be like the outlaw Black Bart, who did time in San Quentin for robbing Wells Fargo stagecoaches before becoming a poet, or Merle Haggard, who did time there for auto theft before making it big in country music. Sam decided he was the 1980s version of these men, a genius artist from the street who slipped up once and did hard time, but gained a lifetime of experience that forged his future greatness.

Sam sold this persona nonstop. He wrote poetry for the prison paper, wrote country songs, and played drums in the prison rock band. His persona as the "joke-cracking burglar hipster artist" had just enough street cred that the other prisoners bought his hype.

And today, Sam Webb is getting out of prison, on April Fool's Day, 1980.

Sam drums on his cell toilet with his sticks, knocking out a light salsa rhythm that echoes off the hollow bowl. His cellmate, Chuck, lying on the upper bunk, grunts a warning that he's about to break Sam's drumsticks again. Chuck is a monosyllabic angry biker version of Mr. Clean, who will attack after two grunts.

"Sorry, Chuck, I got the jitters. I have to get my ya-yas out."

Corrections Officer Mark Garrett hits his keys against the bars. "Your time's up, Webb," he says. He's a tall, thin, African American with a tiny pot belly that looks like he's hiding a football under his pressed brown uniform. "You've baked long enough, time to pull you out of this oven."

Sam stands and hands his drumsticks to Chuck, still lying on his bunk. "Keep them, and everything else," Sam says, gesturing to his books and audio cassettes lining the lower bunk. Chuck takes the sticks and doesn't break them. That's as close to a goodbye that Sam gets.

"Step back, convict," Garrett says, gesturing for Sam to step back six feet.

"I'm not a convict, I'm a free man," Sam says.

"Only until the next time we see you," Garrett says, sliding the door open. Sam tugs his blue cotton prison shirt flat, like he's about to go on stage, then steps out on the red line. Garrett locks the cell behind him. "Walk," Garrett says, and Sam obeys, walking the red line one last time.

Hands holding mirrors come out of the other cells, so the men can watch. They see it's Sam and they clap to celebrate his freedom.

Sam throws his fist in the air as he steps through the metal door. "Elvis has left the building!" he yells, but that's more hyperbole. Sam must go through several steps before a true exit is possible.

Step One is the prison property room. Green fluorescent bulbs light up rows of shelves with hundreds of blue bins. Officer Garrett stands by the door with Officer Koresh, his Caucasian double with his own matching football belly. They cross their arms and sneer.

A female corrections officer, Sandra, carries a bin from the back and lifts it up on the counter, then consults a clipboard as Sam pulls out a plastic bag stuffed with clothes. "Those are the dress-out clothes you bought," Sandra says, nodding at the plastic bag.

Sam rips it open. Inside is a wrinkled blue suit and a white shirt. "I bought this suit with three hundred dollars of my account money! You couldn't keep it on a hanger?" Sam asks.

"This ain't Neiman Marcus," Sandra says.

Sam pulls out new brown wingtip shoes next. "You can't wrinkle these, thank God," Sam says, then pulls out a paper envelope from the bottom, which he rips open. Inside is a brown leather wallet with his California Driver's License, and an Omega watch.

"Hey, my watch doesn't work," Sam says, slipping the timepiece onto his wrist.

"What do you expect, it's been in a paper bag for two years," Garrett says.

"My father gave me this watch. It's an Omega Seamaster, they guarantee the battery for five years," Sam says, holding his wrist up.

"The salt air gets into everything in here," Sandra says.

The next humiliation is in the changing room, where Koresh and Garrett watch Sam strip out of his prison blues and put on his new clothes. Sam must suck in his gut to button his pants, and his wrinkled suit jacket is too tight. "Guess I gained weight in here," Sam says, his arms and chest bulging against the fabric.

"You bought a suit that's too small? What an idiot!" Garrett says.

"You should have spent more time in the library building your brain instead of in the yard building your guns," Koresh says.

The last step is the exit room, where Sam sits across a metal industrial desk from Officer Tom McQuade, a kind middle-aged Santa Claus, but with shorter hair and a trimmed beard.

"You earned eight hundred working in the laundry, plus you receive two hundred dollars in gate money," McQuade says, counting out ten hundred-dollar bills on the table. Sam stares at it, suspicious to touch it.

"It's yours. You can pick it up," Officer McQuade says.

Sam slides the bills in his brown wallet. "Just like Christmas. Thanks, Santa."

McQuade narrows his eyes, and his kind face hardens. "In their limited wisdom but overwhelming kindness, the parole board has granted you release six months early, which means you have a parole officer, Mr. Hal Weinstein. He was your probation officer after your first conviction and suspended sentence. He has made a special request to handle your parole case upon your release, and the board agreed."

"He did?" Sam asks, with honest surprise. "Hal remembered me?"

The guards laugh again. "He's the only one who does. You haven't had a visitor since you got here," Garrett says, nudging Koresh.

McQuade hands Sam a business card. "You meet him tomorrow, at the Hall of Justice on Bryant Street in San Francisco. Here's the time and address. Is anyone picking you up upon release?" he asks.

"Nope," Sam says, then shrugs and smiles as if it doesn't bother him, but it does.

"Then you get an additional twenty dollars for bus fare," McQuade says, handing over an extra Andrew Jackson from his metal cash box. Sam grabs it, but this time McQuade doesn't let go of the other side of the bill. The two men lock eyes.

"Two out of three convicts in California are incarcerated again within three years," McQuade says. "Are you going to be one of those guys?"

"No sir," Sam says, and McQuade releases the money.

"Officers Garrett and Koresh, please escort this man out of prison and drive him to the San Rafael Transit Center."

"Is that it?" Sam asks. "I can go?"

"It is," McQuade says, standing up. "Good luck, Mr. Webb."

Sam exhales with wide eyes as he stands. He grins at the three men, who just stare back.

"Move it, loser, I don't like being your chauffeur," Garrett says.

Leaving San Quentin is a shock to the system, like Dorothy stepping from inside her black and white Kansas cabin out into the paradise of color that is the Land of Oz. The prison is on a peninsula, so as Sam steps out of the last door and into a parking lot, the San Francisco Bay is on three sides. The water is silver and gold under a cornflower blue sky with towering green Mount Tamalpais in the distance. A cool wind hits Sam in the face and flutters his wrinkled suit. A loud honk makes him jump – the Golden Gate Ferry motors by on its way to dock at Larkspur Landing. He heard the same honk six times a day inside, and never knew what it was.

Another honk shocks him back to reality. Garrett is behind the wheel of a prison squad car, and Koresh stands by the open rear door. "Quit staring and get in the car," Koresh says.

Sam is relieved to slide into the backseat and put glass between him and the real world.

"Where am I going?" Sam asks.

"Only you know that. We're just taking you to the bus station," Garrett says.

"Can you take me there instead?" Sam asks as they drive past the ferry landing.

"It's always the bus station. Buy a ticket back here if you want," Garrett says.

"Got to follow the rules," Sam says under his breath, but loud enough for Garrett to hear.

The San Rafael Transit Station is a cement island in a parking lot next to an onramp for the 101 Freeway. There's a row of benches and poles with bus schedules mounted on them and buses pull in and out between long yellow lines. Garrett parks the squad car and he and Koresh exit, but he doesn't open the rear passenger door. With no door handles in the back seat, there's no way for Sam to get out until Garrett opens the door for him.

Sam hears the bus for San Francisco start its engine. Sam taps on the glass. "That's my bus! Open the door!" Sam says.

Garrett opens the rear door but blocks Sam as he gets out. "I have a gift for you, Webb, something I give all my departing prisoners." Garrett punches Sam in the stomach, knocking the air out of him. Sam hugs his gut as he falls back against the car.

"I'm giving you a little extra, for your smart mouth," Garrett says, and winds up for another punch. Sam pushes himself off the car and hugs Garrett like a boxer, sucking hard to get his lungs to re-inflate.

Koresh jams his hands between them and pries them apart. "People are watching," Koresh says to Garrett, holding him in place.

Sam staggers away. "You'll be back in six months!" Garrett shouts after him.

Sam climbs onto the bus and sits in the first seat. The driver closes the door and puts his bus into reverse. "That screw does that too often. Your fare is free," the driver says.

Sam nods his thanks while holding his gut. The other six passengers on the bus stare out the window to avoid looking at him. As the bus zooms past Mill Valley, Sam sits up straight, whistling to keep from wincing, and opens a thick black wallet that he was hiding in his lap. He is impressed by its contents. He takes out a few hundred dollars in cash.

A few miles away, Garrett is behind the wheel with Koresh next to him. He pats his shirt, then rises out of his seat and pats the back of his pants.

"Lose something?" Koresh asks.

CHAPTER TWO

The Sunset District of San Francisco is a grid of stucco box homes built in the 1950s in rows for forty-eight blocks, stretching two miles to the Pacific. To break up the sameness, the developers threw in playful gestures onto each box house, like a castle turret, or a twisting Hobbit chimney or a little balcony under a French window. The owners then painted their homes purple, yellow or pink, to make them stand out in the grey fog that blows in from the ocean.

Sam starts his first full day of freedom at the distant end of the Sunset District, at the Ocean Park Motel on Sloat Boulevard, across the street from the zoo. He takes the bus from San Rafael to downtown San Francisco, and then hopes on the L-Taraval streetcar and rides it to the very end of the line.

He checks in, then walks the two blocks to the beach, sits on the cement wall and stares at the Pacific Ocean. This is his gift to himself on his first day of freedom. On his worst days in prison, he'd visualize this stretch of beach, a place he'd enjoyed as a boy, and he swore that whenever he got out, he'd come here first.

But after only ten minutes, the vast openness of the sky and water overwhelm him, making him feel like an untethered balloon that might blow away. He hurries back to his room and closes the blinds, trying to make his world small again. He orders a pizza delivered instead, and then watches TV in bed while eating his first true pie in years. It's a luxury to stretch out on a queen size mattress, even if it sags in the middle, and Johnny Carson is still as funny as ever. He almost feels happy.

The sound of squeaking box springs and female moaning and male grunting in the next room wake him up in the middle of the night. The man finally groans and the woman giggles. Sam sighs and stares into the blackness, listening to the sound of distant waves on the beach. He wonders how long it will be before he makes love again. How will they meet? Will she be kind? Warm? Pretty? Will she have a nice smile? Then he gets scared. How would he even start?

In the morning, he takes a shower, then stares at his wrinkled blue suit hanging in the open closet. His brown wallet and Garrett's black wallet are on the side table, alongside his father's broken Omega watch. It's all he has in the world. He exhales and gets dressed.

As he exits his room he transfers all the cash to his wallet, tosses Garrett's wallet in the dumpster, and looks for breakfast. He finds it two blocks away at Doggie Diner, which has on its roof the gigantic head of a smiling dog wearing a bowtie and a chef's cap. Sam wolfs down a hot dog on the street, bending forward so the mustard splashes on the sidewalk. A Muni bus roars up, and he tosses the tail end of the hot dog bun to the hovering seagulls as he darts on board.

Sam gets off the Muni bus at the corner of Ortega and 28th Avenue and walks past the green, yellow, pink, and purple houses, then stops at one painted burnt orange, with a black wrought iron balcony and red geraniums on the sill. Sam stares at the house, exhales, and darts up the cement stairs and rings the bell and knocks on the door, but no one answers. He walks down the steps and stares up at the dark windows.

The front window on the neighboring purple house opens and a grey-haired woman in a bright Hawaiian housecoat sticks her head out the window. She has a black patch on her left eye. "They moved away a long time ago," she says, shaking her head.

"Mrs. Wilkenson, it's me, Sam Webb!" He touches his chest as proof.

She spits at him. "I know who you are, you hoodlum."

"I'm looking for Rose, do you know where she went?"

"Are you deaf? I said they moved away!"

"If you know where she is, please tell her I stopped by. It's important."

"She and her boy are better off without you, you prison scum. Don't you dare try to get back to together with her!"

"I'm not, ma'am! We have some unfinished business is all."

"I don't believe you! You're a fake Casanova and you'll ruin her life!"

"I'll come back when I'm settled and give you my phone number. That way she can reach me herself. Okay?"

Mrs. Wilkenson shuts the window. Sam backs away and stares at both houses, a big man in a wrinkled blue suit that's a size too small. The wind blows again, fluttering his suit and pant legs. He flips up his jacket collar and heads back towards the bus stop.

A black Lincoln Town Car, long with straight edges is parked in the bus zone. Sam turns on his heel when he sees it and heads the other way. The Town Car starts up, makes a U-turn, and follows Sam.

Sam grits his teeth and resists looking over his shoulder, but he knows the car is there. He glances at his watch, remembers that it's broken, then pulls out the business card for his parole officer that McQuade gave him yesterday and swears under his breath. He jogs, then runs. The Town Car keeps paces with him but stays twenty yards back.

CHAPTER THREE

T he yellow taxi stops on Bryant Street in front of the grey cube that is the San Francisco Hall of Justice on Bryant Street. When Sam gets out his blue suit is even more wrinkled, with sweat stains under the arms. He dashes inside, but not before spotting the Lincoln Town Car parked across the street with two large men inside.

The San Francisco Adult Parole Department is on the third floor in an open area with rows of metal desks. After ten years of service, you get a cubicle. Twenty years, you get a cubicle next to a window. Thirty years, you get an office with a window. Sam slips past the reception counter, passes the rows of desks, makes a hard right at the cubicles and heads to the first office with a window and leans in. Officer Hal Weinstein, age fifty-nine and rail skinny, sits behind a cluttered desk stacked high with white paper and brown folders, and sips coffee from a Styrofoam cup. He grows his brown hair long on the right side of his head and combs it over his bald white head, then holds it all in place with a dark brown yarmulke. He pats his dome to make sure everything is still secure as he sips and reads. He spills a few drops on the white paper and mops it up with his brown tie.

"Knock knock," Sam says, and Hal spills the whole cup of coffee on the file.

"Don't you knock?" Hal asks as he pushes files off his desk to avoid the spreading pool of brown liquid.

"I did. I said, 'knock knock' instead of knocking," Sam says.

"You're supposed to wait out front," Hal says.

"I was on time but they made me wait an hour, so I walked back here."

"I walked out front at three and you weren't there," Hal says. "I won't bust you for being an hour late on your first day, don't worry. What's worse is that you're already lying to me. Sit down." Hal pulls out paper napkins from his Chinese take-out bag and mops up the coffee.

"Sorry, Hal. We've done this so often I thought we could do away with the formalities."

"When you finish your parole, you can tap dance naked in here. Until then, life with me is nothing but formalities. Understand?" He tosses the napkin and sits back down.

"How much time you got left on this gig?" Sam asks as he sits in the metal chair.

"One year until early retirement, and it's my goal to keep you clean until then. You will be my final project, and proof that my job and the system works, my wiseacre friend," Hal says as he sits back down behind his desk.

"You are such a Boy Scout, Hal Weinstein. You should run for office. You'd be San Francisco's first Jewish mayor."

"Adolph Sutro was San Francisco's first Jewish mayor, a multi-millionaire who served two terms and built public parks, including Sutro Baths, which he donated to The City. Before you mock my faith, know what you're talking about. You look silly in that suit, by the way."

"At least I don't use my tie as a mop," Sam says.

"Good one," Hal says and hands Sam a business card. "Since you didn't give the parole board a home address, that's a hotel in the Tenderloin that takes parolees. Pay by the week and don't move without talking to me first."

"The Taj Mahal," Sam says, reading the card. "It sounds exotic."

"It's not," Hal says, then crosses his arms and leans back in his chair. "Now let's get serious. What are you going to do about getting work?"

"Construction. Maybe work in a warehouse," Sam says. He leans back and crosses his arms too, trying to mirror Hal. He read in a magazine that copying people's body language makes them feel more comfortable.

"Warehouse, huh? Where you can pick up some loose merchandise off the loading dock and sell it to a fence?" Hal asks, riding the back legs of his chair.

"Thanks for the vote of confidence, Hal," Sam says. He rides the back legs of his chair too, until the legs slip out from under him. Sam lurches forward to keep from falling, then tugs at his jacket.

"You will be tempted. I'm just being realistic," Hal says. He pats his head to make sure his yarmulke is still holding his comb-over in place.

"Rose left me, so I lost both my wife and my stepson. I've lost what was left of my youth, plus all my money. All I've got left is my freedom. I'll make it work, Hal. I have no other choice."

Hal slides a piece of paper across the table. "Nice speech. Here's a list of places that hire parolees. There are twenty years of goodwill on that list, and I don't give it to just anybody, so don't blow it for the next guy. Get a roll of quarters, find a payphone and start dialing."

"Minimum wage, here I come!" Sam says, pocketing the paper. "Thank you, Hal."

The men stand up and shake hands…but Hal doesn't let go. He's a smaller man, but he yanks Sam forward until Sam must lean over the steel table. "Stay out of trouble. And stay away from Paul Barnes. He's the worst thing for you. Promise me."

"I promise," Sam says. Hal lets him go and Sam rubs his sore hand. "Damn Hal, you're intense sometimes. Are you this way with all your parolees?"

"I am with you. And you want to know why? Because you have an IQ of 125. It's in your file," Hal says. "They tested you in prison."

"I had no idea. Is that good?" Sam asks.

"It's not genius, but it's up there. It means you could amount to something if you tried. It also means you may be a little too smart for your own good. You did devote your 20s to being a burglar." Hal leans across the desk and pokes Sam in the chest.

"Maybe I'll be your campaign manager when you run for Mayor," Sam says and winks, then backs toward the door.

"Not so fast, I'm not done," Hal says as he darts from around his desk. He blocks Sam before he can get out of the office. "Your jokes are the dust that blinds you from the truth about yourself. God wants you to make yourself clean, remove the evil of your deeds from his sight, cease to do evil, and learn to do good."

Hal is too genuine for Sam to have a snappy response. Sam tries to slip out, but Hal puts out his arm and blocks the door.

"In the Talmud, the Rabbis write that if a man truly repents for his sins, he will be so completely transformed that in heaven his sins will suddenly count as good deeds. That could be *you*, Sam," Hal says, touching Sam's chest. "That could be *you*."

Sam blinks at this skinny middle-aged religious guy with the bad comb-over who's an inch away from his face. His eyes are wide and intense, like a prophet who knows he can save you, and doesn't worry about how dumb he looks as he tries. Even more intense, however, is his breath, which smells like the Moo Goo Gai Pan he had for lunch.

Sam stares at his shoes and tugs at his dirty clothes. The fact that Hal cares so much embarrasses him. "Okay, okay, I'll clean up," Sam says.

Hal drops his arm and slaps Sam on his back. "Good! Stay in touch! Maybe we'll go see a Giants game and watch Vida Blue pitch. He's a great comeback story. Just like you."

"Sounds good. Thanks, Hal," Sam says. He finally squeezes past and runs for the exit.

CHAPTER FOUR

The Tenderloin is a crappy neighborhood, where the denizens of the soft underbelly of The City live in single occupancy hotel rooms and studio apartments. At night, the streets are wet and the air is cloudy with fog. As Sam walks along Turk Street looking for the Taj Mahal Residence Hotel, he notices that the Tenderloin is black and white with shades of grey, just like the black and white classic, *The Maltese Falcon,* which has some scenes set in the Tenderloin. Sam imagines he's like Humphrey Bogart, cool and tough, and it makes him feel like he can handle this place.

Vietnamese immigrants are moving to these sad 50 square blocks. They're bringing their laughing children in bright colored clothes, and they're putting flowers pots on window sills. But in 1980 it's still mostly drunks buying hip flasks of Thunderbird fortified wine, disabled Vietnam Vets with PTSD before we gave their trauma a name, and male and female prostitutes selling their bodies to feed their heroin habits. Sam trades friendly smiles with them as he walks past, but there is no chance of anything happening with any of them, despite his two years in prison. He wonders again how long he must wait before meeting the warm woman with the kind smile who entered his imagination in the middle of the night.

Sam finds the Taj Mahal. It's a narrow three-story grey residence hotel with a big picture window on the ground floor. A small pink sign juts out from above the door with a gold and white image of the Taj Mahal outlined in red neon.

The lobby feels big as he walks in, but that's because it's painted glossy white and the only furniture is two green sofas and an easy chair by the big window. Three retired Merchant Marines in their 80s sit there in their blue wool pea coats – one is Irish, one is Filipino, and one is Chinese, and Sam can tell that this spot is theirs, all day and night, where the aging buddies watch the world go by.

"Hey guys," Sam says and salutes the group, and they salute back.

Sam walks up to the counter. Mr. Amit Pavel stubs out his Beedi cigarette and stares at him from bloodshot eyes, with sockets puffy and black from lack of sleep. Mr. Pavel lives in a cloud of tobacco smoke that stains his teeth, his fingers, and seeps into his curly black hair. He's five feet two inches tall, but he gazes up at you with a silent disdain that announces that you're beneath him.

"I'm Sam Webb. I'd like to check in."

"I'm Mr. Pavel. I own this hotel, as well as The Blue Sapphire on Ellis Street. Show me your identification, and fill out this form," Amit Pavel says, and hands over a check-in form and a pen. "Did Hal Weinstein send you?"

"Yes," Sam says. He smiles as he hands over his driver's license, but Pavel doesn't smile back. Instead, he studies Sam license as if it might be a forgery, while Sam fills out the form.

"You pay in cash. A hundred fifty dollars a week," Mr. Pavel says as Sam finishes.

Sam takes out six hundred dollars. "I'll pay for four weeks," Sam says, handing it over.

"You will want a roll of quarters too," Mr. Pavel says.

"Why is that?"

"There are two payphones and vending machines with sodas and snacks behind you and coin-operated washers and dryers in the basement, Magic Massage units on the beds, and you can buy cigarettes and candy at the front desk," Mr. Pavel says.

Sam writes Mr. Pavel off as a slum lord who makes money coming and going, and sighs and as he hands over another ten dollars for his roll of quarters.

"Don't sigh at me," Mr. Pavel says, as he slaps the roll of quarters on the table. "I am not a criminal like you. I came here with nothing, but I worked. Now I own two residence hotels. I paint, clean, and repair everything here. I am putting two daughters through Stanford. I have no patience for Americans who commit crimes and squander their birthright. If you screw up here, I tell all the other hotels and you can't move anywhere else in this neighborhood. No more attitude. You behave, understand?"

"I understand," Sam says. "I'm sorry."

Mr. Pavel hands over the room key. "You clean. No food, no pets…"

Sam grabs the room key off the white counter and holds it like it's a microphone. "I ain't got no cigarettes! But two hours of pushing broom buys an eight-by-twelve four-bit room. I'm a man, of means by no means…King of the Road!" He backs away, shimmying back and forth across the green shag carpet. "I'll be good, Mr. Pavel, I promise!"

Pavel blinks in shock but still doesn't smile. Sam darts up the stairs.

The upper floors of the Taj Mahal have two long hallways that cross in the middle, and every twenty feet there's a door to another residence room. Each room has a queen-size bed, a small desk, and a chair. There's a closet, and a small bathroom with a sink, toilet, and a bathtub with a shower. Glossy white exterior paint is slathered on all the walls and there's a strong smell of bleach, but it doesn't quite cover the smell of cigarette smoke, take-out food and body odor that has seeped into the walls and floorboards over the decades.

Sam finds that the door to Room 222 is already open, and two men are inside working. A Latino worker in blue overalls screws a box to the headboard of the bed, while a fat white man in blue polyester slacks supervises him. The fat man cinches his belt so tight he looks like a sack of potatoes tied in the middle. His name is Hiram Valosek, he's twenty-eight years old, and he is the sales director for the Magic Massage Corporation. He's also putting himself through grad school at night and is getting a master's degree in a new subject called "computer programming." Valosek can command an IBM computer to follow his orders, using stacks of cards with holes punched in them, which he feeds into the machine, like bills into a money counter. He has written several programs for the Magic Massage Corporation, and each program has over a hundred cards each. The programs he writes can do time-consuming clerical work instantly, like arranging all his clients on a list by their zip codes. Each stack of cards, which represents a program, is held together with rubber bands and stored in his briefcase.

"Excuse me, you're in my room," Sam says.

"We're replacing the Magic Massage unit you vandalized,' Hiram says.

"This is my first night here. Ask the manager."

Wires coming out of the mattress run up into a coin-operated box screwed tight to the headboard of the bed. "She's finished," the worker says.

Hiram points at the unit. "This is a luxury item. It costs ninety-eight dollars to repair and install, which you now owe me."

Sam puffs up his chest, stretching his blue suit. "I am not paying. I just moved in." "You pay me now, or I will have Mr. Pavel throw you out," Hiram says.

Sam ponders the situation. Mr. Pavel already has it in for him, and with the song and dance routine he just pulled, drawing more attention to himself may not help. Plus, he got more cash from Garrett's wallet than he ever expected, and these problems that he's experiencing may just be cosmic payback. *Accept and move on*, he thinks, and hands over a hundred-dollar bill.

"Keep the change," Sam says.

Hiram pockets the bill and points at the unit again. "I suggest you read the warning," Hiram Valosek says, and he and his handyman leave.

Sam moves close and peers at the white warning label with bold red lettering: *Tampering with this unit is a criminal offense and*

anyone vandalizing it will be prosecuted to the full extent of the law.
25 cents for five minutes.

Sam digs in his pocket and finds a quarter, drops it in the slot and lies down on a pink cotton bedspread so soft and old, that little lint particles come off and stick to your clothes. A loud humming fills the room. A man in the next room bangs on the wall.

"You turn that on again and I'll bust it again! You hear me?" the man screams.

The bed stops shaking after only forty-five seconds. So much for five minutes. Sam sighs, gets up and opens the curtain. He's got a big window which lets in a lot of light, but the noise of Muni buses pours in too. Sam glances across the street and sees that the Lincoln Town Car that's been following him all day is now parked across the street and he can see the two large beefy men inside. The driver is a big blond guy with a crew cut and two thick folds of skin on the back of his neck. The other is an even bigger dark-skinned guy with curly hair, a Samoan probably. Both wear red and gold San Francisco 49er football jerseys, in support of a team that, in 1980, has yet to win a Super Bowl. The stocky Midwestern guy looks up and sees Sam in the window and waves.

CHAPTER FIVE

T he next morning, Sam hangs his suit on the shower rod and runs hot water into the tub until the steam takes out the wrinkles. It's still damp when he puts it on, along with being a size too small, but it will have to do. Sam walks down to the lobby with Hal's list, drops quarters into the payphone and starts dialing. Mr. Pavel glances at him and smirks.

"Hello, yeah, my name is Sam Webb, and I got your name from Hal Weinstein and I'm looking for a job and heard you might be hiring," Sam says, then listens to the man talk on the other end about tarring roofs and gluing sheetrock to walls. "I can do that," Sam says.

Sam pauses and listens to the man again, while trading nods with the three old Merchant Marines from last night, still in their pea coats and sitting in their same spots on the two ratty sofas that face the window. Have they moved at all since last night?

"Experience?" Sam asks. "Yes, when I was beholden to the government, I helped tar the roof of San Quentin prison. Hello?" The man hung up.

After working the phones all morning, Sam manages to get a job interview for a brand-new company south of Market Street doing "recycling," which involves separating aluminum cans, glass bottles, and clean newspapers from trash bins at businesses and apartment buildings. Sam goes down to the China Basin building and fills out an application, but he leaves the question blank about whether he's ever been convicted of a crime. Sam assumes the man knows about his record since he got the man's name from Hal, but it turned out it was an honesty test, and the fact that Sam left it blank was proof that Sam was still not honest, and he lost the job.

Refusing to give up or feel bad for himself, Sam spends the evening hours wandering the Tenderloin looking for *Help Wanted* signs, until he spots one in the window of a McDonald's on Van Ness Avenue.

He fills out the application, gets the job, puts on a hairnet and an apron and stands by the fryer ready to be trained by Billy, his pimply faced nineteen-year-old manager. A mist of vegetable grease and beef fat hangs in the air and coats the walls, making everything glisten under the green fluorescent lights.

"You open the bag of frozen fries and dump a bunch in the basket, hit the red button, and lower the basket into the oil. As you're waiting for the bell to ring, you fill the basket next to it with more frozen fries. When the bell rings, you lift the basket out, and dump the cooked fries onto that metal tray, then hit the button again, and lower the second basket into the oil, and then fill the first basket with frozen fries again. You think you can do that?"

"Yes."

"Then do it," says Billy, irritated.

Sam demonstrates that he can follow instructions and is soon sizzling frozen fries and dumping them onto metal trays, ready for scooping into red cardboard fry containers that will help fatten up America.

"So, you were in prison?" Billy asks.

"Yup," Sam says dumping out fries. "I was released three days ago."

"Let me guess. Burglary."

"Commercial burglary. There's a difference," Sam says, lowering more fries into oil.

"What's the difference? A thief is a thief," Billy says.

"I never broke into anyone's home. Only businesses, where I never saw anyone. No one was ever in danger and no one ever got hurt. Insurance paid for everything I stole. Half the time I was hired by people on the inside," Sam says. The bell dings and Sam lifts out another basket and dumps the fries on the metal tray under the orange heat lamp.

Billy moves a step closer and lowers his voice. "I got some friends who work at the warehouse and we've got our eye on some kitchen machines. Big ones. We could use a guy with your savvy."

"Did you just say 'savvy?'" Sam asks. "You want me to clip for you?"

"It's easy money. They won't notice anything missing."

"I'm thirty-two. It's hard enough making fries for you. Stealing for you is just too weird."

"That's the deal. It's the only reason I took you on as a trainee."

Sam stares at the basket of sizzling fries and ponders his situation. Is this his only option? Billy grins and raises his eyebrows, sensing Sam's vulnerability.

The bell rings, bringing Sam back to reality. He takes off his apron and throws it at Billy and walks out. He strides down Turk Street back toward the Taj Mahal, and engages himself in an angry mental conversation with every person who has slighted him in the past three days.

"Nice hat," a Vietnam Vet in a wheelchair says as he walks past.

Sam rips the hairnet off his head and with all his fury tears it into tiny pieces, then throws them as hard as he can. They flutter into the street three feet from him.

CHAPTER SIX

The next morning Sam picks up copies of *The Chronicle*, and The City's two free newspapers, *The Bay Guardian* and the *Tenderloin Times*, and walks a few blocks to Original Joe's on Taylor Street and sits at the counter so he can read the ads while sipping coffee. The chatty hum of the professional men and women around him makes him feel almost normal. He tries to trade glances with some of the well-dressed women, but no one looks his way. That's okay, he thinks, he still feels part of the world, and all it took was a place to go, a chair in which to sit, and a cup of coffee to sip.

He would pay extra for this feeling, he realizes, which leads to a vision. He should open a chain of coffee shops that sell baked goods too, with a few kinds of expensive coffee in different sizes, with some chairs so people can hang out, just to provide this feeling of belonging that he's having. He ponders it, then figures it's too far-fetched, people won't pay extra for coffee just for convenience and the feeling of belonging, and he goes back to the want ads.

He spots an ad he likes – an art gallery wants waiters and bartenders to work art openings, at an address south of Market Street in the warehouse district. That's the job for him.

He walks fifteen blocks south, enjoying the warm sun and blue sky. He finds the two-story brick warehouse on Bluxome Street. A sculptor's studio fills the bottom floor. For the top floor, there's just a steel door, a mailbox with a number and a doorbell. Sam stares at the ad in the paper and then looks up at the warehouse. He rings the bell.

"Come on in!" a woman shouts from the open window above, and a buzzer sounds. Sam pushes the steel door open, steps through and climbs the steep wooden staircase.

The gallery occupies the entire second floor of the building, with walls stripped to the bare red brick. Steel girders crisscross the vast room every ten yards, reinforcing the place against earthquakes. A dozen white wall sections form a maze on the wooden floor, each featuring paintings for sale under track lighting. Couches and low and high tables dot the space, making it perfect for parties. Wide windows look out towards the San Francisco Bay, a southern exposure that lets in a stream of natural light.

Sam tiptoes through the gallery, then stops at a huge painting of a naked purple woman with green nipples giving birth to a rainbow baby. He hears high heels behind him, and spins to meet a beautiful woman in her forties, with short dark hair and wearing a short pink silk dress and a long Hermes scarf around her neck.

"You're not Johnny," she says, stopping short when she sees Sam's face.

Sam freezes like he's been hit in the face with a bucket of ice water. This is the first attractive woman who has spoken to him since he got out of prison, and it's a shock to the system. She smiles as he blinks his eyes back inside his head and finds his footing again.

Sam holds up the paper. "I'm here about the job? Waiter and bartending?"

"That ad is old. I use a catering company for all my party needs now."

"I could work part-time. Do odd jobs, run errands."

"I'm hosting a new art opening next month. Come back on the first."

"I do repair work as well. I'm a great handyman. And an even better bartender."

"Bartender?" She smiles and twirls the edge of her scarf, wrapping it up on her finger. "All right, make me a Manhattan," she says, and nods at the bar in the corner.

It's not even noon yet, but he won't judge. Sam hasn't made a drink in two years, much less sipped one. He goes behind the low bar and finds all the fixings. Sam mixes rye bourbon with sweet vermouth, adds bitters and some maraschino until it turns red, then drops in a thin slice of orange rind. He brings it back to her with a napkin.

She sizes him up, head to toe as she takes the drink, undressing him with her eyes.

"What's your name?" the woman asks, narrowing her eyes at him. Sam figures she's ten years older than him, maybe fifteen.

"Sam."

"I'm Marjorie. You are persistent. I like that in a man," she says, then sips and burns him with her gaze, until the heat makes his eyes water. "Plus, you make a good Manhattan."

It's happening, he thinks. She may be the one, and it's terrifying. Sam slides his hands in his pockets to hide his growing erection, then slides them in his jacket pockets instead, but the pockets are too small, so he puts them in front of him, all while rocking on his feet trying to figure out what to do next. He decides to ask the obvious.

"So, you're an art dealer?"

"You could say that. I ran a lot of galleries in New York," Marjorie says.

"Is this stuff any good?" Sam asks, gesturing at the purple woman with the green nipples.

"Not really. But I convince rich people in San Francisco that it's great, and they think my East Coast sophistication will rub off on them if they buy it," says Marjorie.

"People always need something," Sam says, looking at the art. "Even rich people."

Marjorie laughs, sips her Manhattan, and touches her hair. "So, you're a philosopher."

"I sometimes contemplate the universe," Sam answers, and raises his eyebrow at her. She winks at him. He made the drink strong and it's working on her, but he's not sure he remembers how to handle a woman a decade older than him who's tipsy before noon.

She steps close. "Maybe I do have work for you. Do you enjoy physical labor?"

"I do," Sam says, and steps closer.

"Are you good at it?" she asks. "At being physical, I mean."

"No one has complained yet."

She tilts her head up as he leans down, and they kiss. It's tender, just like Sam was hoping for... and then she bites his lower lip. He gasps and she pulls away.

"You bit me."

She laughs and kicks off her high heels. She moves closer and they kiss again, this time softer, and Sam relaxes into it and puts his arms around her. She probes with her tongue against his teeth, like knocking on a door, and their mouths open and they touch tongues. Marjorie's sucks on his tongue like a vacuum, which excites but scares him. She pulls away and laughs when Sam touches his mouth.

"Whoa. My lips and tongue are aching," he says.

"You're going to ache everywhere after the workout I'm going to put you through," Marjorie says, pulling his belt so that her crotch is against his. "I expect a lot from younger men. I expect stamina from every muscle, you got that, Sean?"

"Sam."

"Whatever," Marjorie says, and pulls him by the belt. He follows her through a maze of white standing wall sections and finds a sofa in an open zone. She pushes him down on it and goes for his pants, but before she can even unbuckle his belt, he grabs at his crotch and groans. She unzips his trousers and sees a spreading stain on his underwear.

"What are you, in eighth grade?" she asks.

Sam spots the napkin he gave her with her drink, and he scuttles over like a crab, picks it up and jams it into his trousers before the stain can spread. He scuttles back to the couch.

"I've been in prison for two years and my only friend has been the widow and her four kids," Sam says, and holds up his thumb and then four fingers.

Marjorie creeps close to him on the couch. "Hmm, prison. That's sexy. Maybe I can help that poor widow of yours," she says. She grabs his right hand and sucks on his thumb, which is neither sexy nor painful. It's just odd.

"Do you have a bed in a smaller room? I don't do well with open spaces," Sam says.

Marjorie yanks Sam to his feet by his lapels then leads him through the maze to the back corner of the vast loft, then through a metal door into a small dark room. Inside is a queen-size bed with a headboard made of thick wood slats of white ash. The bed has black satin sheets and a black comforter. A black and white painting hangs on one brick wall and a large floor to ceiling mirror hangs on the other. There's an open window with a fire escape down to Bluxome Street below, and Sam thinks for a moment of running away.

"That's my bed," Marjorie says, and moves closer.

"A big mirror in the bedroom? That's going to be bad in an earthquake," Sam says.

"Let's make our own earthquake then and make it shatter," she whispers into his ear, and then bites his earlobe. She bites too hard, but Sam can't pull away. They fall onto the bed.

He yanks off his pants while kicking off his shoes and socks. She pulls her dress over her head and tosses all their clothes across the room. All that's left is his dress shirt, and she yanks it open, which sends the buttons flying. They're naked. He is fit and muscular, thick across the chest like a halfback. She is thin with long legs and small breasts, also in great shape. She rolls under him, their mouths meet, they kiss, she opens her legs and waits…

…and nothing.

She rolls on top of him and grinds herself into his pelvis, and dangles her breasts in his face, but still, there is nothing. She reaches down between his legs, but she yanks him too hard and he recoils. "You need the widow and her four kids? See if they can help?" she asks.

"I don't think it'll make a difference," Sam says. He rolls out from under her and sits on the edge of the bed and holds his head in his hands.

"You said you never had any complaints? Consider this your first," Marjorie says. She grabs her dress and underwear and walks out.

Sam stares at his reflection in the mirror. He winces, not liking what he sees.

He steps into the bathroom wanting to take a shower, but he feels too much pressure to leave. Instead, he moistens a hand towel with water from the sink and splashes some rubbing alcohol from a plastic bottle onto it and mops down his neck, chest, armpits, and crotch. It's a "whoore's shower," as his Gaelic grandmother would call it, which is the best he can do under the circumstances.

He puts his clothes back on, but can't find a sock, so he gets down on all fours and sees that it slid under the closet door. He pulls it open and freezes. Inside the closet is a large steel safe, with a big spinning combination ring and a twist handle. Sam stares at it for a long time. He reaches out to touch it – then pulls his hand away as if it might burn him. He closes the closet door so he doesn't have to see it anymore.

Sam finds her in the open kitchen area, dressed in her silk dress and long scarf again, drinking orange juice and blasting Blondie's *Call Me* at full volume while writing in a ledger.

"Can I work your art opening next month?" he asks. "I need the work."

She sighs and hands him her business card. "Call me in a few weeks," she says.

CHAPTER SEVEN

S am goes to Macy's on Union Square and heads past the
perfume counters to the men's clothing department. When he
was a kid, the big Union Square stores always made him feel
good, especially during the holidays, when people were happy and had
money to spend, even if they didn't. The January credit card bill
always brought that truth home to his family, but it was nice when
they lied to themselves and indulged when they shouldn't have.

He touches the grey pants on a mannequin. They have a slight
pinstripe and are cool and light. These would feel good to wear, he
thinks. The jacket has padded shoulders, which he doesn't like; he's
already thick enough across the chest. He touches a black leather
jacket instead. He looks good in black leather.

Then he catches sight of himself in the mirror. His blue suit is even
more crumpled than it was yesterday, with a slight stain on his crotch
area that's noticeable in the light. He feels like a kid again, dressed for
church on Sunday wearing a lousy suit two sizes too small, wrinkled
and stained from playing in the street. He needs a new look.

Should he spend his money on new clothes? He adds up the money
he has left, and then adds up the karmic debt he's incurred. He stole
money from Garrett, so he owes the universe, but Garrett punched him
first, so his karma is even there. Hal Weinstein did him a favor, which
is a plus. Losing a Ben Franklin to that Magic Massage guy is a
minus, he's equal there. Marjorie was both bad and good, so he's still
even. On his fourth day out of prison, his win/loss record is 3 and 3.
New clothes might make the difference.

Something catches his eye at the far end of the aisle. A woman
strides towards him. She's a brunette around his age, dressed in a blue

business suit with a snappy skirt and jacket, a dark red silk shirt and matching red barrette in her hair, set off with a pearl necklace. She's also wearing running shoes, like women do in 1980 in the Financial District. They walk fast from the BART stations to their office buildings, wearing their runners and carrying their office high heels in their bags. Her purse is also open. Does she notice her purse is open?

She drops a pair of brown leather gloves into her purse and snaps it shut, all while in full stride. As she gets closer they lock eyes for an instant and she smiles – and time slows. The three seconds it takes for her to walk past Sam are more like three minutes, like she's being filmed with a high-speed camera and then played back for him in slow motion, so that every muscle twitch and dangling hair curl is brought out in high relief. Her brown eyes sparkle with flecks of gold, and her smile is warm and kind. Then she's gone.

Loneliness sweeps over him. That was the moment he'd been waiting for. He doesn't need new clothes, he needs to see her smile again. He tries to catch up to her, and spots her moving through the perfume department and out the door and up Stockton Street, weaving through the afternoon shoppers. He catches up to her alongside Union Square.

She spots him in a side micro-glance but doesn't slow down.

"You have a fantastic smile."

"Leave me alone."

"You took those gloves in Macy's. But I won't tell anyone."

"I am trying to get back to work. Leave me alone."

"You're not going back to work. Let me buy you a cup of coffee."

The woman crosses Post Street and stops on the corner. "And you're not a security guard for Macy's, so bite me," she says, looking at him from head to toe, catching every stain and wrinkle of his dirty blue suit, then laughs and rolls her eyes. She lets it sink in, then keeps walking up Stockton Street past the Marriott Hotel. Sam could admit humiliation and quit now, or he could ignore her stinging insult and double down. He's feeling lucky and decides to gamble. After all, he's

3 for 3 with the universe right now. He catches up with her as she heads past the Green Door Massage Parlor towards the Stockton Street tunnel.

"I'm not a security guard. I'm like you."

"No, you're not. Go away."

The woman pulls her purse tight to her. Sam knows she's scared, but he's in too deep now, which makes his mouth run faster. "I don't want to bother you, I just thought we have a lot in common."

The woman turns right and heads up the narrow cement staircase that leads up to Bush Street, which runs above the tunnel. She halts midway up the stairs, and Sam tilts back so he doesn't collide into her. She spins to face him, two steps above.

"Really? You mean like maybe you and I share a spiritual connection?"

She exhales on him, like she's blowing cigarette smoke in his face, which surprises Sam and he blinks – and she kicks him in the balls, slams his head against the wall, pulls mace from her purse and squirts him in the eyes. He grabs his face and sinks onto the dirty cement stairs.

"We've got shit in common." She steps on his ankle and Sam howls. She pats his jacket and pulls out his wallet and empties it of cash. "You've got quite a roll here, Slick."

"Give me a break. That's all I got," Sam says, rubbing his eyes.

"Give me that watch too," the woman says when she spots the Omega Seamaster on his wrist.

"My father gave me this –"

She steps on his other ankle until he straightens his arm. She unclasps the watch, slips it in her purse, and disappears up the stairs.

"I just wanted to meet you!" His voice just echoes off the white tile. Blind, Sam rubs his eyes, aware that pedestrians are stepping over him. One of them drops a quarter in his lap.

His vision returns enough for him to stagger to the Sutter Stockton garage where he finds a drinking fountain. He runs water on his eyes until he can see again, but now the entire front of his suit is wet. He's also missing a shoe. As he shuffles up Sutter Street he passes a homeless man pushing a shopping cart, but he's dressed in clean jeans, a shirt, shoes, and a Giants cap. The homeless man laughs at him and Sam wishes he'd just accepted his loneliness and bought the clothes in Macy's instead.

The black Lincoln pulls into a bus zone ahead of Sam, and the large Samoan gets out and opens the rear passenger door. Sam considers running, but the street is too crowded and he's only got one shoe. He opts for conversation instead.

"Who are you guys, anyway?"

"I'm Cliff. That's Dozer," the Samoan says, and points at the large white man sitting behind the wheel. Sam peers inside but Dozer doesn't turn around. All Sam sees are the thick rolls of skin on the back of his neck, like football padding. They almost look like a smiling face, if he added two eyes to one of the top rolls.

"What's with the 49er's shirts?" Sam asks, gesturing at the football jerseys that Cliff and Dozer are wearing. "You think they can actually win?"

"They will if they let the new kid, Joe Montana, play more this season," Cliff says.

Dozer turns in his seat. "Mr. Barnes wants to see you, get in the car."

CHAPTER EIGHT

D ozer drives through China Basin and over the Lefty O'Doul Bridge and into the Mission Bay part of town. There are a few colorful ramshackle houseboats in Mission Creek under the 280 freeway, but as they drive south it's all decaying warehouses, long empty cement piers, and abandoned shipyards with gigantic empty ship locks that are bright red with rust.

Dozer turns left and drives into the ground floor of an old warehouse on the water that looks fresh with new windows and new green paint. A large banner stretches above the entrance: *Mission Bay Health and Fitness – Grand Opening Soon.*

Dozer and Cliff lead Sam through a maze of Nautilus equipment and shiny weights and barbells, all so new most of it is still wrapped in plastic. They lead him down a hall to a wall with a tiny door that is only three feet tall, and there's a constant whacking and thumping from the other side. They point for Sam to go in, so he opens the door, bends down and steps into –

– a pure white room. He stands up just in time to see a squash ball screaming at his face. He ducks, but the ball careens off the wall and almost hits him again. Paul Barnes darts in front of him and whacks the ball with his squash racquet. He's a short man, about five feet and six inches tall, but he's muscular and six-pack fit. He wears a tie-dyed Grateful Dead t-shirt and sports a long brown hippie ponytail. He's a 70s free-love hippie turned 80s sociopathic capitalist, a type common in the San Francisco Bay Area.

Paul aims for Sam as he swings his racquet, and the ball stings Sam on the back of the thigh. Sam dodges a few more hits, then catches the tiny ball as it rebounds off the wall. Paul walks over and takes the ball from Sam's hand. Paul is a half foot shorter than Sam is, but the bigger man is still scared.

"Long time no see, Sam. You got bigger in prison."

"It's weird, Paul, you seem bigger too."

"I am bigger. I am a full inch taller."

"Really? How did you manage that?" Sam asks.

"Rolfing. Let me show you."

Paul leads Sam out of the squash court and through an unfinished hallway to a blue massage room where New Age Muzak plays on the stereo. A tall muscular blonde Nordic woman lights a candle and rubs oil on her hands. Paul points for Sam to sit in a leather chair, then pulls off his Grateful Dead t-shirt and lies down on the table.

"This is Inge. She is a certified Rolfer. Structural reintegration has re-aligned me with the gravity of Earth, releasing so much compressed stress in my skeleton and muscles that I've gained another inch in height."

Inge grabs the flesh on Paul's back, lifts him off the massage table and slams him back down, working him like bread dough. Paul and Sam both grit their teeth and moan – Paul from pain, and Sam from empathetic fear. Inge grins, enjoying their noises.

"Inge is the best bone cracker I've ever had. I call her the Enforcer. I even send her out with Cliff and Dozer sometimes, for guys who are late on their loans."

Thirty minutes later, Paul sits up and wipes his sweat off with a white towel. Sam shifts in the chair, uneasy.

"Found a job yet, Sam?"

"I got some leads."

"That's bullshit. Look at you. You're one step up from a street person." Paul laughs, and Inge joins in but laughs too loud, like she wants to please Paul. Sam smiles to hide his humiliation.

Paul gets up, puts on a fresh Dead Head shirt and gestures for Sam to follow him.

"A lot has happened since you went in. I bought this property for the long term, waiting for the neighborhood to change. I've up-scaled. I move half the stuff I used to. Nothing big. I love electronics and these personal computers people are buying. I think that's going to be big. And I buy exercise equipment. I love being in shape. Fitness will be huge too."

They walk back into big open gym area. Light streams in through the wide warehouse windows, shining off the bright metal of the exercise machines, barbells, and weights.

Talking about computers while walking past exercise equipment gives Sam an idea. "Maybe someday they'll put computers into actual treadmills, combining your two big loves. The computer will be on the treadmill and tell you how your workout is going."

Paul scoffs. "That's stupid. Still love being the smartass, eh Webb?"

Sam blinks. He wasn't joking; if a computer can be on a desk, why can't it be in a machine, or a car, or a stove or a refrigerator? Sam chooses to flatter Paul instead. That's always worked better than trying to communicate with him.

"What you're building here is amazing. You're legit," Sam says.

"Not quite. I'll go totally legit when I have ten million. That's what the Kennedys did. I want to be mega-rich before I'm middle-aged. You don't want to middle-aged with no gravitas, Sam. And money is how you gain power and authority."

Paul leads him out a sliding glass door onto a balcony that overlooks a line of broken Southern Pacific rail cars rusting on railroad tracks that run alongside the water, from the era when ships and railroads intersected here. Paul leans against the railing and stares across the bay.

"I want you to work for me again. You were a great safe cracker."

"I'm pretty rusty. I'm sure I'd mess up.'

Paul laughs. "Like you did last time, you mean?"

Sam sets his chin and stares hard at Paul. "That's exactly what I mean, Paul. Except I didn't mess up. You did. The information you gave me was wrong, and I got caught and went to San Quentin for two years."

"There was $500,000 in that safe. Half a million dollars. I need that cash," Paul says. He stands as tall as he can, twisting the towel in his hands as he stares up at Sam.

Sam straightens his own spine, trying to get taller too. "And I deserve my cut. But the safe was empty and the cops were waiting for me. Someone tipped them off."

"What are you saying? Are you accusing me of something?" Paul asks.

The salty wind from the bay blows across their faces. They stare at each other like two twitchy gunfighters ready to explode.

Dozer and Cliff appear on the interior side of the sliding glass door. Sam glances at them and they cross their arms and glare, letting Sam know that if he shows any anger towards Paul he will be punished. Sam smiles and waves back at them.

"At my trial, the lawyers said I stole $500,000 from that safe, money that insurance paid back to the company, money that was never in the safe anyway. Maybe you told the company your plans to rob them. Maybe you planned it all with them. Maybe they took all their cash out of the safe before I showed up, and then insisted I stole it. I go to prison, and you split the insurance money with them," Sam says.

"That's a good story."

"I had plenty of time to tell it to myself over the past two years. But I never said it out loud. I kept my mouth shut. Not one peep."

Paul leans against the balcony and looks down at the red boxcars and the green water of the San Francisco Bay. He puckers his lips, calculating. "It's true, the police found you kneeling in front of an open safe with nothing inside. After hours of hard work, they happen to walk in at the precise moment that you opened the safe? You didn't hear them coming? And it's empty? That's hard to believe. I think if you had the time to get it open, you had time to pass off everything inside to someone, who disappeared with the money. Like Rose. That's the story I've been telling myself for two years, and now I'm telling it to you." Paul looks back over his shoulder at Sam, to see his reaction.

Sam shrugs. "That's a good story too. But they investigated Rose and found nothing."

"You went to her old place. It's the first place you went," Paul says. "I knew you would, too. That's why I put Cliff and Dozer out front, and the day after you got out of prison you show up there. Why would you go visit your ex-wife anyway? I thought she dumped you."

"She's the only family I got. I was hoping to see them again."

"You think she'd take you back?"

"I don't let myself think that way."

"Or maybe she has my money. You could have been paroled to another city, but you came back here."

Sam gestures at the renovated building. "Look at this place. You're doing better than ever. And me? Rose divorced me and she and Carl disappeared. I lost everything for you, Paul. Can't we just leave it at that?"

Paul motions for Cliff and Dozer to come outside. They slide open the glass doors and step onto the balcony, and the wind snaps at their football jerseys as they move into place on either side of Sam. Inge then moves into the doorway, blocking Sam's potential exit. Paul smiles. "If that's the truth, I have to help you get back on your feet."

"That's okay. Let's just never see each other again. My parole officer would prefer that."

Paul gestures for Inge, and she steps out wearing just her white jeans and white t-shirt, her blonde hair back in a ponytail, which the cold wind whips. Goosebumps appear on her skin, but she doesn't shiver. Her Nordic blood loves the cold. She stands next to Sam, two inches taller, staring down at him.

"I insist that I make it up to you. I'm offering you a job," Paul says.

"I can't. I'm going straight."

Inge pinches Sam's shoulder nerve so hard that Sam drops to his knees to try to escape her, but she just tightens her grip.

Paul sighs. "Who are you to refuse my charity? If you live in this city, you work for me."

Sam motions that he accepts his offer. Inge releases him and steps back, letting Sam rub his injured shoulder. "How long will this charity last?" Sam asks.

"Until you get on your feet. I owe you that much for being such a stand-up guy."

"Thanks, Paul." Sam pulls at each metal rung of the balcony railing, hauling himself to his feet.

"I can even help you find Rose again, if you miss her that much," Paul says, and then gestures to Cliff, who pulls out a thick envelope and hands it to Sam. "In the meantime, that's my gift to you. Go buy yourself some decent clothes."

Sam opens the envelope, and inside is a thick stack of hundred-dollar bills, the favored legal tender for criminals around the world. Sam smells that weird dirty scent that hangs on cash that been touched by too many people. He puts the envelope in his suit jacket pocket. Next, Paul holds out a gun for him to take. Sam shakes his head, refusing to touch it. Paul waves it under his nose, even pushes it against his face.

"Take it."

Sam glances at Dozer, Cliff, and Inge, and they all stare back at him with stone faces. Sam takes it and becomes one of them. Four days out of prison and he's already holding a gun.

CHAPTER NINE

Sam admires the new clothes laying across his hotel room bed – blue striped suit, dress pants, and dress shirts, plus dress shoes in brown and black. He wears black jeans, boots, a white shirt and a cool black leather jacket. He smiles at his purchases, then glances at Paul's gun on the bedside table, next to Sam's wallet, thick with cash. His smile disappears. He picks the suit off the bed and little pieces of pink cotton from the old bedspread stick to the wool on the back.

"I'm so sick of this dump," he says out loud, but inside he's grateful he's not in prison.

He hangs the clothes in the closet, pulls off the bedspread and throws it in the corner, and then falls back on the bed. The gun gleams on the side table, inches from his head, forcing him to look at it. He runs his hands through his hair and exhales hard. It doesn't help. Then he notices the Magic Massage unit on the headboard behind the gun, finds a quarter in his pocket and drops it in.

The bed vibrates. He lays back and closes his eyes, trying to relax…and the man next door bangs on the wall again. Again, the bed sputters to a stop after only a few seconds.

"I'm trapped!" Sam screams.

"We're all trapped, asshole! Shut the fuck up!" the voice yells through the wall.

A car honks. Sam looks out the window and sees a white van parked in the bus zone across the street. Dozer sticks his hand out the driver side window and waves for him to come down.

Five minutes later, Sam is driving the car while Dozer sits in the passenger seat. A small black box the size of a deck of cards vibrates in Dozer's hands.

"What's that?" Sam asks.

"It's a pager. It's got a phone number. People call it, then punch in the number they're calling from, and their digits show up on the screen here, and I call them back," Dozer says, pointing at the green-lit pager screen. "Have you been living under a rock?"

"Kind of," Sam says.

"Pull over, stop at that payphone," Dozer says, pointing. Sam pulls the white cargo van over in front of Hamburger Mary's on Folsom Street, and Dozer darts out and grabs the phone handle just before a bearded man dressed in only black leather chaps, boots, and a black vest can reach it. Dozer drops in his quarter, dials, listens, then hangs up and hops back into the van. "Make a left here, and head down to 3rd and Bryant."

"Wouldn't it be easier if the pager were a phone too? And then you could talk on it, and even type messages to each other on it?" Sam asks.

"Don't be stupid," Dozer says. "Who needs that when there are payphones everywhere?"

Sam drives, making left-hand turns on the one-way streets south of Market Street until he finds 3rd and Bryant. A skinny brown-haired kid bounces on a street corner in the blustery fog, wearing just a thin blue t-shirt, shivering and waving. Dozer motions for Sam to pull over. The kid opens the back door and hops in onto the furniture pads lining the cargo area.

"Go one block under the 280 on-ramp. Hey, a new guy! How is it, new guy? I'm Vinny!"

Sam waves at him in the rearview mirror but doesn't speak. A few turns later, Sam finds the dark surface street that runs under the freeway and pulls over. Vinny jumps out of the back and rummages through the thick bushes and comes back carrying a teetering stack of five VCRs in their cardboard boxes, pushes them deep into the van and climbs back in. Sam pulls away as Vinny slams the back door of the van.

"Yo, new guy, slow down! I almost fell out, dude!" he yells towards the front." I got five JVC 900s. That's fifteen hundred dollars for me, motherfuckers."

Dozer peels off ten crisp Ben Franklins from his thick roll and holds them out to Vinny. "Try a thousand. When you hide them in a fucking bush the boxes get soggy," Dozer says, pointing at the stained cardboard. "They're so wet they're falling apart. The cardboard it comes in is as important as the product, jackass."

Vinny stares at the bills but doesn't take them yet. "Come on, Dozer. I worked hard for those VCRs."

"No, you didn't," Dozer says, and holds out the money.

"When do I meet Barnes?" Vinny asks. He scratches at his bare arms as if wiping away an army of invisible ants.

"Never heard of him. Is a VCR in every box, or do I have to check?" Dozer asks.

Sam stops at a red light on South Van Ness Avenue. Vinny scowls, grabs the money, and hops out the back. He slams the van door hard.

"Enjoy your next fix!" Dozer shouts out the window.

As Sam pulls away he looks at the fading image of Vinny, hunched over in his thin t-shirt, darting through honking traffic, clutching his money. Sam then catches his own eyes, then looks down at his new black leather jacket and pin-striped wool pants. He was just a few hundred dollars and a few days away from being Vinny himself.

Dozer's pager goes off again and he smiles when he sees the number. "Screw that junkie. This is the best clip there is," Dozer says.

"You want me to find a payphone?" Sam asks.

"She's always at the same spot. Take Mission to the Embarcadero," Cliff says.

She? A female thief? Sam wonders to himself. He follows Mission Street as it curves parallel to Market Street toward downtown. The looming grey two-level Embarcadero Freeway comes into view. Sam can almost see the lights of the Ferry Building and the Bay Bridge between the gigantic cement pillars. Dozer whacks Sam's arm and gestures for him to pull over to a corner bus stop. A woman leaves the Muni bus shelter, opens the back door and climbs in onto the furniture pads. She's dressed in a long cashmere coat, a blue beret, a green silk scarf, and she carries a purse on a long strap.

"How's it going, Kath?" Dozer asks, with the tone of a high school geek who's got a crush on the unattainable cheerleader.

Sam glances at her in the rearview mirror, as she takes off her beret and shakes out her long brown hair. He knows her. She's the woman shoplifter from Macy's, who smiled at Sam and froze time. A shiver of cold humiliation and then hot anger runs through him.

"Head for 2165 Howard Street. It's a garage," Kath says, then looks around. "These Chevy vans are disgusting. You guys are making money, can't you get something better? Or at least put some seats back here? Fix the suspension?"

"These get the job done just fine," Dozer says. "Whaddya got?"

"Five hundred heartbeat monitoring kits."

"Paul's going to love that. That's just the stuff he's looking for."

"Good. Then you can tell him to put a couch back here," Kath says.

Sam makes a hard right, tilting the van onto two wheels long enough for Kath to slide across the back and bang her head on the wheel well.

"Hey! Watch it!" Kath yells.

"What are you doing, she could get hurt back there!" Dozer yells and hits Sam on the arm, his schoolboy crush a little too obvious. Sam waves his hand in apology but says nothing.

This section of Folsom Street in a semi-industrial neighborhood stuck between South of Market and the Mission District. 2165 Folsom Street is a one-story garage with a bow and truss curved wooden roof. Sam backs the car up against the sliding garage door, leaving Kath enough room to hop out the back. Sam kills the engine and gets out too, but not before putting on a pair of black Ray Ban Wayfarer sunglasses and a black fedora hat with a red feather in the silk band.

"I'll help you carry the boxes," he says, tilting his head down to hide his face.

"Suit yourself. You can lift this door then too," Kath says, and points at the heavy metal sliding garage door she just unlocked. Sam sets his feet, grabs the handle and lifts from his legs. The heavy door rolls up easily.

"Wait here," she says, and goes into the dark garage and turns on one light. She returns with a cardboard box full of smaller boxes – the small but expensive heartbeat monitors.

"There's more," she says and hands them to Sam, who puts them in the back of the van with the VCRs. She goes back inside…and Sam disobeys and steps in and follows her.

Sam eases through stacks of office furniture – metal chairs, tables, and desks – and stacks of cardboard boxes full of new blenders, food processors, coffee makers, and electronics.

He finds Kath in an open section of the cement floor under a single dangling lightbulb.

He steps into the circle of light, and she jumps back with a gasp.

"I told you to wait outside," she says.

Sam grins from behind his dark glasses.

"Moon too bright for you tonight?" Kath says. "Give me a break, please."

"You and I know each other," Sam says.

"Can it, Romeo. Just carry the boxes please," Kath says, holding out another box.

Sam doesn't take it. "We met downtown the other day," Sam says. He takes off his glasses, tilts his head and flashes his lopsided grin that he practiced in the mirror for two years.

Kath grabs a lamp and swings it at his head. Sam ducks and plants a foot against Kath's stomach and pushes her hard against an office desk. Before she can get back up, and before Sam even thinks, he pulls out the gun that Paul gave him out and aims it at her face.

She gasps and holds her breath, which makes Sam regret his move. Paul forcing him to take the gun was still in a grey zone but pulling the gun out and threatening her with it moves him past grey and straight to jet black. This qualifies as assault and battery with a deadly weapon, he realizes, and as an ex-con on parole, he's just earned himself multiple years in prison, if he doesn't handle this just right.

"Don't hurt me," Kath whispers, her eyes still wide.

"You mean like how you hit me?" Sam asks. He puts the gun away and helps her up. "I still can't breathe right since you kicked me in the ribs."

"I kicked you in the balls, not the ribs," Kath says, sitting on the table.

"Whatever," Sam says. He pushes open her cashmere coat, checking for weapons, then grabs her purse off the table. He rifles through it and pulls out just a few dollar bills. "That's all you have?"

"I don't like carrying a lot of cash, for this very reason."

"Where's my watch that you took?"

"I'm wearing it," she says, and takes the gold and silver Omega Seamaster off her small wrist and hands it to him. Sam takes off his sunglasses so he can examine it, and notices the second hand is moving.

"Hey! You got it working!" Sam says.

"It seemed like it was worth fixing," Kath says.

"This is great! This was my father's watch!" Sam says with happy pride as he slides it onto his wrist.

"He had good taste," Kath says.

Sam admires the watch, then smiles at Kath, who smiles back, embarrassed. That initial moment of mutual attraction again passes between them, until Sam remembers how angry he is.

"Give me your money!" he yells, his voice breaking.

"I just did, idiot," she says.

Embarrassed, Sam looks around for more damage he can inflict. He spots a cassette carrying case on the adjacent desk, the zip-up kind with a handle that's the size of a small briefcase that can hold forty music tapes for any road trip. He grabs that instead, along with the second box of heartbeat monitors for Paul.

"That's all my music!" she shouts.

"You borrowed my watch, I'll borrow your music," he says, and backs out of the circle of light. He dashes out of the garage, pushes the monitors in the back of the van, slams the rear door, jumps into the front seat and tosses the cassette case on floor between him and Dozer, then starts up the van.

"What's going on?" Dozer asks.

Kath slams two empty whiskey bottles against the windshield. They both shatter and the windshield cracks, creating two intersecting spiderwebs of silver light.

Dozer screams, and Sam slams the car into gear and tears off down Folsom Street.

Sam giggles as he makes a right on 17th Street and then another right onto Shotwell, then pulls over into an open parking spot.

"I like that girl's energy," Sam says, while Dozer hyperventilates.

"Let's see what kind of taste in music she's got," Sam says as he pulls out a random cassette and pops it into the van's cassette player. Iron Maiden's debut album sounds like a bomb going off, and Dozer screams again. The bass vibration from the speakers makes the already soft broken windshield fall into the car, shattering into a million tiny pieces. Dozer's eyes roll back into his head and he passes out. His forehead hits the dashboard and he stays there, lost in the deep sleep of narcolepsy.

"So that's why they call you, Dozer, huh?" Sam asks the sleeping man.

Sam stares at the streetlights through the open front of the car, listening to the blasting music and waiting for Dozer to wake up.

CHAPTER TEN

I t's a bright, fresh spring morning in the Tenderloin of San Francisco, and Sam finishes his breakfast and coffee at Original Joe's and darts back up Turk Street to the Taj Mahal.

"Morning, guys!" Sam says to the Merchant Marines in their pea coats, and they all wave hello back. Sam almost gets past the front desk, but Mr. Pavel sticks two pieces of pink paper under his nose.

"You got two calls. Your parole officer wants to see you and a man named Barnes. Here are their numbers and their addresses where they want you to go," Pavel says, and then wags the pink phone message notes until Sam takes them. "I don't like it when the payphone rings so much, and I don't like taking your messages."

"Why don't you get a phone answering machine then?" Sam asks.

"What is that?" Pavel asks.

"It's a machine that answers the phone for you if you don't want to answer it."

"Why wouldn't I answer it if I am right here?"

"If you are away from the phone then, it will answer for you."

"If I am away from the phone, I wouldn't hear it ringing so it wouldn't matter anyway."

"What if the call is important though?" Sam asks. "In fact, aren't we supposed to have phones of our own by now, that we can carry with us, so we can call people anytime? And even then, if we don't want to answer, it will record a message for us."

Pavel shakes his head and walks away. Sam looks at the two messages, deciding which he should deal with first. It's a choice between the Saint Francis Yacht Club and the grey monolith that is the Hall of Justice on Bryant Street.

"Yacht club first, Justice second," Sam mutters. He's afraid of Paul Barnes, but considering what he's been doing, he's much more scared to see his Holiness the Amateur Rabbi Hal Weinstein right now.

An hour later, Sam wanders down a dock alongside the St. Francis Yacht Club, strolling between the boats. Paul Barnes appears on the deck of a Gulf Stream motor yacht called *Irish Mist*. He holds up a glass of champagne. "Hey, Sam! Over here!" Paul yells. "Glad you could make it!"

Sam walks down the dock and stops in front of the three steps that lead up to the deck of the black and white two-level yacht, which has a captain's crow's nest on top. He hesitates before getting on; after all, a moving yacht combines the two sensations he dislikes the most. First, on a moving boat, you can't just step off – you're trapped until someone brings the boat back to shore and sets you free, just like a moving prison cell. Next, you're in the vast wide open, like a floating cork on an endless sea. He's still not used to that much openness.

"Come on," Paul says, gestures to him from the railing. Sam exhales and climbs on board. Paul signals to the crow's nest and the pilot puts the boat into gear and backs out of the slip. Sam stands at the railing watching the dock recede, missing his chance to jump back onto land.

"Relax! You act like you'll never see dry land again. You want a drink?" Paul asks.

"Jack Daniels," Sam says. "And water."

"Still a bourbon drinker, huh? I like that," Paul says, then shouts through the open glass door into the main cabin. "Hey, Troublemaker! Get out here! And bring me a Jack Daniels and a glass of water!"

Paul drops into a plush easy chair on the open back of the boat. It's arranged like the patio, with black and white outdoor furniture and a gas barbecue, but instead of being next to a pool you're next to the San Francisco Bay, with just a metal and wire railing between you and miles of moving green water.

Sam shuffles in place unsure what to do with himself, until Kath comes out of the main cabin holding his drink and his glass of water. First, relief sweeps through him. Seeing her is a guarantee he won't be killed. Paul still might hurt or humiliate him, but Sam now knows that at least he won't die. Second, he feels a little rush of joy in his heart, happy to see her again.

"Why, it's Little Miss Head Banger! How's the Heavy Metal groupie today?" Sam asks, relaxing into his cocky persona. She puts the drinks on the table in front of Paul.

"Like I'm seasick and need to barf," she says.

Paul opens a cooler next to him and pulls out a Pabst Blue Ribbon in a bottle, pops the top and hands it to Kath, then hands Sam his drink. "Here we are, the coach and his star players. It's a beautiful day, and a great meal is coming. Do I take good care of my people, or what?"

Paul pops a cassette into the stereo and the Grateful Dead comes through the four large quadrophonic speakers on the back deck. Paul sips his own drink, a green smoothie concoction. Sam and Kath stand like wallflowers at the junior high school dance, refusing to move.

"It's a party! Drink! Drink!" he shouts at them, and they obey.

Inge walks onto the back deck wearing a one-piece white bathing suit with black combat boots and black glasses, a perfect match with the black and white decor. She lays a tray of sandwiches and sliced fruit down on the table.

"What a nice lunch. Thank you, Inge. And keep that outfit on, I like it," Paul says.

Inge smiles but makes no sound, then disappears back inside. Paul bites into a turkey sandwich and turns to Sam and Kath.

"Let's talk business. Kath, you can't beat men up in the street for hitting on you. It embarrasses them. Sam has low enough self-esteem as it is. Not to mention that you can get arrested for both shoplifting and beating people up," Paul says.

"What I do on my own time is my business," Kath says.

"Everything you do is my business now," he says, then points at Sam. "And you, give her money back."

Sam sips his Jack Daniels. "Not until she gives me back my money first," he says, crossing his arms and puffing up his chest – until the yacht goes over a swell and he must throw his hands and legs out to steady himself. Half his drink lands on the white deck.

Paul yanks a roll of cash out of his pocket and peels off hundred-dollar bills and throws them in Sam's face. "There's your money! Happy now?" Paul yells.

Both Sam and Kath scramble to catch the bills skittering across the deck before the wind blows them into the water. "You brats got what you need? You're both worse than kids! You're lucky I put up with you!"

Sam and Kath each count the bills they grabbed, then look at each other. "I'm square if you're square?" Sam asks her, gesturing at her wad of money.

Kath nods. "Yeah, I'm square," Kath says, and pockets her windfall.

"Good! Because I have a brilliant idea," Paul says, plopping down into his chair to finish his sandwich. "I'm hooking you up together. From now on you'll be working for me as a team," he says, then bites and chews as Sam and Kath launch their verbal assault.

"Her? Dirty Harriet? If psychos could fly, she'd be their squadron leader!"

"Him? Mr. Scratch and Sniff? He leaves a scent trail fifty yards wide!"

Paul laughs, then glances at the main cabin. Inge stalks out, growling at them like a rabid Amazon. She reaches for Sam's shoulder and he knocks her hand away, terrified of the pain she can inflict. Paul raises his hand and Inge falls into place behind her boss.

"Hear me out. Kath, you bring me the best high-end merchandise, but always in small quantities. You never get inside a warehouse for a bigger haul. Sam, on the other hand, can break into buildings and into safes, although the last time you did it, you did get caught," Paul says, glancing from Kath to Sam. "By yourselves you're not that much. Together you might add up to one decent criminal. What do you think?"

"Here's what I think," Kath says. She guzzles her beer and then burps like a trucker in a Peterbilt talent show, long and hard, in a rumbling rising note like a honking eighteen-wheeler speeding past. Paul and Sam stare at her, shocked. "I have brothers," she says and shrugs.

"They taught you to be disgusting?" Sam asks.

"Yes, they did. Just like your San Quentin boyfriends taught you to be an obedient little pillow biter," Kath says. She grabs a cloth napkin off the table and holds it against her mouth, as if she were stifling a scream.

"I don't think we're interested in your offer," Sam says to Paul.

Paul slaps the table as if they were. "Good! This is the deal then. We'll each pick one job. First Kath, then Sam, then me. You two do the work, and I'll pay for all the expenses – cars, tools, bribes, cover – and we split each payday three ways."

"What happens after the three jobs?" Sam asks.

"If you like the arrangement, we keep working. Or you walk away. All debts to me erased. You owe me nothing," Paul says, his palms up like he's Jesus offering them the loaves and the fishes. Kath and Sam look at him and each other, suspicious.

"Too easy. There's got to be a hitch," Kath says.

"Why do you say that? I want my people to be happy, and I know neither of you loves working for me. I want to change our situation, so we can all benefit. And if my idea doesn't work and you decide to move on, I'll know it wasn't meant to be," Paul says. His voice is low and earnest like he's quoting a church poem on a fabric wall-hanging.

The pilot steers the speeding bouncing yacht on three long loops past downtown, under the Bay Bridge, around Alcatraz and then past downtown again. By the third loop Sam is sick and Kath is laughing.

The Jack Daniels didn't help. Paul takes pity on him and parks the yacht alongside the docks at Pier 39, so Sam doesn't have to endure the bouncy ride through the choppy waves all the way back to the St. Francis Yacht Club. Paul and Kath stand at the railing and watch Sam walk a slow crooked arc up the dock with his hands stretched out as if he were a drunk in the dark just hoping to touch a wall to keep the world from tilting away from him.

"He might need this, but I don't," Kath says.

"I know. Neither do I. But I can make it worth it for you."

"I knew something else was coming," Kath says. Sam reaches dry land and waves at them in triumph, then disappears into the tourists crowding Fisherman's Wharf.

Paul leans close. "Sam likes you. Play along with my offer. Talk to him."

"What are we supposed to 'talk' about?"

"Where he put five hundred thousand dollars of my money. He's got it hidden someplace and I want to be there when he gets it," Paul says, and then explains the whole safe cracking story. "I've got too much tied up in the health club, and in real estate. I have no liquidity. I need cash, right now, and he has it."

Kath hears it all, then shakes her head. "This game's not for me. I'm no Mata Hari."

Paul glances over his shoulder to check if Inge is watching, then reaches out and rubs the back of Kath's neck. She recoils at first, then closes her eyes, bites her lip and endures his touch.

"I remember a time when you'd do pretty much anything I asked you."

Kath shakes his hand away. "That's before I knew you better."

Paul walks back to his chair. He pulls out a cigar from a cedar box on the table and lights it, blowing the smoke towards her. "Don't get ugly with me. I found you dumpster diving at age seventeen. You used to huff paint thinner until you passed out in the gutter. I changed all that," he says, then sucks on the cigar until the tip lights up red.

"And you won't ever let me forget it," Kath says.

"You miss me sometimes. You miss all this," he says, gesturing at the yacht. "Admit it."

"I don't. And quit bringing it up," Kath says, crossing her arms. "Or I'll tell Inge."

Paul holds up his hands in surrender, and laughs. "Then I admit it. I remember the fun we used to have, and I miss it. Just do me a favor and have fun with Sam for a little while."

"You want me to fuck him?"

"If that's what it takes. Or plan burglaries with him. With this business arrangement, you have a reason to spend time together. Just work your magic and find out what I need to know."

Kath paces the deck like a caged tiger. "Why me? Why not some other girl?"

"Because you still owe me money. Remember all that cash I've given you over the years? You're still paying interest, you're not even into principal." Paul plops back down in his black and white easy chair. He puts his feet up on the table.

"I've been paying my debt off. Your math is funny. It always has been," Kath says. "And you could get any girl to do this. Girls with more professional talent than me. It doesn't add up."

Kath faces him, her legs apart and her arms crossed. The fog horns blow under the Golden Gate, announcing the incoming marine layer that rolls in during the late afternoon. The wind whips her hair and raises gooses bumps on her bare arms, but she doesn't break her gaze. Paul puffs on his cigar and crosses his own arms, his stare matching hers.

"Because you look like his wife."

Kath's eyes widen as Paul grins. "What? He's got a wife?" Kath asks.

Paul signals to the pilot up top, and the yacht pulls away from the Pier 39 docks. Paul walks over to Kath, circling her. "He had a wife, until he trashed it. A real looker too, just like you. Different hair color, you're taller, but your eyes, mouth, and chin are the same," Paul says, pointing at Kath's face and hair like she was his model. "It's probably why he followed you out of Macy's, whether he realizes it or not."

Kath blinks, unsure what she thinks about this new revelation. She picks up a thick green blanket off another easy chair and wraps it around her shoulders. It's emblazoned with the name of the yacht, *Irish Mist*. She shivers and stands by the railing and looks out over the water. They are coming up on Alcatraz Island, and the old decaying federal penitentiary.

"What's in it for me?" Kath asks.

"One hundred thousand, and all debts forgiven. And you'll be done with me forever."

"These burglary jobs are a sham then," Kath says.

"They don't have to be," Paul says. "We can all still make money."

"I want them to be shams. No risk, no one gets hurt, no one gets caught," she says, still staring straight ahead. They are now parallel with rocky Alcatraz and the lighthouse atop the old Federal prison. Paul sighs and shakes his head.

"Your job and mine can be shams. I can set that up easy. But the job he picks must be real," Paul says. "But I bet you'll find out what he did with the money long before he ever takes that chance," Paul says.

They stare at the old prison passing by, a yellowing matron whose broken windows look like accusing eyes. "I'll think about it," Kath says. "But if I do it, you and I are done. Forever means forever."

CHAPTER ELEVEN

B
ay Meadows is the oldest racetrack in the United States, a beautiful one mile oval next to a green grandstand, thirty miles south of San Francisco. It was torn down in 2008, so they could build a high-tech community for Silicon Valley, but in 1980 you can watch the jockeys in their multi-colored polka dotted satin shirts ride the giant thoroughbreds four times a week.

Kath rides Caltrain down to Bay Meadows every Sunday, to visit the Meadow Song Retirement Community, a two-story U-shaped building just two hundred yards away from the race track parking lot. One arm of the "U" provides assisted living and has an Alzheimer's ward with a locked door so the patients can't wander. The other arm holds small one-bedroom apartments with rooms so small you can't fall without hitting a wall with a hand railing to grab first. This is the side Kath visits every week, and she says a little prayer as she passes the green locked double doors of the Alzheimer's ward, thankful that she doesn't have to visit there yet.

She rides the elevator up and knocks on the brown metal door to apartment 201. She knocks, then rings, then knocks again, and just as she's about to get the manager with a passkey, a tiny woman in a pink bathrobe pulls the door open. She is Kath's great Aunt Bella, she's less than five feet tall, she is in her eighties, and she wears a brunette wig that looks more like a helmet than hair.

"Didn't you hear the bell, Aunt Bella?"

"Yes, I heard it! The door is unlocked, just come in! I don't want to stop what I'm doing for every damn person who knocks on the door!"

Kath kisses her on the top of her wig and follows her into her tiny apartment. Aunt Bella is a pack rat who collects old *National*

Geographic magazines, cans of food, playing cards, cribbage boards, and poker chips. Kath joins her aunt at a tiny kitchen table. Bella likes to eat her breakfast while playing Solitaire. Aunt Bella bites into a piece of homemade cinnamon toast.

"Want some?"

"No thanks," Kath answers. She slides a small pink gift-wrapped box across the table.

Bella puts down her half-eaten piece of toast and rips the package open. Inside are the gloves that Kath stole from Macy's.

"You said the department store billed you for gloves they never sent, right?" Kath asks.

Bella's eyes light up as she remembers. "Yes! I called them on the phone and told the saleswoman exactly what I wanted from the catalog, and then they sent me the bill, but the gloves never came! Can you believe that? How long will it be before I can order something while sitting in my home and trust that it will arrive?"

"Maybe someday, Auntie," Kath says, and takes off her green scarf, blue beret, and cashmere coat. "It's warmer down here than in The City."

"That's why I live here, because there's sunshine. You've got 'hat head,' run your fingers through your hair," Bella says, pointing at Kath's brown locks. Kath fluffs up thick brown hair as Aunt Bella stares at her and sighs.

"What?" Kath asks.

"You are so beautiful. I wish I still had hair like you."

"I know," Kath says, and reaches out and holds her aunt's sugary hand.

"You shouldn't have wasted your money on me."

"The gloves were a bargain. I even got a pair for myself."

"They are beautiful calfskin. Thank you," Bella says. "Put them next to the stack of canned beans next to the window."

"Why do you keep a stack of canned beans leaning against the window?" Kath asks as she places the gloves next to a four-foot-tall stack of cans.

"If the bad guys climb up the rain gutter and try to break in at night, I'll hear the cans fall over," Bella answers.

"Want to go to the track when it opens?" Kath asks.

"I'd love to. I have a system. Boys who wear pink always win big for me."

She watches her aunt play Solitaire for several minutes. Kath sits but then stands again. She paces, then stops, then runs her hands through her hair, and then goes back to watching.

"You just cheated. You put red on black," Kath says.

"Arrest me. Sit down, you're bugging me with your hovering. What's wrong with you?"

Kath sits down, clears her throat, and spits out her thoughts. "Speaking of cheating, the director said you were taking people's social security money again," Kath says.

"I won their money fair and square. No one forces them to play poker with me," Bella says. "Is that why you came down today? To bust my chops about my gambling?"

"You used to cheat on me to get me to do the dishes, Auntie. Where's the money you won?" Kath asks.

"This is my apartment, and it's my money! You stay out of my business! And that director makes a fortune off me for this place, and off the medicine I buy from him!" Bella screams, spittle flying from her mouth. Her sugar-coated cards spill off the table and her wig tilts back on her head, exposing her yellow hairnet.

"Let me handle your bills. He's serious about the money. You want to keep this place, don't you?" Kath says.

Tiny Bella faces off against her grandniece, curling her nose as if she's ready to toss out an Italian gypsy curse. She gives in instead. "It's behind the television set."

Kath walks two steps and reaches behind the oven-sized wooden box of a TV set and pulls out a thick envelope of cash and thumbs through the bills. "Are your track winnings in here?"

"I keep that separate. Track money is crisp and fresh. That money smells like old socks."

"You've got fifteen hundred here. You're a busy old lady, Bella."

"And you're not busy enough if you have to worry about an old lady like me. Don't you have any men to occupy you?" Bella asks as she starts another game of Solitaire.

"No one worth talking about."

Bella stops laying her cards down and stares at Kath as she puts the envelope of cash in her coat pocket. Kath looks up, and they lock eyes. "What?" Kath asks.

"There is someone."

"Let's just say someone is trying to set me up with someone and I can already tell that I don't like the guy. It's awkward."

"You can't give him a chance?"

"There's no spark, Auntie. Trust me."

Bella goes back to her Solitaire game, carefully laying red on red and black on black. Kath watches her for a few seconds, then sits down across from her, her eyes welling with tears.

Bella looks up. "Katerina, what's wrong?"

"I'm not a bad person, am I?"

Bella reaches over and grabs her hand. "You appeared from nowhere to take care of me, my sister's granddaughter. You're the only family I have left. You pay all my bills with money that comes from I don't know where. I don't deserve you."

"I'm not that wonderful. I've hurt people. And I'm afraid I'm going to do it again."

Bella moves her chair closer to Kath. The old lady with the helmet wig runs her tiny fingers through the younger woman's thick locks.

"It's impossible to go through life without hurting or being hurt. You can't sit on the sidelines. You just jump in and do your best and follow your heart," she says. "And be honest."

"Be honest?"

"It's the most important and hardest thing. Be honest with yourself, and others."

Kath nods, not saying how impossible that is for her right now. She sniffs and smiles instead. "What is it about you and me? How come we get along?" Kath asks.

Bella gathers the deck of cards, shuffles them and splays them face up on the table with the speed of a blackjack dealer, and pulls out the Queen of Spades and the Queen of Clubs. "Birds of a feather flock together, and we're both dark-haired ravens," Bella says, holding up the cards.

She then grabs a Jack of Hearts and holds him up.

"Now see if you can catch the Jack of Hearts," she ways, and then bends the cards slightly and moves the three of them on the table, back and forth, faster than a hustler playing three-card monte on a cardboard box on Market Street.

"Follow my hands, watch him close, see if you can catch him..."

Bella stops moving the cards, and Kath points at the card in the middle. Bella turns it over, and it's the Jack of Hearts. "Got him," Kath says.

"This time. But sometimes us ravens end up alone, like me. Don't let that happen to you. You don't have to take crap but be honest and forgiving. You don't always have to win."

The two women reach out and grab hands across the tiny kitchen table, surrounded by *National Geographic* magazines with tin cans stacked against every window.

CHAPTER TWELVE

S am gets off the Noriega Muni line and takes a rambling walk for several blocks, making turns on streets past bodegas and Chinese restaurants just to make sure Dozer and Cliff aren't following him in their Lincoln Town Car. He turns up the collar of his jean jacket to both hide his face and to protect himself against the fog.

He cuts back to 28th Avenue and Ortega Street, passing all the little houses with their bright colors, and stops again at the stucco house painted burnt orange with the black wrought iron balcony and the red geraniums on the sill. It's where he and Rose and her son used to live, in another life so long ago it feels like it didn't happen, but it did. Sam stares at the house for a minute and then realizes that either the geraniums are fake, or someone is living inside and watering them. He walks closer and stands in the driveway and stares up at the tiny balcony and sees dirt on the underside of the pots, and a few red petals are falling off.

They're alive. Someone cares about the geraniums, which means someone cares about the house. Maybe Rose is there. Maybe Rose is coming back, or Mrs. Wilkenson is going in and watering them for her. If Rose had sold the house, someone new would answer. He darts up the stairs and knocks on the door, then rings the bell. There are no lights on, and there's no window he can use to peek inside. He can't decide whether no one answering is a good sign or a bad sign.

He pulls an envelope from his pocket and darts up to Mrs. Wilkenson's house, next store. These homes in the Sunset have their mail slots on the ground level, next to the garage door, right under a tiny square window that helps illuminate the inside of the dark garage. That way the mailman doesn't have to dart up hundreds of staircases a day. But before Sam can drop the envelope in her mail slot, Mrs. Wilkenson dumps dirty water on him from her front window above, drenching his new stonewashed jacket.

"Did I surprise you, punk?" She still wears her black eye patch and her bright Hawaiian housecoat.

"I have a letter for Rose," he says, holding up the still dry envelope.

"Get away from my house, or I'll drop hot bleach on you next."

"Don't throw my letter away. Rose will want it," he says, waving it.

"She'll never call, and I'll never call her about you, understand? Not after what you did to her, and her boy Carl!"

But you'll still water her geraniums for her, Sam thinks, and darts up to the mail slot and drops the letter in, while Mrs. Wilkenson spits her curses down on him.

CHAPTER THIRTEEN

Sam leaves the Taj Mahal and walks down Turk Street until it almost reaches Market, and then makes a left on Mason and walks uphill. He has a lunch meeting in North Beach but doesn't want to take Muni. The sun is shining, and the air is cold and brisk, so he decides to walk over Nob Hill. He's lost weight since prison because he's walking more and lifting weights less, and he's not overeating crappy food out of boredom. He wants to keep the momentum going, so he takes off his leather jacket and throws it over his right shoulder, transfers his leather briefcase into his left hand, and then powers up one of the steepest streets in San Francisco. He passes pretty girls with big coiffed hair and colorful padded jackets, and bright bandanas around their necks or in their hair. He and a cute blonde make eye contact as he passes Geary Street, and she smiles. He's ready, he realizes. He can put his mistake with Marjorie behind him now. Something is bound to happen, and soon.

Memories flood through him as he walks up Mason, past Post Street and the Olympic Club where the Catholic cops, firemen and union bosses are members, then past the Marines Memorial Club, for veterans, and the Metropolitan Club, a social and athletic club for women. Then he walks up the steepest part of Mason to the top of Nob Hill and past the most exclusive club of them all, the Union Pacific Club for the rich WASP businessmen who once controlled The City. They built this club first, then denied entry to everyone else. So, the Catholics started the Olympic Club, the veterans started the Marines Memorial Club, the women started the Metropolitan Club, the Jewish citizens started the Concordia Argonaut Club, the successful writers, artists and musicians started the Bohemian Club, and the lowest of the low on the social ladder, the journalists, started the Press Club. Sam's half-Irish, half-Mexican family couldn't get into any of them, but they would hire him, and he got jobs handing out towels and robes at their pools, working as a bartender for their parties, and cleaning their bathrooms. He also saw how easy life was when you had enough money that you could stick with your group and never think about what anyone else was doing.

He walks across the top of Nob Hill then heads down the other side toward Russian Hill. The cars that had passed him as he walked uphill, he now passes as he walks down, mostly because they're circling the block looking for parking. It's absurd, he thinks. He'd pay each of these drivers in cash to carry him to his destination, especially if the ride cost him less than a taxi fare. He could organize a few hundred drivers to circle the neighborhoods and give short lifts to people, which would cut down on the number of cars, free up some parking and get people places faster. It would be a good business, and it could work in other places, like New York. All he needed was a way for the drivers and the riders to contact each other quickly. He stores it in the back of his mind with his "phone the size of a pager" idea and his "friendly expensive coffee shop" idea, for the future.

He jumps onto a passing Powell and Mason cable car, pays the fare, grabs a transfer ticket and rides into North Beach. He checks the numbers on the transfer and they add up to 21, which always meant good luck when he was growing up.

He hops off at Joe DiMaggio playground and walks another block north to Fior d'Italia, the restaurant next to the San Remo Hotel. He puts his leather jacket back on, checks himself in the beveled mirror outside, then goes inside and spots Kath in one of the two leather booths. It's only noon, so they're the only ones in the restaurant. She's wearing a black leather jacket too, and she sports the same blue beret as the last time he saw her. She stubs out her cigarette as he slides into the booth across from him.

"Look at you with your briefcase, you look so important," Kath says.

"Look at you in your little beret, like you're some underground spy," Sam says. He flicks open his briefcase and takes out her cassette case and slides it across to her. She unzips the case and opens every plastic cassette holder to make sure the music cassette is still inside.

"Prince is missing," she complains.

"Who's Prince?" Sam asks.

"My Prince cassette," she says, holding up the cassette box, showing a half-naked prince on the cover. "There were 34 cassettes in here, and now there are 33. Hand it over."

Sam reaches into his breast pocket and hands over the missing music. She just shakes her head. "You'd steal from your own mother."

"Should we order? I remember the tortellini here is good."

Kath puts her Prince music back in its case. "I'm not breaking bread with you. I'm having an iced coffee just to stay awake, you bore me so much," Kath says.

"Then why am I here? Paul said you need help planning your job," Sam answers.

"I'll tell when and where, but that's it. Your job is to get us inside, nothing more. If you can manage that, then I take over. You do as I say, and you'll get your cut. Understand?"

"Why so harsh?" Sam asks, his feelings hurt.

"Your reputation precedes you. You're too much of a risk. You'd get caught breaking into a dog house," she says.

"Thank you for your honesty, but I think *you're* the one who is too much of a risk, Little Miss Angry Headbanger. We're working on this job together."

"Fine. But if you screw up and get caught again, I'm not hanging around to save you."

A young male waiter with curly hair, wearing a black bowtie and a long white apron arrives with Kath's iced coffee. "Anything for you, sir?" he asks Sam.

"I'll have the same as her. And some of those almond cookies, in the twisty paper wrappers?" he asks.

"Amaretti di Saronno cookies, yes sir," he says, and disappears.

Sam leans across the table as Kath sips her coffee. "Listen, Katherine –"

"– my name isn't Katherine. Get it right, Chuck."

"It's Sam, not Chuck."

"I know that."

"Then why did you call me Chuck?" he asks.

"Because you called me Katherine. Don't do that," she says.

"What is Kath short for then? Catheter? That would make sense. I had a catheter inserted once for a kidney problem and it was damn painful, just like you are."

"My name is Katerina. Kath is a nickname my mom gave me because she didn't want to call me Kat."

"How about Lady K? Can I call you that?" he asks. "We all have reputations, Lady K. Before you lecture me about getting caught on jobs, I know something about you too."

Kath downs her coffee and stares hard at him. "Listen, Chuck –"

"Sam. My name is Sam."

"Let me tell you something, Ground Chuck. You'll never know what it's like to be me, not until you've gone through what I've gone through."

The young waiter returns with Sam's iced coffee and a plate of cookies. Everyone smiles as he places the cookies between them, then leaves.

"Let me tell you something, Lady K," Sam says, as he untwists a cookie from its paper. "You'll never know what it's like to be me having to listen to you talk about how I'll never know what's it's like to be you, going through what you've been through."

Kath blinks and shakes her head. "What?"

Sam dips his cookie in his coffee, bites, then sips. He unwraps another cookie and pops it into his mouth, then flattens out the wrapper on the table. "Why do you work for Paul, anyway?"

"I don't," Kath answers. "I'm my own boss. I sell what I clip to the fence who pays the most, and that happens to be Paul Barnes."

"No way. He's got something on you. That's why he stuck you with me," Sam says, not looking at her. He sips his coffee instead and flattens out another almond cookie wrapper.

Kath laughs. "I owe him money, that's why. But nowhere near a half a million like you."

Sam looks up and locks eyes with her. He folds up his cookie wrappers and pockets them in his jacket but says nothing.

"How much was really in that safe? It must have been a lot if you were willing to go to prison for it," she says, but Sam doesn't even shrug. He just keeps staring at her.

Kath pulls out several pieces of paper from inside her padded jacket and lays them on the table. "Don't talk then, just listen. Dozens of Japanese computer crystal display monitors, small and super high-end, are sitting in this warehouse in South San Francisco. They cost a thousand dollars each, and there's sixty to a case," Kath says and points at the paper. "Your job will be to get me on the roof, get me in, and then help get me out."

"That's it? I'm just muscle?"

"You can use your awesome brain power on your own heist, Chuck Roast."

"Can I take these papers? Is this the address?" Sam asks, taking Kath's drawing.

"Yes, it's the address, and no, you can't take them. Memorize them," Kath says, and holds them out. Sam stares at them for two minutes and then nods. Kath pockets her papers, finishes her coffee and stands up. Sam holds his hand up to stop her.

"I need to know one more thing," Sam asks, and Kath is already impatient. "Do these guys deserve it? I used to not care, but now –"

Kath interrupts him. "No, they don't deserve it. Nobody deserves getting robbed by us. But we're both stuck, the poor stealing from the rich, okay?"

Sam nods and sighs. "See you later, Lady K."

"And remember to pay the waiter. I come here a lot so don't make trouble."

She pushes open the big wood and glass doors and walks out onto Mason Street. Sam waits for a beat and then glances out the window to check out her ass in her tight jeans as she strolls away. She's got a nice figure to go with that sharp tongue of hers, he thinks. He finishes his coffee and smiles.

He wonders if he should get the tortellini but decides against it. The cookies were enough, and it's always tough for his palate to go from sweet back to savory. But he will walk back on Mason Street and through four neighborhoods to get back to his Tenderloin hotel and keep his lucky 21 Muni transfer in his wallet, and his cookie wrappers in his pocket. He knows he'll need some luck in the next few weeks.

CHAPTER FOURTEEN

South San Francisco is an industrial town with little similarity to her painted sister to the north. The town is bordered by 280 on the west and the Bayshore freeway on the right, and the tiny town of Brisbane to the south. The airport, the Union Pacific Railroad, the warehouses and the storage yards are all here, the moving guts that make the city to the north work. Just like New York City uses the open space of northern New Jersey, San Francisco uses the open space of South San Francisco, then takes her for granted.

Sam and Kath cross through the dune grass that ekes out a living between all the broken asphalt, cross railroad tracks, step through a break in a cyclone fence, and dart up to a parking lot behind a two-story warehouse. It's one of six grey buildings that line this half-mile stretch of soil between the freeway and the San Francisco Bay.

Sam drops the black canvas bag he's carrying, and Kath pulls out her new calfskin gloves and puts them on. They both stare up at the backside of the grey warehouse, which has one decorative red stripe around its middle. The moon is low on the horizon, there's a distant train whistle, and the planes lining up to land at SFO create a tiny row of lights in the sky. The dull roar of the freeway is the background noise that covers everything.

Sam and Kath stare at each other. This is their Rubicon; they each have one die to cast, and it will determine their future. Sam hesitates a bit too long.

"I knew it. You're not even ready."

Sam smiles as he takes out a pair of yellow dishwashing gloves from his jacket. He puts them on, then steps back through the hole in the cyclone fence. He walks a few yards through the white yarrow and into a wild blackberry bramble growing up the backside of the fence. He comes back with a fifteen-foot extension ladder. He guides it through the hole in the cyclone fence and leans it up against the building.

"Can you help me extend this, please? If I do it alone, it will make too much noise," Sam says, with a thick layer of sarcasm.

"This is planning?" Kath asks.

"How do you think the hole in the fence got there?" Sam asks. "I watched this place for 24 hours straight, both on a weekend and a Saturday. Did you?"

Kath doesn't answer but helps him extend his ladder instead. They carefully pull out each section, so it moves past each joint with a tiny click. Sam then leans the ladder up against the building, and it clears the top by a foot. He holds it for Kath and gestures for her to climb. She obeys. Once she's at the top, he throws his canvas bag on his shoulders like a backpack and climbs.

Sam steps onto the roof next to Kath, takes off his canvas bag, and then leans over the building and grabs the top rung of the ladder. In an impressive show of strength made possible by two years lifting weights in prison, Sam lifts the ladder up by the top rung, then grabs the next rung and lifts again, until he has enough of the ladder above his head that he can lean the ladder against the lip of the building. He then guides it down so it's flat and perpendicular to the parapet, making a cross. Sam swivels the heavy ladder so it's parallel with parapet and then lifts it and lays down onto the gravel and tar roof without a sound.

Kath raises her eyebrows. Sam made it look like he was lifting bamboo, not aluminum, and she feels a tingle in her fingertips, toes and the back of her neck. She's impressed but hates that she is.

"Muscle head," she mutters instead.

Kath starts to walk across the gravel, but Sam stops her with his yellow-gloved hand. He opens the black canvas bag and pulls out a roll of toilet paper. He unrolls it a bit and holds the edge, then tosses the heavy end of the roll across the wide roof. The paper unfurls and flutters down to the gravel top – except in four places where the paper forms miniature tents across four invisible trip wires. These are attached to an alarm box with a direct line to the security company.

Sam and Kath carefully step over two of the four wires and get to the center of the roof. They both kneel. Sam unzips his canvas bag again and pulls out a battery-operated buzz saw. He lays it against the roof but does not start it. He glances up and sees the first light in the row of lights in the sky getting larger until it splits into two lights, one on each wing of the huge jumbo jet landing on one of SFO's two parallel runways a half mile south. As the rumble reaches its peak, Sam starts the buzz saw and cuts an inch into the roof. The loud scream of metal cutting through gravel, tar, paper, and wood is drowned out by the landing plane, but he can only cut for twenty seconds before the rumble has passed and he must stop.

"How long is this going to take?" Kath asks.

"They're landing every minute. I'd say three hours."

They stare at the line of lights in the sky to avoid staring at each other. Another tiny light appears in the distance as another plane drops into the last place in line.

"Nice night. With no moon, you can see more stars," Sam says and winks at her.

She rolls her eyes. "Just get me inside, please."

Another rumble begins, and Sam lays the buzz saw against the roof. He cuts another quarter inch cut, holding the spinning saw steady against the vibration until his hands and arms lose all feeling – and then he stops. Sam must replace the batteries every hour, he must shake his hands every five minutes to get feeling back in them, and he must close his eyes when the sparks fly because the spinning teeth hit spraying wood and bits of nail, but he keeps going.

Three hours later, his buzz saw stops.

"Why are you stopping?" Kath asks.

"It's dead and I'm out of batteries," Sam says, staring at the saw in his hand.

"You are such an idiot," Kath says.

"How many hours have I been doing this?" Sam asks.

Kath looks at her watch. "Three hours."

Sam puts the buzz saw back into his canvas bag and pulls out a crowbar, wedges an end into the cut, then pries open the hole he's cut. There's a crunching of wood and metal, but it opens, like a hatch to a buried tomb. He then puts the crowbar back and looks at Kath.

"You were saying?"

"Bravo. We still need to get down onto the warehouse floor, Chuck Roast. I'm not Spider Woman, I'm not going to jump thirty feet down."

"Spider Woman. That's a good name for you," Sam says, then motions for Kath to step back. "Hold your venom, Spider Woman, and let Chuck Roast finish cooking."

Kath wants to hit him with more poisonous darts, but thinks better of it and backs up a few feet. Sam stands up, shakes out his legs, and walks back across the gravel roof, careful to step over the trip wires. He grabs the long ladder and easily lifts it over his head despite it being fully extended and lays it on his shoulder. He whistles as he walks back toward her, stepping over each trip wire with ease, like a fisherman with his pole on his shoulder, stepping from rock to rock in a stream.

Kath sees his strength and grace and feels that same tingle in her feet and neck again but refuses to let it rise to a full thought in her mind.

Sam lays the ladder across the hole so that two rungs frame either side. Sam kneels back down by his canvas bag and pulls out a rope. He ties one end to one rung, then loops the rope around the opposite rung, creating a simple pulley. He holds the rope, stands up and nods at Kath.

"The rope has a loop in the bottom. Put your foot in, slide through the hole and I'll lower you down," Sam says. "Sorry. Putting the ladder down there would make too much noise."

Kath stares at the contraption he created. "Is it going to work?" she asks.

"I sure hope so."

Kath stares at him and then at the hole, not trusting.

"I'm an Eagle Scout. Our motto is 'be prepared.'"

Kath sits on the ladder, hooks her foot in the knotted loop, lowers her feet through the hole in the ladder, grabs the rung with her hands and drops down. Sam pulls the rope taut and lowers her slowly.

"Hold onto the rope now," Sam says as her head disappears inside the hole.

Kath grabs the rope and Sam lowers her down by inches until she's on the warehouse floor.

Kath looks around. Rows of metal and plywood shelves line the big open warehouse. The overhead lights are off, and the only light comes from the exterior lamps in the parking lot shining through the high windows on the building.

"Hey," Sam whispers in her ear.

Kath jumps and that electric tingle shoots from her feet right up to the back of her neck again. She punches him in the chest. "No one said you could come down yet," she says.

"You want me to set up an exit for you, don't you?"

"Do whatever you're going to do, just stay out of my way."

Kath pulls out a small penlight and heads off into the stacks. Paul set up this job, he picked the warehouse, he promised the alarm system would be off, and he told her where the display monitors would be. There's nothing as easy as an inside job, she thinks, and so far, it's been as smooth as promised, even with Sam around. Not that she'd ever tell him that.

Sam watches Kath walk away and shakes his head. He doesn't want to be here either, but he's worked for days taking every precaution he could imagine, then trying to imagine more. He doesn't want to go back to San Quentin, especially for this Spider Woman with the poison mouth. He calms his beating heart by concentrating on prepping the exit.

She finds the third row of shelves, just like Paul told her, and starts looking for thin boxes of expensive crystal display monitors.

Sam finds a hallway alongside the south wall, and an office with six-foot-high windows. An exit here will put them closer to the hole in the fence he carved two nights ago. He grabs a chair and stands on it and examines the window. A strip of electrical security tape runs in a pretty square on the inside of the glass. It's silver and decorative, but it's also metallic and conducts electricity, completing a circuit that will cease if someone opens the window or breaks the glass, thus setting off the alarm.

Sam reaches into his pockets with his yellow latex gloves and pulls out a long strip of plastic-coated electrical wire with an alligator clipper on each end. He clips one end onto the spot where the silver tape runs onto the window, and then the other end where the decorative strip leaves the glass pane, creating a new circuit loop that bypasses the window.

He twists the handle and pushes open the cantilever window – and no alarm goes off. He steps off his chair and pushes a desk up against the window and then puts the chair on the desk and admires his work. They have a way out. Sam looks at his watch and exhales. He moves back into the warehouse.

Kath is not doing as well. She's made her third loop through the shelves, and the monitors are not out where they are supposed to be. She stops in front of a locked metal cabinet at the end of the middle row, convinced the display monitors are inside. Someone saw them out on a shelf and must have locked them up again, she thinks. She doesn't want to leave here empty-handed and have Paul force her to do this again. She shakes the locked metal cabinet like a kid shaking a vending machine trying to loosen a hanging candy bar.

What she doesn't realize is that the heavy, locked cabinet has a motion sensor attached to the back. It's designed to go off whenever someone moves it, in case someone tries to steal the whole cabinet. That silent alarm has begun to ring.

She takes off her left glove and lays it on the shelf and pulls out a picking tool from her backpack and tries to jimmy the tiny metal lock. She almost breaks the tool and then stabs herself in the hand. The rhythm of the night is changing, and she's getting the terror sweats now.

"You can't open a lock?" Sam asks, making her jump again, but with no tingle this time.

"If you're so smart, you open it."

Sam runs his hands along the top of the cabinet and finds a key hidden along the outside edge and unlocks it. He opens the metal doors and reveals a cardboard case of sixty super thin crystal display monitors in unopened boxes.

"That's cheating,"

"Isn't that the point?" Sam asks. "We should get out of here."

"Go ahead, Chuck Roast, leave if you want to," Kath says, and starts shoving boxes of LCD monitors into her empty oversized backpack.

Sam goes back to the office and paces in the weak light coming in the window until the noise of a car engine makes turn on his heel. He climbs up on the desk and sees an Ace Security Service car drive by. He's already halfway out the window when he freezes. He eases back inside.

Kath closes the metal cabinet and zips up her bag just as a side door to the warehouse opens. She ducks just before a flashlight beam hits the wall above her. Two voices whisper as Kath scurries on her hands and knees down between one set of shelves and then another, and then rolls onto a bottom shelf and hold her breath as a set of uniformed legs walks past.

She closes her eyes and prays to God, whom she only remembers only during her worst "foxhole" situations. Like all the times before, she promises the Lord yet again that if she gets out without getting caught she'll change her whole life, handle her debt to Paul somehow, while still taking care of Bella. She'll become a nun, even.

Then she thinks she's so horrible that even the nuns won't take her and that she doesn't deserve rescue. She'll never get out now anyway, since she doesn't even know where her escape exit is. She was too busy being cruel to Sam to worry about it, and now she wishes she hadn't called him a chuck roast and told him he could leave if their situation went south.

A hand grabs her arm while another hand goes over her mouth. It's Sam, lying on his belly on the floor, motioning for silence. He pulls out a handful of small marbles from his pocket and rolls them across the open floor, and when they hit the far wall they make enough noise to make the uniformed legs and whispering men to run towards it – and Sam pulls Kath the other way.

They scurry across the floor and dart into the far office. Sam lifts her off the floor, but Kath needs no help. She yanks herself away from Sam, flies up on the desk, onto the chair and leaps for the window like a high jumper leaping to get over the bar. She slides through the opening – until her ass gets stuck in the window.

Sam stares at her peach-shaped bottom wrapped in black denim, amazed at a sight he hasn't seen up close in two years. He wonders if he has permission to touch, but when he hears the shoes in the hallway behind him, he seizes both cheeks and pushes her the rest of the way through, tosses her backpack out next and then dives out himself, head first.

Sam rolls across the asphalt like a paratrooper and pops to his feet, grabs the backpack, grabs Kath's hand and yanks them into a dash for the hole in the fence.

A warehouse door bangs open behind them.

"Stop! Or we'll shoot!"

They get to the fence as an explosion rips the blackberry bushes next to them. Kath ducks and runs through the hole, with Sam right behind. They tear through the grass, down across the railroad tracks, while the two faceless men behind them scream and give chase. Sam and Kath reach another fence and Sam throws the backpack over.

"Don't throw them, you'll ruin them!" Kath yells.

Sam rips off his jacket and throws it so it lands on the barbed wire on top. He climbs and throws his leg over, reaches down and grabs Kath's hand and pulls her up so easy it's like he's pulling a fish out of the water.

She gets half her body over the fence when one of the guards reaches them and grabs her foot. He's not a cop, but he's dressed in blue pants and a white shirt with a shiny gold badge on the front pocket. Kath grabs the top of the fence with both hands and tries to tumble over, but the barbed wire slices her left palm open because she's only got a glove on her right hand.

Sam spots the other guard, back by the railroad tracks. He's too overweight to chase them, but Sam sees a glint of metal in his hand. He's the one shooting, and he's moving closer. Sam tumbles over and tries to pull Kath with him.

Kath hangs halfway over the fence with her head upside down, but she can't shake off the guard pulling on her leg. The guard lets go with one hand and grips the fence for balance, and when she spots his fingers looping through a square in the cyclone fence and she bites hard on his knuckle. He screams and lets her go. She tumbles the rest of the way over, pulling Sam's jacket off with her.

She lands on Sam, knocking him to the ground. He pulls them both up, she grabs the backpack, and they run. Sam and Kath must run across railroad tracks, but a slow-moving train is coming.

"I can't make it!"

"You have to!"

The fat guard gets to the cyclone fence, aims through a space and pops off three more shots, which zing by Kath's head. It gooses her speed, and she and Sam dart in front of the rumbling train. The light blinds their vision and the horn blasts out their hearing. They get across the rails in time, but the front edge of the train catches a tiny edge of Kath's boot heel, which sends her spinning like a kid's toy top. She collides with Sam and takes him down. They lie on the gravel of the railway embankment and stare up at the stars and the bright line of jets lining up above them. The mile-long train rumbles on past, six feet from their heads. They gasp, catching their breath.

Sam lifts his head and looks at the length of the train.

"I've got a Ford Fiesta parked five hundred yards south of here," Sam gasps. "But let's lie here for another ten seconds."

Kath gasps for air and nods.

CHAPTER FIFTEEN

A foghorn blasts. Sam and Kath lean against the hood of the blue Ford Fiesta, which he parked on the steep part of Bryant Street, right under the massive cement and steel superstructure of the Bay Bridge. There's a dirt slope with broken bottles and debris that leads up to the bridge on one side of the street, and darkened warehouses on the other, but in front of them they can see the lights of Red's Java House on empty Pier 30 down below. The Bay Bridge above them stretches across the water to the twinkling lights of Oakland.

Sam places large Band-Aids, alcohol, and Neosporin out on a towel on the hood of the car, and gets to work on Kath's hand.

"Good thing there's an all-night Walgreens," Sam says, and then pours alcohol on the wound. Kath winces and inhales through her teeth. Sam dabs the cut dry with the corner of the towel, adds a spot of Neosporin and then stretches a large Band-Aid across her palm. She flexes her fingers, but the bandage stays in place. She pulls her leather jacket tight around her and shivers.

"You want to get back in the car?" Sam asks.

"I hate that car. Fiestas are junk."

"They're anonymous. That's why Paul got it for us."

"They give me the creeps. Bad memories."

"You hate Chevy vans, you hate Ford Fiestas. Why? It's just the getaway car."

She looks at her hand, then at the bridge, avoiding the question. She asks one instead.

"Why'd you come back for me?" Kath asks.

"You would have done the same for me," Sam answers.

"No, I wouldn't have. I already told you that."

"Maybe I just want you to admit I'm not such a bad guy after all," Sam says.

Kath looks at the twinkling lights across the water so she doesn't have to look at him.

"Why don't you leave town? Paul will be after you if you stay here."

"I'd ask for a transfer to another city, but it'd break my parole officer's heart," Sam says. They stay quiet for a moment. Sam can hear the dull roar of the cars streaming onto the Bay Bridge far above them.

"Something is keeping you here. Why else would you go through all this?" she asks, and looks him in the eyes, waiting for an answer.

"Not something. But maybe someone."

Sam leans forward to kiss her. Kath lets his lips come within a half inch of hers, and then pulls away. She puts her hand on his chest. "Back off, Romeo."

"Why?"

"Because I don't date losers."

"Yet here you are with one, all the same."

"And I wish I were anywhere else in the world but here."

"We all wish for a lot of things."

"True. But wishes never come true," Kath says, with a sad defeat in her voice.

"It's the wishing that matters, not whether they come true or not," Sam says.

"That's the dumbest thing I've ever heard," Kath says, trying hard to make him hate her.

"Is it?" Sam asks, and he reaches into his inside jacket pocket and pulls out the two Lazzaroni cookie wrappers from the restaurant. He rolls each up each tissue into a cylinder and places them on the asphalt in front of them. He reaches into his other pocket and pulls out a book of matches.

"A wish is just a spark of hope. Can you still make a wish? Or is there no more spark left in you?" he asks.

Kath stares at him as if deciding whether to insult him or play along. She finally blinks and nods. "Okay, I have my wish."

"That one's yours, this one's mine," he says, nodding at the two cylinders of paper on the ground in front of them. Sam kneels, strikes a match and lights the top of each paper.

Each cylinder lights up with a blue flame that descends in a ring down the cylinder of paper, illuminating the green Lazzaroni printing as it blackens. When the flame reaches the bottom, the burning cylinders rise off the ground and float into the sky. They touch ten yards up, their red lights go out, and the embers float away on the salty breeze.

"What did you wish for?" Kath asks.

"I can't say. If I did say, it'd be a lie anyway."

"Why is that?"

"If you tell the truth about your wishes they never come true."

Sam stares at her without blinking. She stares back. He leans in for a kiss –

"Let's celebrate!" she says, pulling away. She opens the car door and hops into the passenger seat.

"You couldn't keep up with me," Sam says. He opens the driver's door, slides behind the wheel and starts up the Fiesta.

Sam bangs a U-turn and heads through the South of Market neighborhood. In two minutes, they find the Hotel Utah, which has a bar that hosts a live band. It then takes them twenty minutes to find parking, which they finally do, six blocks away.

"'It's better to be lucky than good,' as my mother used to say," Sam says as he parallel parks his tiny toy car. Within ten minutes they get past the security guard, order drinks and are listening to Stark Naked and the Car Thieves thrash their country-punk music on the tiny stage in the corner.

Kath doesn't wait for the drink Sam is ordering. She hits the dance floor and pogos in the minuscule mosh pit with four other punks to the song *I Ain't Gettin' Any*. Kath is thinking three things – she's thrilled she got away with most of the LCD monitors intact, she's terrified that Sam is going to hit on her again, and she hopes that if she dances all night, she can exhaust him into giving up.

Meanwhile, Sam is thinking three things as well – he's thrilled he got away with most of the LCD monitors intact, he hopes he gets lucky with some girl soon, because two years without sex is too long for any man under eighty, and he'd love to have a real drink.

"Jack and Coke, please," he tells the bartender, and pays his two dollars and takes a long sip of the sugary alcohol. A lonely barfly sits on the corner chair and stares at the six dancers pile-driving up and down in front of the screaming band. Sam can see him focusing on Kath, one of only two girls in the mosh pit. He's a young blond guy with acne scars and muscles, cauliflower ears and he's missing a front tooth, which tells Sam everything – he's bad with girls, he's angry about it, and he makes up for it by getting into fights. He met plenty of dim bulbs like him in prison.

"That bitch can dance. Is she yours?" the barfly asks, confirming Sam's assessment.

"She's here with me, if that's what you mean."

"Damn, that bitch is hot, you lucky SOB. Do you nail that ass on a regular basis?"

"Nope."

"How about I take her from you then? Let me borrow her for a few hours? I could teach her a lesson for you," the barfly says, then points at Sam and slaps the bar, laughing hard at his own hysterical joke.

"She needs it, let me tell you!" Sam says, laughing even louder. He laughs so loud he must gasp for air and slaps the barfly on the back. He trips and almost yanks the barfly off his stool but pulls himself up by yanking on the barfly's lapels instead. "Sorry, dude. How about I buy you a drink first? Then you can hit on her." Sam says.

"Now you're talking! Buy me another vodka and grapefruit and give me your woman!"

"Bartender! A vodka grapefruit for my new friend and bring us a bottle of champagne! On ice! With three glasses! He's stealing my woman!" Sam holds up a credit card.

The bartender is an older guy with a paunch and grey hair who's been working four nights a week at the Hotel Utah for a dozen years, and the dull stare he gives Sam proves he hates the Saturday night crowd the most. He prepares Sam's beverage request.

"Thanks, pal. You're all right. I may not kick your ass now," the barfly says.

The barkeep plops the drink down on the bar, sending a small wave of sour alcohol spilling out the top and onto the wood. He then smashes an ice bucket down on the wooden bar with a bottle of Veuve Clicquot inside. "There you go, boys. The best we got."

Sam hands the bartender a credit card, then pours three glasses of champagne and holds up a glass of bubbly for Kath to see.

Kath spots his offer at the peak of her pogo leap, ponders it as she slows, and then moves towards the bar. She figures free champagne is too good to pass up, even coming from Sam. She did feel that tingle up her spine when he was swinging that ladder around like a baseball bat, but she won't allow that tingle of attraction to turn into a fully flowing electrical charge. One sip is all she'll allow herself, just to be polite. Maybe two, but that will be it.

Kath dances over and takes the glass from Sam. They clink flutes and sip.

"I'm going to nail you," the barfly says, grinning at Kath. "He said so."

"Not too hard, okay, superstar?" Kath whispers, which makes the barfly blink. Kath shoots Sam an evil look as she tilts her head back and swallows the whole glass. Sam slaps his new companion on the back. "Drink, my friend, drink! You deserve this!" he says, and pushes the full glass towards his new friend, gesturing him to sip.

The bartender returns and puts the bill down in front of Sam. "That'll be 49.33, Frank."

The barfly's eyes widen in almost tearful friendship. "Frank? My name's Frank too!" he says, and he's so excited he grabs the bill and the credit card and reads it. "Frank Ryan? That's so weird, my name is Frank Ryan too! Let me show you!"

The barfly goes into his pocket for his wallet and feels nothing. He's scared as he pats his jacket pockets, and then confused as he checks his pant pockets, and then angry as he realizes what Sam has done to him.

Sam holds out a glass of champagne to him and smiles. "Who just taught who a lesson?" he asks. "But you can still try to kick my ass if you want to."

Frank hits Sam in the face, but Sam ducks the punch enough that it's a glancing blow off the cheekbone. Sam kicks a barstool onto the floor and pushes Frank so he tumbles backward over it. As Frank falls, Sam grabs his heels and flips him onto his head. The Hotel Utah has a cement floor and the loud bonk of Frank's cranium bouncing off it makes everyone in the bar stop, including Stark Naked and the Car Thieves.

"Am I bleeding?" Frank asks, lying on the floor, touching his head everywhere.

"Nope. You're fine," says the bartender, with a tone that betrays that he wishes Frank's head was more of a melon and less of a bowling ball.

Kath grabs the bottle of champagne from the bucket just as a security guy plows into Sam from the right while Frank Ryan pops up and plows into him from the left. They careen around the small bar like three pinballs with flailing arms and hands, their punches barely connecting while they collide with all the tables and chairs.

"Want to give me a hand here?" Sam asks Kath.

"You look like you're doing fine," Kath answers as she sips champagne from the bottle while backing toward the door.

The three men collide again, but now Frank is as mad at the security guard as he is at Sam and swings hard at him instead. They grab each other's throats. Sam ducks under them like he's playing London Bridge, and rushes out the door.

He and Kath run down the street. Sam reaches out and grabs her hand. Kath laughs, her voice echoing off the wet pavement. They run across traffic and blend into a crowd of people outside an underground nightclub. They move into the people and pause to catch their breath. Everyone around them is also in black jeans and black leather, and they find a brick wall against which they can lean.

Kath takes one more swig of champagne and offers it to Sam, who tilts his head back and chugs it too fast, and fizz shoots up his nose. Kath laughs as he coughs and wipes his mouth, and Sam grins and hands the bottle back. The bruise on his face where Frank Ryan punched him has swollen up to the size of a golf ball, making his boyish grin even more lopsided.

"I think we've had enough." Sam puts the half-full bottle on the sidewalk.

The crowd of youngsters surrounding them eye them but don't approach, like a circling school of curious fish. Indie rock blasts from the second floor above, and the doorman behind the red velvet rope lets in only four people at a time.

Sam and Kath smile at each other, not sure what to do next.

Sam wonders if he should try to kiss her.

Kath wonders if she should let him, if he tries again. All memory of her promise to herself to resist him has been wiped clean by the bubbly alcohol.

Sam leans in, and Kath stops him with a hand on his chest. "I don't trust you."

"That's okay. I don't trust you either."

"But you are cute."

"What should we do about that?" Sam asks, and flashes his crooked grin.

"I think we should call it a night," Kath says, and pulls him away from the crowd.

They meander down the street, hands in their pockets, not daring to hold hands again but bumping shoulders occasionally instead. They find their way back to the Ford Fiesta, but as they get closer, they see the front passenger door is open, and two short legs are sticking out.

Sam leaves Kath four steps back and sidles up to the open door. A small African American kid has popped off the ignition cover and is trying to hotwire the car.

"Finding everything you need?" Sam asks.

"Leave me alone," the kid mutters.

"Forget it, kid, we still need the car for a couple more hours," Sam says, shaking the keys loud enough for the kid to hear, then yanks him out of the car by his heels. The kid's butt hits the pavement right on his tailbone, and he rolls over and moans. Sam reaches in and pulls out the hammer, screwdrivers and wire strippers the kid left on the front seat and dumps them on the pavement next to him.

"What's your name?" Sam asks.

"Muhammad Ali," the kid says, rubbing the back of his jeans.

"What are you trying to steal a car for? You're a baby."

"Because I'm hungry, that's why."

"You want to eat a Ford Fiesta? You must be pretty hungry."

"You people aren't cops, fuck off," Muhammad says, and gets to his feet and walks away.

"Hang on a second," Sam says, and pulls out his wallet and hands the kid a twenty-dollar bill, but when Muhammad reaches for it, Sam pulls the bill away. "You want me to tell you what you were doing wrong?"

The kid nods. Sam hands him the twenty, and then pulls out the yellow plastic dishwashing gloves he used in the robbery and hands them to the kid. "First off, wear these, otherwise you'll get shocked. On this car, you should have just banged the flat head screwdriver into the ignition and twisted it. That usually works, and it's the fastest way to go."

"Okay," the kid says.

"If that doesn't work, you use the Phillips to undo the panel and expose the wires. On a Ford Fiesta, you'll see red lines and brown lines going into the ignition cylinder. The red lines are the electrical power for the lights and the radio, which you need. The brown wires run to the starter, which gets the engine going. You want to bypass that ignition cylinder, because you don't have a key, right? Cut the red power wires first, strip the ends, then touch them together to get power to the system without needing a key to complete the circuit," Sam says, and holds up the key. "You can then twist them together if you're wearing the rubber gloves. Then you can cover them with cheap black electrical tape. Got it?"

"Got it," says the kid.

"Then you cut the brown wires, strip the ends, and just lightly touch them to each other, and the car should start. You do need gloves for that because that jolt can hurt. But you don't have to twist them together, because the car is now running. Just like you don't have to keep turning the key in the ignition. But you do have to tape off the ends. Want to try?" Sam asks.

"Are you serious?" the kid asks.

"If you do it in less than two minutes, I'll give you something worth a lot more than twenty bucks, Mr. Muhammad Ali."

Muhammad shrugs and nods. Sam looks at his watch, then at Muhammad…and points for him to go. Muhammad picks his tools off the ground and climbs back in the car.

"Why are you doing this?" Kath says, walking close.

"You got something better to do? If you want to go, I'll give you taxi fare."

Kath doesn't have anything better to do, and Sam's odd behavior is intriguing enough that it sends another light shiver up her spine.

The car roars to life, and Muhammad comes out, proud and grinning.

"One minute, fifty seconds," Sam says.

"What do I get?" Muhammad asks.

"Another two twenty-dollar bills, along with my professional assessment," Sam says, and holds up two bills for Muhammad to see. When Muhammad reaches for the money, Sam pulls it back.

The kid rolls his eyes. "This is jack."

"You can listen to instructions, understand them, and then quickly implement them, which means you have a high IQ. Crime, however, does not pay, especially for young black men. If you stay in this line of work, you will be in prison in less than five years. If you stay in prison for more than two years, your life will be ruined. Or, I can take you to my parole officer and he can place you in a work/study program. The kind of program that I ignored when I was your age. He's a religious zealot, so he really would try to help you."

"I'll take my chances, chump," Muhammad says. He grabs the bills and runs.

Sam watches him run around a corner. "You think I made a difference?"

"I think you made it worse," Kath says.

Sam's face falls with regret. "How do you figure that?"

"You make people *pay* for advice, you don't pay *them*. Otherwise, it has no value."

Sam blinks at this nugget of wisdom, then nods and stares at his feet. "That makes sense," he mutters. He sticks his hands in his jacket pockets and shrugs, trying to warm himself up in the cool fog.

Kath looks at this man, so smart and capable, and wonders how he got here. He's smart and he has good intentions, yet he makes dumb mistakes. Maybe he was born in the wrong place and then started down the wrong path. Maybe he made a few wrong turns at key moments. Now he's here, stuck on this one-way street in cold San

Francisco at three in the morning. Then she realizes that's it's her own story that she's pondering…but it may be his story too.

"I wish we still had that champagne," he says.

"I've got champagne back at my place."

Sam turns to her and they share a smile. He moves close, shuffling inch by inch, waiting for her to stop him. She doesn't. He leans down and kisses her, and she kisses him back.

CHAPTER SIXTEEN

Kath lives in a small one-bedroom apartment on the bottom floor of a pink clapboard duplex on 29th Street, just below Diamond Street. It's one of the steepest blocks in The City, with a 30% grade. When you're walking the block, it's smart to turn around halfway up and walk backward the rest of the way, just to give your thighs a break.

Sam makes sure he curbs the wheels of the Fiesta and yanks hard on the parking brake, so the tiny car doesn't roll down the hill and smash into St. Paul's on Church Street. He and Kath push their doors closed and then lean against each other as they cross sideways against the steep street, like tipsy mountain goats. They reach level ground when their feet touch the first pink painted cement step that leads up to her door. They give each other a victory kiss.

She's on the ground floor while the landlady, Mrs. Sanchez, has a door that opens to a narrow, steep staircase that goes up to a bigger living space above. Kath unlocks her door and they tumble inside, still kissing.

Kath pulls away and shuts the door. "Put on some music," Kath says, and pushes him down onto the black leather couch. Sam spies a turntable with some records leaning against the brown coffee table, and picks out George Benson's *Breezin'*, lays it on the platter and drops the needle into the groove for the first track. Kath digs through her refrigerator and finds a half-finished bottle of Perrier Jouet and pours half-flat champagne into two plastic breakfast glasses.

"You really do like champagne," Sam says, standing up and taking the cup from her. They clink plastic and then down their beverages, then move close and slow dance, pasting themselves against each other. They kiss long and hard, and Kath pulls away again.

"I'll go get ready," she whispers in his ear, then bites his earlobe a little too hard before stumbling into the bedroom and slamming and locking the door behind her.

Kath's bedroom is a monster rat's nest. She darts around picking up piles of dirty clothes and flings them into an already full closet, and pushes hard to get the door closed, cracking the painted plywood. She finds a dirty dish on her writing desk, scrapes the food with a fork into the bubbling ten-gallon fish tank by the window and sticks the dish and fork inside a drawer. She finds air freshener and gives the canister a long squeeze, ensuring the destruction of a cubic meter of ozone. She takes off her leather jacket, yanks off her turtleneck and throws them both over a chair, getting down to just her bra. She rifles through her underwear drawer and finds a negligee and lays it against her upper body and looks in the mirror. She is lean and muscular, but when she sees her messy hair and the freckles on her upper arms, she exhales, disgusted with herself.

Sam goes into the kitchen and splashes water on his face. He wets a dish towel and wipes under his pits, trying to mop up the terror sweats he's got flowing. He spots his reflection in the dark window over the kitchen sink. "You can do this, Sammy," he whispers, then exhales slowly. He cups his hand over his mouth and tests his breath and finds it gross enough that he picks a lemon out of her fruit bowl, cuts it open, squeezes some into his mouth, rinses, puckers, and spits into the sink.

Back in the bedroom, Kath pulls on a white t-shirt instead and lays across her bed – a waterbed, and she rocks gently on the waves. She coughs, then gets up, opens the door a crack and lies back down, sending another ripple undulating through the water.

Sam pushes open the door and comes in. He's still wearing all his clothes, even his leather jacket. He stares at Kath, lying on her bed wearing just a white t-shirt and black panties.

"Wow. You look great."

"Thanks. I don't know about you, but I think you should take your clothes off."

Sam sits on the edge of the waterbed and kicks off his shoes. He leans forward and kisses her, and she wraps her arms around his neck and pulls him close. The waves bob them up and down so much their lips barely connect, smearing Kath's lipstick across both their faces. He rolls on top of her, crushing her arm until she yelps.

"I haven't done this in two years, you know."

Kath pulls herself out from under him and rolls on top instead. "That's okay. You relax."

Kath pins down his arms and kisses him. It's working. Sam's excitement grows and he kisses her back. He smashes his mouth against hers, until their teeth bang against each other, making her wince, and then he grabs her butt cheeks too hard, making her yelp in pain again.

That ends it. He rolls out from under her and retreats to his starting position sitting on the edge of the bed. Kath sits up and leans against her headboard.

"Is it me?" she asks.

"No. I shut this part of myself off for such a long time that I don't know how to flip the switch back on again," he says and reaches for his shoes.

Kath comes from behind and breathes in his ear and rubs his chest and back. She wraps a leg around him and slides her heel between his legs and gently rubs back and forth. She smiles.

"It seems to me that your switch works just fine."

Sam comes alive. They collapse back on the bed. Kath giggles as he straddles her. She reaches up and unbuttons his shirt and his belt buckle, while he struggles to get off his tight leather jacket. He tosses out all the contents of his pockets – the yellow dishwashing gloves, the marbles, the alligator clips, the pen flashlight, and then tries to yank off the jacket, but it gets caught on his thick arms. Kath has his shirt and pants open and she touches his hard six pack abs, tracing the outline between the muscles with her fingers.

"You have a fantastic body," she says, grabbing his butt cheeks now.

Sam yanks both the jacket and shirt off over his head, and he holds his clothes aloft and twirls them, triumphant. They both laugh as he tosses them onto the bed.

And a gunshot rings out. Sam falls on top of Kath, hugging her.

"Are you okay?" he asks.

"What was that? Did someone follow us?" she asks, until she notices they are sinking into a growing pool of water.

"That was the gun Paul gave me. I forgot it was in my side pocket," Sam says.

"You shot my bed!" Kath screams.

They leap up, but their weight tears a longer rip in the plastic. A wave of water flows out from below too, since the bullet tore through the top and then exited out the bottom, leaving two holes. They sweep away rugs and clothes and furniture, but they can't move fast enough. Over two hundred gallons of water rush across her floor, into her living room, soaking the hardwood floors.

Kath runs into the living room and opens the front door, and the wave of water flows over her two pink cement steps and down steep 29th street towards St. Paul's Church. Kath stands on her stoop, then looks down at the flowing water covering her cold shivering feet.

"I'm sorry," Sam says. "You must really think I'm an idiot now."

She points at her feet and the stream of water flowing across them, then points inside the apartment, and then points at Sam. Her mouth is open as if she was screaming, but nothing comes out. She's like the child who falls so hard on the playground but can't even cry yet, and Sam is the anxious parent waiting for the wail that proves that she's alright – but it never comes.

Sam wishes she'd punch him or insult him again, but she stays silent.

The water subsides. She, too, wishes she could dig up the anger and disdain that she had for him just twelve hours ago, and throw it in his face, but she can't. Instead, she sits down on the wet cement step…and finally cries.

CHAPTER SEVENTEEN

The morning sun shines through the sheer white curtains hanging in the front bay windows. Everything above the floorboard is still damp from the water surge that flowed through the apartment. Kath is asleep on the black leather couch, while Sam sleeps curled up in the futon chair with the round wicker frame. Damp towels are piled up by the front door along with a broom. They spent an hour pushing water out the front door and then mopping up the remaining dampness until exhaustion overtook them.

Kath opens her eyes and glances at her watch. It's 9 a.m. She sees him asleep, and eases off the couch and into the bedroom. She closes the door behind her, locks it, and then finds his wet jacket at the bottom of the wooden waterbed frame. She manages to slide out his wallet without touching the gun, then sets the jacket back down.

Inside the wallet, she finds an expired driver's license, a parolee card, cash, and then a photo of a beautiful young woman with red hair and green eyes. On the back of the photo is a woman's handwriting: *Your gypsy for life. Love, Rose.* In another slot, she finds a photo of a younger Sam posing outside with a red-haired boy in a baseball uniform, and both wear baseball gloves. On the back is written: *Carl's 5th Birthday.* There's one more photo of the three of them together wearing red sweaters, the kind of photo you get done for Christmas. They look happy.

Back in the living room, Sam opens one eye and sees that Kath is in the bedroom. He touches his shirt as if hoping to find his jacket, and he knows immediately what Kath is doing, and decides to do the same thing. He darts over to a chest of drawers and a bookcase against the wall. She has a lot of self-help books: *I'm Okay, You're Okay, The*

Games People Play, The Prophet, and *The Road Less Traveled.* He opens a drawer and finds a pile of stickers and decals from all 50 states, plus famous U.S. landmarks, like the Grand Canyon, Yosemite, Yellowstone, and Mt. Rushmore. Under that pile is another pile of roadmaps from different regions in the United States.

He closes that drawer and opens the one below it and finds a much neater pile of old photos of a girl. Sam picks one up. The girl is Kath, he realizes, and she's about eleven. She wears bell bottom jeans, platform shoes, and a purple tube top, and she's posing in front a green AMC Gremlin parked on the rugged Oregon Coast. He turns the card over and there's a girl's handwriting on the back – *1972 AMC Gremlin, Cannon Beach.*

In another photo, she's posing with an older woman with the same wavy dark hair and the same smile as Kath. It must be her mother. They are wearing matching yellow summer dresses with black sunglasses in front of a Ford conversion van in Death Valley, next to a big outdoor thermometer that reads 110 degrees. There's a tall man with them, with dark hair and a big thick mustache. He's wearing a camouflage t-shirt and looks mean. Sam turns the photo over and reads the back. *1973 Chevy Van, Death Valley with Jim the Jackass.*

In another photo, Kath and her mother pose in front of a gunmetal grey Cadillac in the parking lot of Disneyland. They are dressed in blue jeans and white button-down shirts tied in the middle, and they both have red bandanas in their hair. The man with them this time is older and has thin greying hair, with a pot belly hanging over blue polyester slacks. Sam turns the photo over and reads the back. *1970 Cadillac Sedan de Ville, Disneyland, with Pete the Perv.*

Sam leafs through the dozens of photos, all of them showing Kath and her mom on different road trips in different cars at different American destinations, all with different men, and young Kath cataloging the cars while despising the men who owned them.

He hears rustling from the bedroom, closes the drawer and eases back into the weird round futon chair, just as Kath exits the ruined bedroom with his jacket on her arm.

"Careful, there's a loaded gun inside," she says as she hands it to him.

He takes the wet jacket and puts his finger through the bullet hole in the breast pocket. He slides it on and moves his shoulders. The damp leather smells like sour milk.

"I had a good time last night," he says.

"It was just the champagne talking," Kath says. "I shouldn't have had any."

"I'm sorry about your bed. And your place."

"I'm glad, actually. It's good that things didn't go any farther."

"You can take whatever you need from my cut to pay for the mess I made," Sam says, then walks out the front door, leaving Kath to survey her ruined home.

Sam crosses steep 29th Street and sees a familiar Lincoln Town Car parked behind the ugly blue Ford Fiesta. The driver's window lowers and Dozer sticks his head out. Cliff sits in the passenger seat. Both men still wear their 49er jerseys.

"Did you score?" Dozer asks him. "You look like you slept in the tub."

Sam doesn't answer him. He gets in the Fiesta, releases the parking brake, backs his wheels off the curb and coasts down the hill.

CHAPTER EIGHTEEN

Sam swings open the door to Room 222 in the beautiful Taj Mahal Hotel on Turk Street, and finds Hal Weinstein sitting on his sagging bed with the fraying pink bedspread. Hal wears the same brown slacks, white short-sleeved shirt, and brown tie. His brown yarmulke is still pinned to the thinning brown hair he combed over his bald dome. Hal stares at the Magic Massage unit bolted to the wall, then looks up at Sam.

"Does this thing work?" Hal asks.

"Not really. You drop a quarter in and the mattress shakes for less than a minute. My neighbor threatens to kill me whenever I turn it on," Sam says.

Hal pushes the glasses back up on his nose and moves around the room. He checks under the mattress, opens the drawers of the tiny desk and bureau, and opens the closet door. Sam's old clothes hang inside.

"Finding everything you need?" Sam asks.

"Not yet," Hal answers.

Sam goes to the windowsill where he keeps a bottle of bourbon and two shot glasses. He pours two drinks and hands one to Hal, who shakes his head.

"It's ten in the morning. The day just started."

"Mine just ended. I was working all night cleaning up water damage in a warehouse down in the China Basin Building. Their fire alarms went off."

Hal stops and looks up at him. "What's the name of the company?" he asks, pulling out a pen and a tiny pad of paper from his breast pocket.

"Bayside Remediation. I worked there three days this week. Call them."

"I will," Hal says, and writes it down on a pad and slips the pad back in his breast pocket, along with his pen.

Sam sips his bourbon. "You like snooping in people's closets?"

"I'm always trying to establish an accurate picture of the parolee," Hal says. He walks close and examines the clothes Sam is wearing. He runs his hand down the jacket's front lapel.   "Your jacket is wet."

"Like I said, water damage clean-up. I dropped my jacket in it by accident."

Hal runs his hands down the lapel and sees the bullet hole in the breast pocket. He touches the hole and raises his eyebrows at Sam.

"Cigarette burn. I bought it second hand."

Hal takes a step back, crosses his arms and eyes him top to bottom. This diminutive brown and white parole officer can make Sam's heart race with one sideways look.

"You stagger in here at 9 a.m., looking like an *ekidik balagan*. You're up to something."

"Make your calls, Hal," Sam says, and then opens a drawer and pulls out a business card and hands it to him with the name of the company on it. "Ask for Dwight. He hires me."

Sam is smart enough to prepare an alibi before every burglary. He bribed Dwight at Bayside Remediation to say he'd been working there, and even coached him on how to answer the phone in case Hal or anyone called. What is pure luck, however, enough for Sam to think his lucky streak is still going, is that he'd picked someone at a remediation company to bribe, which is the perfect excuse for his overall dampness.

Hal takes the card and snaps the white edge with his thumbnail. "How did you get the job?" Hal asks.

"I went through every want ad and found nothing. Then I just started walking. I saw these guys drying wet rugs out on Pier 32, and I walked out and asked if they needed help. They said to call every day, and when they had a job that needed an extra guy, they'd hire me. That's how I met Dwight," Sam says, then holds up his drink. "Do you mind? I just got off work, I've had my cocktail and now I need to sleep."

"Do I need to check the bathroom?" Hal asks.

"Check it if you want," Sam says and collapses on his bed.

Hal stares at him, then narrows his eyes and walks out. "See you in a few days!" Hal shouts as he slams the door.

Sam jumps off the bed and goes into the bathroom. He pulls open the plastic curtain across the tub and reveals the sharkskin suit he bought, along with his nice silk patterned shirts and slacks, all hanging on the rod. He then checks behind the toilet and pulls out a wad of money that he had taped behind the bowl.

He sits on the edge of the tub and sighs. He slides back into the tub and closes his eyes, relieved that he's safe and the long day is finally over – so relieved that he falls asleep within seconds with his head against the hard porcelain and the wad of money against his chest.

CHAPTER NINETEEN

Kath pulls her jean jacket tight and lifts an old brown suitcase up the stairs and through the glass doors into the Mission Bay Health Club. The *Grand Opening* banner hangs up high in the tall atrium. The windows are clean, and there's a new carpet and new paint smell. Dozer sits behind the high, white counter.

"Hey, Kath! We're open, what do you think?"

Kath looks around. There's a dance exercise room with hardwood floors and mirrors, and inside there's a Jane Fonda workout happening with a dozen men and women dressed in tight shiny spandex with colored bandanas tied around their foreheads.

"I don't get it," she says.

"Neither do I, but look at them," Dozer says, and gestures at the people on the workout machines and stationary bikes and in the exercise room. "Paul is a smart guy and he can spot a trend a long time before anyone else does. Maybe he's right about this one."

"Is he around?" Kath asks.

"Yeah, but Inge's giving him a treatment. I wouldn't risk going back there," he says, and nods at the long white hallway that leads to his office.

Kath heads down the hall anyway. When she gets close to Paul's office, she can hear muffled cries and moaning. She leans close and listens. Are they having sex? Is he whipping her? Is she whipping him? She then realizes she doesn't give a damn and knocks as loud as she can.

Inge yanks the door open and stands in the door frame, panting, with beads of sweat running down her face. She's wearing her Mr. Clean white t-shirt and white jeans, but all the perspiration is making her clothes a little too see-through for Kath, and she tilts her head back so she can keep eye-to-eye contact instead of nipple-to-eye contact with the Norwegian Amazon.

"Is Paul here?" she asks.

Inge allows Kath to enter the room with her suitcase. In the middle of the room is a flat piece of wood with wooden slats and leather straps that looks like a cross between a massage table and a medieval torture rack. Paul is strapped down in the middle of it, wearing just navy-blue bikini underwear, and he's drenched in sweat too. Inge kisses him long and hard on the mouth, and then undoes the straps holding down his waist, ankles, and wrists.

"Inge was just working on my spine." Paul steps off his torture rack and grabs the towel that Inge offers him. "Thank you, Inge, that will be all for now."

Inge growls at Kath as she leaves the room. Kath smiles and waves as she goes.

"I can see the hair on her back through her t-shirt, she's sweating so much," Kath says.

"Don't be mean," Paul says.

"You make a cute couple. You suit each other."

"Of course, she loves me to death," Paul says. "But something's missing."

"Like the ability to speak?"

"If I want snide conversation, I can always talk to you." Paul takes his time putting on a terrycloth robe, making sure to show off his only somewhat defined muscles and abs.

He thinks he looks better than he does, which is why he lingers as he slides on his robe like a narcissistic idiot., Kath thinks to herself. He's still short, and Sam has a much better body, Kath starts to think — she then drives that thought from her mind.

She puts the suitcase on the floor in front of Paul, then backs away, like a supplicant delivering an offering to the king. Paul grins, unzips it and pulls out sixty thin boxes of the LCD monitors.

"Where are the rest? They were supposed to leave two cases for you," he says.

"We encountered some problems. No one left any cases out."

"I'm not impressed," Paul says, and motions for her to follow him. They leave his torture room and walk back down the white hallway.

"Neither am I. You didn't hold up your end of the bargain at all. You said the alarm system would be off, but it wasn't. You said the goods would be left out, but they weren't. You said no guards would show up, but they did," Kath says, following close behind.

They get to the main workout area and another male employee in a white t-shirt and white jeans hands him a mango protein smoothie, then pushes open the glass doors for him. Paul and Kath step out onto the balcony overlooking the rusting red rail cars and the blue San Francisco Bay in the distance.

"It was supposed to be a sham, and it wasn't."

"Relax. They were in on it too. It added realism, for Sam's sake," Paul says, and sips.

"They shot at us. I almost bit one guy's fingers off," Kath says. "This is too dangerous, we have to call it quits."

She also wants to scream that he's a lying sack of shit, but she knows that he's enough of a psychopath that she'd regret it. Most of all, she just wants out of the agreement they made, and the best way to do that is to use all her verbal skills to push him right to the edge.

"The bullets didn't hit you, did they? I 'm telling you, they were in on it," Paul says, and glares at her with an eyeball stare that insists that she not dare contradict him again. "What I'm more concerned about is the rest of the case of display monitors I already paid for on this 'inside' job."

"So now I owe you for your mistake? Fine, take it out of my cut, I don't care," Kath says. "You're going to deny your fuck-up no matter what I say, so it's safer for me just to walk away."

Paul starts to micro-shake. His face and hands tremble almost imperceptibly, but enough for Kath to know she's getting to him. She loves it.

"Don't blow up, Napoleon. People can see you through your big glass windows. You'll look bad in front of your slaves."

Paul grins a big fake smile. "Take it out of your cut? You did such a bad job, I may not pay either of you anything," Paul says. He sips his smoothie and puts it down on the metal railing of the balcony.

"Fine. I'll tell Sam that you decided to *short* us. That you don't *measure up*…"

"Leave, before I throw you over this railing."

Kath turns to go. "Fine. The deal is off."

Paul grabs her wrist. She can see from his crazed eyes that he's fighting to control his rage. They stand frozen, staring at each other, until the cold breeze from the Bay raises goosebumps on her skin. With his free hand, Paul reaches into the pocket of his robe and pulls out an envelope, and then turns her wrist hard and slaps the thick envelope into her palm. It's full of cash. "That's all of it, paid in full," Paul says. "You can't use your sour tongue to get out of arrangement. Not this time."

Kath wants to rub her sore wrist, but she sniffs back a tear and counts the money instead.

"Thank you," she says, suddenly realizing she needs the money.

"You're welcome. And the money is not the real issue. What's more important is what happened between you and Sam."

Kath puts the money in her jacket and shrugs. "I tried everything. Clingy lingerie, perfume, dancing, champagne. Nothing worked."

"What's his problem? Is he gay?" Paul asks.

"I don't know, but I have an idea."

"Yeah? What is it?" Paul asks, with true curiosity. Kath realizes he has already forgotten about his strange cruelty to her just a moment before, which makes her despise him more.

"He's still in love with Rose," Kath says.

"So? He's a guy, he still needs to get his rocks off," Paul says, gesturing at Kath's body like it's the most convenient receptacle for that male requirement.

"Not all men are like you, Paul." She means it as an insult but Paul nods, taking it both as truth and a compliment.

"Did he tell you he was in love with her?" Paul asks.

"No, but he keeps a picture of her in his wallet. And when a woman gets rejected, she hopes it's because there's another woman, and it's not because of her."

Paul grins. "You like him a little. I knew it. Keep trying. Trust me, he likes you."

She bites her lip. Now it's Paul who has Kath on edge, and he's pushing her, which she doesn't like. "I'm the one with him, not you. I can tell, nothing is going to happen."

Paul moves close. The wind blows Kath's hair across her eyes and Paul pulls it away, then he smiles and touches the breast pocket of her jean jacket and feels the envelope in the pocket underneath. "Then *make* something happen."

"I don't want to go through another heist with him. It's too much," Kath says.

"Then don't. These heists are just an excuse to force you two together. Just make him love you and find out what he did with the $500,000 and your job is done, no risk necessary. It's all up to you, sweetheart," Paul says.

He picks up his smoothie off the railing and gestures that Kath can go. She does.

CHAPTER TWENTY

The next day, Kath puts on a yellow dress and a straw hat and hops on a Caltrans commuter train going south and visits Bella at the Meadow Song Retirement Community. After a slice of cinnamon toast, Bella gets dressed up in her best pink polyester pantsuit, puts on a floppy hat, and they borrow a golf cart from the gardener and zip across the street to watch the afternoon horses at the Bay Meadows race track. Both women wear dark sunglasses and carry purses full of cold hard cash.

They head to the paddock and relax on white bleachers in the shade under oak trees. Kath reads the racing forms while Bella checks out the jockeys and their horses circling the paddock.

Bella likes pink; she wins big with pink, and she goes for any jockey and horse that wears pink, be it polka dots, solids or stripes. Kath goes for the odds. She likes a horse with 7 to 1 odds or below and always bets that horse to show, which is a decent payoff for a horse landing in either first, second or third, without a big upfront risk.

The gals have a great time. Bella uses her age to sneak them into the Thoroughbred Club where they seize the sweetest spot in the grandstand. They pay for their beers and hot dogs with big bills and leave big tips, so no one cares. It turns out that both of their systems work, and each of them turns five hundred dollars into a thousand. They're in a fantastic mood when they cross the parking lot and head back upstairs.

Kath swings open the door to Aunt Bella's tiny apartment, and in the middle of the small kitchen table is a huge bouquet of flowers.

"Aunt Bella! Someone sent you flowers!"

"Again? They're from my secret admirer," Bella says as she takes off her hat and glasses and sticks her winnings in her ceramic Winnie the Pooh cookie jar.

"Since when do you have a secret admirer who sends you flowers?" Kath asks.

"I can't say. That's why he's a secret."

The bouquet is pink roses and tulips, which proves to Kath that this admirer knows Bella well. Kath reads the attached card while Bella puts the kettle on for tea. "'To the most amazing creature on Earth.' He sounds like he's quite a catch," Kath says, snapping the little card in her hand.

"He's very romantic. A little too romantic, if you know what I mean," Bella says.

Kath corners her great aunt in the kitchen as she plops bags of mint tea into two mugs. "This Meadow Song place is pretty racy," Kath says. "Maybe I should move in."

Bella pulls the whistling kettle off the burner and pours the hot water for the mint tea. "First, you tell me all about your man. The one you work with," Bella says.

"He can't be trusted."

"What else is new? That's true about all men," Bella says, waving her hand.

"I don't tolerate lying. We don't have to live that way anymore," Kath says.

Bella hands her the brown mug of mint tea, then crooks her finger, beckoning Kath to lean close to listen. "Don't be too picky. You're only young once, darling, trust me."

CHAPTER TWENTY-ONE

The Hall of Justice on Bryant Street is the law enforcement guts of The City. Superior Court is on the ground floor along with Traffic Court, and the main headquarters of the San Francisco Police Department ramble everywhere else in the building, which is the size of a city block.

Police detectives are on the fifth floor, which is where Detective Alden Stone sits. His desk is in the third row of ten desks each, right in the middle, and he's a good cop who works harder than the rest. He is six feet tall with sandy brown hair and he is in decent shape. He's stressed, however, all because of his new computer. All the detectives must use them now, and if the captain wants him to use it, he's going to use it, damn it.

Originally from Boston and a family of cops, he moved west ten years ago with his wife and ten-year-old son and joined the SFPD, where he moved up to detective within five years. He also gave up his love of the Red Sox and adopted the Giants instead (which he never dares admit to his East Coast buddies), but the Giants aren't destined to win a World Series until 2010, thirty years from now. In the meantime, he likes his job, loves his family and sometimes goes to watch baseball in blustery Candlestick Park, even sneaking away for an afternoon game with Hal Weinstein, a parole agent on the third floor who likes the national pastime as much as he does.

Stone pecks at his computer console, wishing he could just bang out the report on his old IBM electric typewriter instead. The computer screen is black, and the letters are green, and he gets lost when he tabs too far and enters data in the wrong panel, or cell, or whatever the computer consultant calls it. He wishes he was outside watching a game or investigating a burglary.

His boss, Captain Han Yee, a middle-aged officer with twenty-five years on the force, wanders through the maze of desks, pulls up a chair and sits down. "Captain Han" oversees all the detectives and runs a tight ship. The lean and lanky captain is also one of the best tennis players in The City, dominating the public courts in Golden Gate Park at least four times a week. He leans back and exhales, until Stone finally looks up.

"Sorry, Captain Han. I get lost in this stuff."

"Everyone's behind. When we have a real database, everything will go faster," he says.

"Yes sir," Stone says, but he lets doubt seep into his voice.

"Did you look at that South San Francisco warehouse robbery?"

"But isn't that San Mateo County?"

"Chief thinks we should take the lead. It keeps good relations."

Stone smiles and opens a drawer. He pulls out a plastic bag, and inside is a woman's brown leather glove. "This is all we got. It's Italian, top of the line. Only sold at the San Francisco Macy's, nowhere else, so the woman probably lives in The City and went south for the job. We got a fingerprint from the warehouse, and we're beginning to cross-reference it with the computer files, but the database isn't fully built so it will still be a while."

"Anything on the male?" Captain Han asks.

"Nothing except for the description the two guards gave us. Stocky guy, brown hair, good athlete. He's built like a halfback, but he scaled and flew over that cyclone fence like a kid."

"I have to tell the Chief something more than that the female burglar bought gloves at Macy's," Han says.

"If these two are pros, then her print is going to come up. And they'll probably try another robbery. If they're as sloppy as they were on this one, we'll catch them," Stone says.

CHAPTER TWENTY-TWO

S am stands on the corner of Divisadero and Geary Street, waiting for Cliff and Dozer to drive up in their Lincoln Town Car. His leather jacket is dry, but it doesn't look so new anymore. The leather is cracking, and the bullet hole in the breast pocket makes it look cheap, but it's the warmest jacket he's got. It's the middle of June, the month when the rest of the country is heating up, which means San Francisco is beginning to plunge into a wet, blustery cold.

He's early, which gives him time to think. He feels like he's in a burning house with one window that's still open, and he must dive through it to escape. Paul is the fire who wants half a million dollars. Sam is holding those flames in check, but Paul can flare up at any moment and burn him. Rose is his escape window; when she shows up, so Sam can dive through to safety. That's when he'll get a parole transfer from Hal and move to another town. But Rose has gone missing, and now Sam is committing crimes for Paul, and Hal is getting suspicious. His escape window is closing, and one slip up could trap him inside where the fire will consume him.

Then there's Kath, who is a complete distraction from what he must accomplish. They have a weird attraction/repulsion thing going on, which is tough to figure out while planning a heist, while also trying to find Rose. It's too hard on the brain.

Prison was easy compared to this, he thinks. Then he remembers what prison was really like, and he changes his mind. Enduring ten times this madness is better than going back to prison.

Sam spots the Lincoln coming up Geary Boulevard and waves. Dozer pulls over into the bus zone, and Sam hops in the back. Dozer re-enters the flow of traffic heading towards the ocean. Cliff points at a black duffel bag on the rear passenger seat next to Sam.

"That's everything you asked for," Cliff says. "You must have something big planned."

Sam unzips the bag and goes through the contents. There are electronic supplies, a small vacuum, a blow torch, duct tape, marbles, zip ties, and more. Sam zips it back up.

"I also need a getaway car parked for me in front of this address," Sam says and hands Cliff an index card with an address on it. "Nothing flashy. Leave the key on the front left tire, under the wheel well."

Cliff and Dozer look at each and smirk, evidence they don't think much of him.

"Anything else, superstar?" Dozer asks, looking in the rearview mirror at Sam.

"Yeah, I need a thousand dollars."

"Don't you already owe Paul five hundred times that?" Cliff says. "What for?"

"Expenses. Paul's job is to give me what I need and to cover expenses."

"Paul isn't going to like this," Cliff says, peeling off ten Ben Franklins from a wad of cash he pulls out of his front pocket. He hands it over like he's doing Sam a favor.

"Pull over here," Sam says and grabs the cash. Sam opens the passenger door while the car is still pulling into the bus zone at Geary and Arguello Street. He jumps out with the duffel bag, slams the door without a goodbye, heaves the bag on his shoulder and walks away. Cliff and Dozer honk, wanting him to turn around, but Sam ignores them.

Across the street at the Coronet Theater, *The Empire Strikes Back* is playing. He knows Cliff and Dozer will be trailing him all day if he doesn't do something, so he dashes across the four lanes of traffic on Geary Boulevard, pays his $2.00 matinee price and goes inside. He watches the spaceships and the aliens go at it for a minute, then sneaks out the back door.

He jumps on a 38 Geary bus heading back downtown.

He rides it all the way to the end of Market Street near the Ferry Building, then walks to Pier 30 and heads to Red's Java Hut and buys himself a hot dog. He hasn't had a dog since his first morning out of prison, down at Doggie Diner by the zoo, and he got a hankering for another one when he was leaning against the Ford Fiesta with Kath the other night. He spotted the Java Hut lit up on the dark pier, and decided he'd go there when he got the chance.

Now it's noon on a crisp late spring day, the warm sun is breaking through that marine layer, and he's got his hot dog, his black coffee, and he's sitting at the picnic table listening to the seagulls squawking overhead as the ferries cruise by on their way to Oakland and Larkspur.

Simple pleasures, he thinks to himself. It's nice to have your heart set on something, and then make it happen. He remembers being eight years old and wanting to buy a Blackberry Soda. Saving 35 cents and then buying one at Davy Jones' Liquor Locker on Taraval Street was the highlight of his summer. Life was easier then.

Sam is halfway through his second bite when Kath appears, interrupting his reverie. She drops an envelope in front of him and crosses her arms. She wears dark glasses, except for a jean jacket, and a Raiders baseball cap.

That makes sense, Sam thinks. She's got to be the rebel.

Sam opens the envelope and checks out the thick wad of cash. "Water damage wasn't so bad, huh?" Sam asks.

"Bad enough," she answers. "It'll smell like wet wool for a long time, thank you."

"How's your hand?" he asks, and Kath answers by holding up her palm and revealing a thin red line where the cut is healing.

"Are you going to tell me your plan?" Kath asks.

"To buy another hot dog maybe. Want one?"

"I meant for your job."

"Oh yes! For that, I'm going to need to take you shopping for clothes. Interested?"

Kath's eyes widen behind her sunglasses, but she keeps her lips pursed. "Sure," she says.

Sam waves down a taxi, and they find their way to a chic boutique on Post Street, near Jones, called Clairo. Kath walks into the long narrow boutique, which sells wrap dresses and circle skirts and mermaid gowns, along with the jackets with padded shoulders and the oversized shirt dresses that are hip in 1980. She heads straight to the rack of expensive dresses against the wall, and rifles through them. Kath finds a blue and white striped dress with a mermaid silhouette. Sam watches as she holds the dress against herself and gazes into a mirror.

"I thought you'd pick from these dresses over here," Sam says, pointing to the discount rack on the other side of the boutique.

"I can pick out my own clothes, thank you."

"But I'm dressing you for a job. You have to look a certain way."

"You want me to look sophisticated, right?" Kath asks, then pushes him into a man chair close to the dressing room. Sam falls back against the leather back with a plop.

"Fine. Just make sure you can move and run in it, in case we're being chased. You tend to get yourself into those situations," Sam says, and when Kath glares at him, he shrugs.

Kath puts the mermaid dress back and grabs a Marilyn Monroe *Seven Year Itch* circle dress in light purple with tiny pink polka dots.

The young hip blonde shop girl with the big earrings steps forward. "I'll open a dressing room for you," she says. She's been watching their interaction since Kath walked in, hanging back and waiting to swoop in and help close the sale. "Don't step into it. Put it on from the top and pull it down, it'll go on easier," she whispers.

Kath winks at her as she opens the first dressing room door.

Kath strips down to her bra and panties and holds the dress up against her body. She sighs. It's going to be a tight fit. She puts it over her head, gets the straps adjusted, exhales and tugs it down over her hips. She opens the dressing room door, and when Kath turns her back, the gal zips her up. They are two women who don't know each other but they are working in tandem to get Kath the dress she wants. Kath turns back around and looks at her with a question in her eyes: *Am I hot in this?* The shop girl nods and smiles.

Sam sits in his man chair and stares at his feet, bored. Kath steps out of the dressing room and coughs gently, and when he looks up, she smiles and swings the skirt for him. He freezes and stares at her long smooth bare legs, tighter waist and high bosom, all created by the magic of a perfect fitting dress. He mutters something.

Kath turns to the shop girl. "I think that means we'll take it."

CHAPTER TWENTY-THREE

Five hours later, Kath is back in her little house with the pink cement stairs and the musty smell of wet wood. She's got fans blowing on the hardwood floors and the baseboards, and every piece of furniture is moved away from the walls, to help dry the place out.

She searches through her water-damaged shoes and finds a box with a pair of pink pumps that still look new, plus they fit. She puts on a lapis lazuli necklace and bracelet and her mother's thin Cartier watch. It's a knockoff, but a damn good one.

She checks herself in the mirror. She goes to touch her hair and then stops. She looks great. She should just dip herself in amber and preserve how she looks right now, she thinks. She's thirty years old, she's smart, in great shape, and she's got style. Five years ago, she was a naive kid with big hair and bad taste who liked disco. Five years from now she may be fighting hard to hold on to what she's got now. She's peaking, and she knows it.

She wonders who she's trying to impress. The men in her life? Or just herself? Because the men in her life sure don't seem to be moving up in the world. But Sam did buy her a chic dress. And he did save her ass the other night. And everybody can have an accident. Then again, Sam may be accident prone.

A long honk outside makes her break her gaze with herself.

She steps outside and finds a black limousine in the street, with its nose pointed up the steep hill. Sam stands by the open back passenger door, looking handsome, trim, and sophisticated in a blue pinstripe suit. Her opinion of him goes up a notch. As she moves closer, he hands her a rose and helps her into the back seat. Tick – he goes up another notch.

He slides in beside her, closes the door, taps on the glass, and the chauffeur drives on. Ray Charles plays on the tape deck, as Sam pours two glasses of champagne.

"What do you think?" Sam asks.

"I prefer Cadillac limos to Lincolns, but this one is nice."

"What's your favorite car anyway?" Sam asks, handing her a glass.

"A convertible Porsche. A '64 blue Roadster would be perfect for me."

"Duly noted," Sam says, finishing pouring his glass. They clink glasses and sip.

Kath makes sure it's a tiny sip. Champagne and Sam are not a good combo.

"You haven't said what the job is. I'm not quite dressed for a break-in," she says.

"We're going to a party. The limo just gets us there," Sam says.

The limo driver heads south of Market Street, turns down narrow Bluxome Alley and stops by Marjorie McKale's art gallery. The heavy metal door is propped open, and music flows out of the second-floor windows. Sam and Kath fall in line behind two older art patrons walking up the steep wooden steps. "Just go with the flow," he whispers.

They stop at the top of the stairs. Five people mill around the bright abstract paintings on the white panel walls, the bronze statues on pedestals and the serving tables filled with hors-d'oeuvres. Track lighting creates pools of light that people move through, and the lights of The City and the Bay Bridge twinkle outside the arched windows.

Gallery owner Marjorie McKale wears a loose copper-colored silk dress with a plunging V-neck and a matching silk scarf and silk headband in her short hair, like a flapper from the 20s. She even has a long black cigarette holder to complete her look.

She spots Sam and smiles as she walks over, and then frowns as she sees Kath.

"You're late," Marjorie says.

"No, I'm not. You told me 7 p.m. It's 6:45," Sam says.

"And I didn't say you could bring someone," Marjorie says.

"I'll pay her from what you pay me," Sam says. "And you want them loose, right? They'll buy more if they drink more, and people will drink more if she's serving. Makes it better for everyone," Sam says, and he flashes his tilted grin.

Marjorie eyes Kath from head to toe as if she were a lousy painting she had to sell, then waves her hand at Sam. "It's an open bar, but no tip jar. That's tacky. And add plenty of ice," Marjorie says, then exhales smoke in his face, spins on her heel, and stalks off.

Kath's Italian blood goes from cold to a hot simmer as she watches the older woman walk away. She then glares at Sam, wanting to punch him.

"You'll get the last laugh," Sam says.

Ten minutes later, Sam is behind the bar with his jacket off and his sleeves rolled up, slinging drinks for the dozens of people who are coming into the party. He's making the hard drinks while Kath carries a tray of wine glasses through the party.

Sam hands a gin and tonic with a twist of lime to a puffy man in a velvet tuxedo jacket. "Here you go, sir, enjoy your evening," Sam says. The man sips as if Sam were invisible.

Kath returns with a tray full of empty wine glasses, then moves behind the bar and stacks them in the sink while Sam fills clean glasses with Cabernet. "I can't believe I put on a five-hundred-dollar dress to be a cocktail waitress," she says.

"It'll be worth it, trust me," Sam says, as he slides the last full glass onto her tray. Kath sighs with disdain, then picks up the tray and walks away. As she goes, Sam stops to sigh with admiration, watching how good Kath looks from behind in the expensive dress he bought for her.

Kath offers a glass of wine to a woman in a pink pantsuit chatting with two friends as they admire a bronze statue. She takes the glass from Kath's tray without a glance at her.

Marjorie stands with two women and their husbands admiring the painting of the purple woman with the green nipples giving birth to the rainbow-colored baby. Kath offers them wine, which they all take without acknowledging her either.

Kath likes this anonymity. Being so close and yet so invisible allows her to stare at the women's jewelry and the men's wrist watches without suspicion. She wonders what Sam has planned. There's plenty of money in this room.

Marjorie pinches Kath on the arm, making her jump. Marjorie raises her eyebrows at her and nods at four men laughing two paintings down.

"Make sure you serve them, I'll go talk to them in a few minutes," Marjorie says, then turns her back on her.

Kath assesses the four men before walking over. Three of them are young men in their late twenties, wearing the preppy uniform that is becoming popular in 1980 – penny loafers with no socks, LL Bean pants, and Brooks Brothers button down shirts under blue blazers. An older preppy man with tortoiseshell glasses and thinning blond hair holds court over the three younger men. They are all similar except the older man can't button his blazer over his paunch. Kath reaches the group as the older man finishes his story.

"...and he asked me, 'Julian Schnabel? Isn't he a tailor on Montgomery Street?"

The three sycophants all laugh on cue. Kath holds out the tray to them all.

"What about you, darling? Do you have an opinion about the newcomer, Mr. Schnabel?"

"I wouldn't know," Kath says, and holds out the tray. All four men take a glass, leaving her tray empty.

"Of course, you wouldn't. What about this painting? Any opinion?" the aging preppy asks, and gestures to the painting behind him, an abstract painting that is different streaks of red from top to bottom, in one big block.

"It's very red," Kath says, deciding to state the obvious.

"A stunning critique, my dear. You should write it up for *Idiot Savant Art Review*. I'm sure they'd publish it," the man says, and his three courtiers laugh.

"Why are you making fun of me?" Kath asks.

"Darling, I'd never make fun of you! Do you like Monet?" he asks.

"Money?" Kath asks back. "Are you asking me if I like money?"

All four men start laughing and the paunchy man with the thinning hair laughs the loudest. "Darling, your face is as red as the painting. What's the matter?" he asks.

Kath smiles, turns, and walks back to the bar and plops her empty tray in front of Sam. "Whatever you have planned better happen soon, or I'm going to kill somebody."

"Robbing them will make you feel a lot better," Sam says.

As Sam loads more wine onto Kath's tray, Marjorie sweeps back to the bar and lifts a glass and sips. "I just sold a worthless piece of shit, thank you very much!" she says.

"We are running out of champagne," Sam says.

"That's impossible," Marjorie coughs.

"People are drinking, just like you asked," Sam says. "There's a liquor store four blocks down. People are drunk enough that I could just buy some Korbel at this point."

"You can't leave," Marjorie says.

"You promised me a ten-minute break every hour," Sam says.

"Then go get some and hurry back, I must tend to my sheep." Marjorie says, then walks over to the four preppy men and gestures at the red painting behind them.

Sam takes two still full champagne bottles and empties them into the sink.

"It's happening soon," Sam says. "And when it does, it will happen fast."

Kath hears him, but she's also watching Marjorie working the four preps, especially the older one who likes to humiliate people. Marjorie keeps gesturing at the big red painting, hoping for a sale, but the older guy just shrugs. But then he whispers in her ear, and Marjorie laughs, and they both look back at Kath and the prep points at her.

Kath knows what's up. For Marjorie to close him, Kath must be part of the deal.

When she turns back to Sam to complain that the evening is about to become a lot more complicated, Sam finishes filling ten glasses of champagne and puts out a card: *Gone to get more champagne, back in ten minutes.*

"You can't leave now," Kath says.

"I won't be gone long. In five minutes, go to the bedroom in the back corner of the loft, and open the window to the fire escape. I'll be outside waiting," Sam says. He wipes down every counter and every glass and everything either of them touched.

"Then what?" Kath asks.

"I stay busy in the locked bedroom, while you come back out here. Just make sure to keep Marjorie and all the guests tanked up and away from that back bedroom. When I'm finished, I'll come back up here with a few more bottles of champagne, as I promised, then grab you and we leave," Sam says. "She won't notice that we're gone for thirty minutes and won't think to go into her bedroom for an hour. By then we'll be long gone. Got it?"

Before Kath can express her worry about Marjorie and the rude preppy guy, Sam darts down the stairs and is gone. Kath looks at her watch, and then at Mr. Prep, who is still eyeing her. She hopes she can dodge him for five minutes.

Sam runs over to the blue dumpster in the alley and pushes it under the fire escape below Marjorie's loft. Sam opens the dumpster top and pulls out the black canvas duffel bag that Cliff and Dozer gave him, puts it on like a backpack and vaults onto the dumpster. He jumps and reaches the bottom ladder of the fire escape, yanks it down, and climbs to the second-floor landing outside the bedroom window, then pulls up the ladder behind him.

He catches his breath, pulls his favorite yellow dishwashing gloves out of the black canvas bag, pulls them on, wipes down all the metal railings he touched, then glances at his watch. No one saw him and he's outside the window with a minute to spare…and he waits.

Kath eases through the party, avoiding Marjorie who is closing a sale with a small group of Japanese businessmen. She passes the open bathroom door, then finds the bedroom six yards down a dark hallway. She slips inside and moves toward the window –

and the light pops on. It's the old preppy with the paunch and the thin blond hair standing by the light switch.

"I didn't catch your name," he says.

"Barbara. I didn't catch yours," she says.

"Fredrick Constantine Hauser," he says. "Marjorie would be livid if she knew you were in her bedroom, Barbara."

"I was looking for the bathroom," Kath says.

"You passed the open bathroom door as you came in here," Frederick says, and then lies down on Marjorie's white ash bed with the black silk comforter. "This is not a good situation for you, Barbara, but I want to help you. I like finding solutions to problems that benefit everyone."

Kath doesn't dare glance at the window.

Outside, Sam hears voices inside the bedroom, but a curtain blocks his view.

Frederick leans back against the headboard in just the perfect spot so that the track lighting illuminates the red bald spot on the top of his skull. "See if you can follow this, Barbara. Marjorie wants to sell me a painting. I want to buy it. You say you like money, and I want to give you some of mine. Marjorie and I have already talked, and she agrees that the serving wench would be a wonderful add-on to close this deal. So, can we all help each other?" he asks, then leans back and unzips his pants and undoes his belt buckle.

Kath stares at this big balding bag of dog poo stuffed into tight clothes. Why doesn't he wear socks? It's not like his pasty ankles with gross tiny black hairs is somehow more attractive than black cotton.

He raises his eyebrows at her, which makes Kath feel like she just drank spoiled milk. Why are some men such pigs? And why do the worst pigs seek her out? There was the endless parade of slime balls who disappointed her mother. Then she caught the same slime ball bug, it seems, and she ended up with a jerk like Paul. And now this clown is making his power move on her. What makes them pick her to be their play toy to abuse? Is it the way she dresses? The way she walks? The way she smells? All she wants to do is run away.

"You can take off that silly outfit for a start. What do you say?" Frederick asks.

Except Kath is stunning in this dress, and she knows it; in fact, that's why Frederick is insulting her outfit, so he can make her doubt her confidence. Sam bought her the dress precisely because she looked so good in it. In fact, Sam is the only guy she can remember who didn't try to make her feel bad about herself. He teases her sometimes, but she also can tell he's got a real crush on her, and not some weird macho desire to dominate her.

"Hello, Barbara? What's the delay here?" Frederick asks.

Kath smiles. In one instant, she sees a beautiful solution to her problem with Frederick, which will also give her and Sam the time they need to accomplish whatever Sam has planned. She gets on the bed, crawls up to Frederick and kisses him on the lips.

"Do you like martinis, Frederick?" she asks in a whisper.

"I love them," he says, but blinks, betraying his nervousness at her new boldness.

"Get comfortable while I get us two ice cold ones, with one olive each, shaken, not stirred," she says, making sure she slides her hand across his crotch as she gets off the bed. "We can discuss price over drinks."

Kath blows a kiss and closes the door behind her, then heads into the party. She spots Marjorie, still with the Japanese businessmen. Kath steps behind the counter and starts making a martini. Marjorie walks over.

"Refill those men's drinks, they're having whiskey straight," Marjorie tells her.

"I want the money you owe us now," Kath says as she grabs the martini shaker and fills it with ice.

"I beg your pardon? How dare you even speak to me like that," Marjorie says, glaring as she chews on her cigarette holder.

Kath pours the gin into the shaker, then adds a spoonful of vermouth to the top.

"Let me break it down for you, just like Frederick did for me. You want him to buy that shitty red painting, which costs ten thousand dollars. I saw the price when that paunchy prick was humiliating me," Kath says, and starts shaking the shaker. "Frederick told you that he'd buy it, but he wants me to be part of the sale, and you agreed. So, if you want to sell him the painting, you'll pay me the money owed for both the bar service and for servicing Frederick, then leave me alone in that bedroom for one hour," Kath says.

"Frederick should pay you for your professional services, not me," Marjorie says, eyeing her up and down like she has a disease.

Kath wags her finger. "Sorry, boss lady. You must pay what's due. Let's say one thousand, all in. Otherwise, I go back into that bedroom and bite his dick off." Kath puts the martini shaker and two glasses onto a tray, and drops an olive into each glass, then smiles at Marjorie and rubs her hands together. "Just think of that ten thousand," Kath says, and holds out her palm.

A tiny smile bends up Marjorie's razor straight lips – a begrudging respect for a worthy adversary. Marjorie's small gold purse hangs from a long chain over her shoulder, and she snaps it open and pulls out ten hundred-dollar bills and lays them in Kath's hand. "You have an hour, and if I don't get that sale, I get this money back," Marjorie says.

Kath slides the cash into a small pocket on the side of her dress, picks up the tray with the martinis and heads back towards the bedroom.

She just bought herself an hour. She hopes that's enough time.

CHAPTER TWENTY-FOUR

S am sits on the fire escape outside Marjorie's bedroom window and stares at his watch. He's supposed to be halfway through this job by now, and he's not even through the window. He can hear someone in the bedroom. It sounds like a man humming.

He wishes he had a way to communicate with Kath. He imagines a pager-like device, like a phone, but one that allowed you just to write a short message. The numbers on a phone also have letters, which means you could write a short amount of text and send it. It could even have a visible screen, like the ones he and Kath just stole the other night, but smaller. He could write a short note, and then send her that message, just like you would to a pager, and she could read it and then write something back. No conversation, just some info about what's going on. That would be perfect for this situation. The technology couldn't be that complicated, he thinks. It could even go with a portable phone. Maybe he should find an engineer to help him work on it.

He looks at his watch. He'll give this job another five minutes – and then he hears Kath's muffled voice from inside the bedroom. He can't understand what she's saying, but he knows it's her.

Kath pushes the door open with her foot. "Hello, Professor," she sings.

"Professor? I like that," Frederick says as he sits up. Kath slides the tray onto the sheets, and then climbs onto the bed and straddles him. He inhales and grabs Kath's bum cheeks as Kath gives the martinis another long shake.

"I think a martini is perfect foreplay, don't you?" she says, shaking her torso as much as the shaker. She opens the martini top and pours two martinis into the two glasses sitting on the nightstand. She brings a cold glass close to his lips.

"Doctor wants you to open up, Professor," she coos. He does, and she slowly pours the whole cold biting cocktail into his mouth, filling it until it overflows down his cheeks. "Swallow, swallow, swallow if you want me," she whispers, and he gulps the drink down, and she follows one martini right away with the other.

Frederick can't keep up with the swallowing as the second drink spills out the sides of his mouth. He fights to sit up. "Slow down, hang on," he sputters.

Kath yanks hard on his unfastened belt, pulling out the leather strap from his pant loops so fast that it cracks like a whip. Frederick's eyes bug open, and he grabs his chest.

"That's right, baby, you're in over your head," Kath whispers and pushes him back down so hard his body bounces an inch off the mattress. Kath kisses him hard, jamming her tongue down his throat. She then reaches between her legs and into his pants and squeezes his erection. Frederick groans and his eyes roll back inside his head. Then, faster and smoother than a Las Vegas dealer shuffling a deck of cards, Kath loops his belt through the wood slats of the headboard, grabs his wrists, jams them together and pushes them into the belt loop and pulls the leather taut. As Frederick opens his mouth to speak, Kath jams the napkin inside.

"Be good now, and the doctor will make you feel better. Okay, Professor?" she asks.

Frederick shakes his head and tries to spit out the napkin, but it's jammed too far down his throat. Kath jumps off the bed and smooths her dress flat. Sam was right, she needs a dress she could move around in, and this one is doing the trick. She pulls aside the curtain and undoes the latch and lifts the window.

Sam hands her the black duffel bag, steps through the window into the room and sees Frederick with his wrists tied to the headboard, fighting for air on the bed. He's kicking his legs in the air and thrashing from side to side, trying to get free. His face turns from red to purple.

"What the hell did you do to him?" Sam asks.

"I kissed him. He couldn't handle it."

Sam opens the black duffel bag and pulls out a long white cord. Kath stands on the bed and steps on Frederick's shins, drawing from him a long, muffled scream. Sam ties his feet together and then ties the other end of the cord through the wood at the base of the bed, stretching him out flat. Sam checks the belt loop holding his wrists to the headboard and decides that Kath did a good enough job. Frederick can't slip out.

Sam stares at Frederick's inflated purple face. "I've never seen a face that color before."

Frederick gurgles and gestures with his eyes towards his jacket. Kath searches his inside breast pocket and finds a bottle of pills. She shakes the bottle in his face. "You need these, Professor?" she asks, and he nods vigorously.

Kath pops open the top, pulls the napkin out of his mouth, places two pills onto his tongue and slowly pours the watery remnants from the shaker into his mouth. He groans his gratitude as his eyes roll back. Kath and Sam step back and trade nervous glances.

The pills must work fast because his skin color turns from purple to pink within two minutes. His eyes pop open, and anger floods his face again.

"Help!" he shouts, but Kath dives on top of him and gets the napkin back across his open mouth before he can get the second word out.

"Oh baby, that's it! That's the spot, oh my God, keep going!" Kath shouts, as she and Sam yank Frederick's head up and tie the napkin behind his neck, gagging him. He groans as loud as he can, but Kath groans right along with him, disguising his anger as mutual passion.

Frederick shakes his head and pulls at his straps, but there's no escape.

Kath looks at her watch. "You have about forty-five minutes."

"I won't need that long," Sam says, and opens the sliding closet door, revealing the safe inside. "This is a Herring-Hall-Marvin, about 40 years old."

"Does that mean it's easy to open?"

"It means it's easy to cut. This thing will melt like butter," and he makes a cutting motion with his yellow-gloved right hand.

Sam unzips the duffel bag and pulls out four hand towels and hands them to Kath. "Put each of these under each corner," he says, and then pushes hard on the safe. As he gets one corner off the floor, Kath slides a towel under the claw foot. After putting towels under all four corners, Sam squeezes into the closet. He gets behind the safe, gets his back against the brick wall and pushes. He only moves the steel box a few inches, but there's now enough space for Sam to squat down, secure his back against the brick wall and get his feet on the metal back of that big boy. He pushes with his thick legs like a powerlifter, and the safe slides across the hardwood floor into the middle of the room.

Sam and Kath kneel behind the safe, leaving Frederick groaning on the bed. Sam digs latex gloves out of the duffel bag and hands them to Kath. "Put these on, and then wipe down everything you touched," Sam says, holding out another hand towel.

While Sam unloads all his equipment, Kath wipes down the glasses, the serving tray, the bed frame, the doorknob, and even Frederick's pill bottle. Frederick glares at her with hatred, and Kath kisses him on the forehead. "I won't tell anybody, Professor. Your tiny little secret is safe with me," she says, and squeezes his crotch through his pants.

Kath kneels next to Sam and all the gear he pulls from his bag. Sam holds up a long metal prod with a bent tip. "This is an electrical welding torch," he says. Next, he holds up a heavy metal vacuum with a canister like a circular bullet holder on an old Tommy Machine Gun from the 1920s. "And this is a vacuum with a charcoal canister to suck up the smoke. And these are goggles," he says, and holds up two sets of goggles with smoked glass to wear.

They each pull goggles onto their foreheads. Sam plugs in the electric welding torch, turns it on, and then tapes a wire from the torch to the metal of the safe. "Your job is to suck off any smoke with that vacuum, but be careful, the metal on the safe is electrified now," he says.

Kath plugs the vacuum into the socket. Sam lowers his goggles over his eyes and nods at Kath, who copies him. Sam snaps the welding torch on, and a blue spark appears, and Kath turns on the power vacuum, and a loud hum fills the room. Sam lays the blue flame against the metal, and a red line appears. Kath holds the vacuum just above the rising smoke, and it gets sucked right into the canister. Within a minute, they've already cut one long line in the metal.

Kath hears a high tune. Where is that coming from? Kath then glances at Sam. He's whistling. Her heart is racing, she's so scared. But Sam? He seems to be having the time of his life. He loves the planning and the details, with all his tools and tricks arranged just right, yet when there's a bump in the action he can roll with it, no problem. He's smart, he's good-looking, he has all the qualities to be a success, he's funny –

– but he's still a lying criminal, Kath reminds herself. Remember that. And remember what Paul wants from him, and from her. Sure, he's good tonight, and sure, he's saved her ass before, but it's his jackass mistakes that made Paul stick them together in the first place.

Sam's already cut three sides of the square hole when there's a knock on the door. Frederick moans louder. "Frederick? Are you in there?" Marjorie asks through the door, shaking the doorknob. Sam and Kath turn off their devices and look at each other with wide eyes.

"Unzip me," she whispers to Sam and turns her back to him. Sam zips down the zipper on the bodice of the circle dress. Kath jumps up, drops the spaghetti straps off her shoulders, exhales and pushes the dress down to the floor. She steps out of it, leaving her wearing just her pink heels and black panties. She darts over to the bed, grabs Frederick's open pants and yanks them and his underwear down to his knees, and then rips his shirt open, leaving him naked from his chest to his thighs. He howls in anger through his gag as Kath then tosses her beautiful dress over his flaccid paunchy nakedness.

The knocking gets louder. Kath steps to the door. She exhales and cracks it open, making sure that her nakedness fills the opening. She catches Marjorie's evil eye and glares right back.

"You said we had an hour," Kath says.

Marjorie stares at Kath's perfect small breasts, then catches herself and peeks past her and sees the half-naked Frederick tied up on her bed, with Kath's dress making a little tent over his groin. He groans at Marjorie, his eyes glancing down at the foot of the bed, where Sam kneels just out of view.

"What's wrong with him?" Marjorie asks.

"He's mad that you interrupted us," Kath says, putting her hand on the door jamb to block Marjorie's view into her bedroom.

Sam holds his breath. It will be a hasty and naked exit if she pushes the door open.

"Why are you wearing plastic gloves?" Marjorie asks, looking at Kath's hand on the door.

"He gave them to me," Kath whispers, nodding over her shoulder at Frederick. "We're playing doctor, and he wants me to give him a prostate exam."

Marjorie furrows her brow as if she's confused, intrigued and disgusted, all at the same time. She shakes her head, exhales, and stares back at Kath. "Your partner is not back yet with the champagne. He's been gone thirty minutes," she says with a teacher's stern voice.

"What, you want me to look for him? I'm a little busy in here," Kath says, and then wiggles her gloved fingers at Marjorie. "Or do you want to take over and finish the exam?"

Marjorie rolls her eyes. "Carry on," she says, and walks away.

Kath closes the door, locks it, and leans her back against it and exhales. When she opens her eyes, both men stare at her in silence – Frederick lying on the bed tied and gagged, and Sam kneeling in front of a ruined safe with an electric welding torch in his hand. Kath feels her nakedness and grabs her dress off Frederick, steps into the middle, yanks it up and gets the straps in place. She tosses the hand towel over Frederick's crotch to hide that most unwelcome hairy sight and kneels back down next to Sam. She snaps her fingers in his face, like a hypnotist ending a spell, and he blinks back to life.

Sam pulls his goggles back over his eyes and sparks the torch back up, and Kath turns the vacuum back on again. Sam lays the torch against the metal and cuts the last line of the square, and the hot metal drops into the safe. Sam turns off the torch, then sticks in his hand and pulls out smoldering stacks of money. Kath tries her best to suck up the smoke pouring off the burning bills.

"The money is burning!" she hisses.

"A little charcoal never hurt anybody," Sam says.

"It's money, not steak on a barbecue. Do something," Kath says.

He grabs another hand towel, sticks in his hand inside the safe, pulls out the blazing hot piece of metal and tosses it onto the floor. He flicks the heat off his burnt fingers, wincing. He then reaches back into the hole and yanks out wads of hundred-dollar bills. "I figured right. Marjorie likes to be paid in cash," Sam says as he shovels the bills into the open black duffel bag.

The fistfuls of cash flying past her face make Kath put down the vacuum and help Sam load the duffel bag, but with the vacuum off, the room begins to fill with the smell of burnt paper from the burning bills still in the safe. Sam zips up the bag, then pushes aside the curtain and steps through the window back onto the fire escape. He waves his hand at Kath. "Come on!"

Kath darts over to Frederick and kisses him on the forehead.

"Do you need another pill, Professor?" she asks, but he just blinks his red-eyed fury at her. The smoke sets the fire alarm off. Bells ring throughout the building.

"Come on, the firemen can help him more than you can now!" Sam yells, and she steps through the window onto the fire escape.

CHAPTER TWENTY-FIVE

The fire alarm blasts a wave of noise down the alley as dozens of people dash out of the building. Sam and Kath lower the bottom ladder of the fire escape, but no one looks up at them. The ringing alarm, in fact, gives them a perfect reason to be using the ladder.

Sam climbs down first with the duffel bag on his back, then looks right up Kath's dress as she comes down the ladder after him. As she dangles from the last rung he grabs her by the waist like she's a leaping ballerina and helps her jump down to the ground.

He tugs her hand and they run down Bluxome Alley, then turn right on 4th Street, and then they keep turning and running down the short tiny streets south of Market Street until they are on yet another short alley with a dead end. The whine of the fire engines fades in the distance, and Marjorie's loft seems a long way away.

Sam walks up to a small purple car and finds the keys on the front left wheel, as requested. He unlocks the car, pops the hatchback, throws the bag in, slams it shut, slides behind the wheel…and notices that Kath is still standing in the middle of the street.

"That's a 1975 Pinto. I'm not getting in that," Kath says.

Sam looks at the odd wedge-shaped car with the sloped hatchback. "I didn't pick it. This is Paul being cheap."

"Well, you should have picked it!"

"I brought you here in a limo. That was the 'date' part of the evening. This is now the 'robbery' part. The getaway car is supposed to be cheap and anonymous, okay?"

"You don't get it! I can never be in a Pinto! Never again!" she shouts.

Kath regrets shouting the moment she does it. She must already seem crazy to him, and she doesn't want to confirm it all by dragging up her boring childhood. She spent years riding around in the backseats of cars like this, speeding across empty American landscapes. Her desperate yammering mom was always in the front seat, throwing herself at yet another loser behind the wheel who was somehow going to change everything for them.

Kath waits. This is the moment, she realizes, when a typical man would scream at her until spittle flew from his mouth, or throw something, or even hit her. That's what Paul would do. That's what her mother endured.

Sam gets out of the car, grabs the black bag from the back, pulls off his rubber gloves and sticks them into his jacket pocket, and heaves the bag onto his shoulder. "Let's find a taxi," Sam says and walks back up the alley towards 4th Street.

Feelings of relief and then worry sweep through Kath. Relief that Sam isn't pressing her, and worry that they'll now get caught because of her.

It's not even midnight yet, so 4th Street is busy. They hear police sirens but see no squad cars, and there are plenty of taxis cruising the South of Market neighborhood looking for club hoppers. Sam hails a red and green Veterans Cab, and he and Kath slide in the back. A Vietnam vet with a long grey ponytail and granny glasses sits behind the wheel. Sam tosses a fifty-dollar bill onto the front seat for the man.

"Take us to the zoo. We're staying at a motel out by the Great Highway," Sam says.

The veteran nods and pulls back out into traffic. Within a minute, they're on the onramp for 280 Freeway heading south. As they rise above The City, Kath spots the flashing red lights from the fire trucks and squad cars that are clogging the narrow streets below. We caused all that madness, she thinks, with a mixture of mischievous pride and adult shame.

Her heart flip-flops in her chest. That was too much of a risk, she thinks. If they got caught, she wouldn't last a day in prison, and Bella would lose her apartment in a minute. She must make Sam reveal his secrets. Sam's a nice guy and Paul's a pig, but she can't keep having these close calls. Hell, she's thirty years old and smart enough to be doing a lot more with her life. She must make a change.

They exit the taxi at the Ocean Park Motel. The fog tastes like salt and is so thick it puts rainbow halos on all the street lamps. Waves crash in the distance. There's no traffic on the street at 11 p.m. on a Saturday night. Sam walks up the stairs to the second floor of the motel, and stops three steps from the landing and starts feeling under the handrail.

"What are you doing?" Kath asks. "Looking for gum?"

"Getting the room key. I wasn't going to take it with me. That wouldn't have been smart," Sam says as he unpeels a room key that he taped there earlier.

Kath is nervous again. There's only one key. Does that mean there's only one bed?

Sam spots her worried look. "The motel was supposed to be for just me. If I was driving the Pinto, we could have counted the money at your place and I would have left you there. But you don't want a taxi driver knowing where you live, right" he asks, and tosses her the key, which she catches in mid-air. "It's room 24. Go make sure it's to your liking."

Kath pushes past him on the stairs, finds the room and opens the door. Despite it being an older motel built in the 1930s, the upper floor rooms are refurbished Art Deco suites with a small kitchenette. At one time this motel was a beach vacation destination long before the neighborhood and the zoo were even here.

Kath flips on the light and walks through the suite while Sam leans against the door. There's a pull-out sofa bed in the living area. The bedroom has a queen size bed and a door that locks. Kath opens the refrigerator and sees that he's stocked it with eggs, bacon, beer, and fruit. There's also a bottle of champagne chilling in the back, but she doesn't let the possibility of drinking it rise too high in her consciousness. She slams the fridge door and spots bread, butter, jam and potato chips on the counter, and a red and white tin of Lazzaroni cookies, the ones with the paper wrappers. She remembers lighting them and the wish she made for Bella.

"I was planning on laying low here for a few days," Sam says. "I already paid in cash."

"It'll do," Kath says, and Sam drops the duffel bag on the floor and shuts the door.

Ten minutes later they each sip beers at the round kitchen table while stacking one-hundred-dollar bills into piles of ten, until they cover the linoleum with piles of cash.

"Eighty-four thousand," Sam says. "That's twenty-eight each for you, me and Shorty."

"Money always stinks. Too many people have touched it," Kath says. She holds up a fat wad of charred bills from their cash barbecue back at Marjorie's loft. They have small burn marks on one side. "What about these?"

"I wouldn't spend them. It raises too many questions," Sam says.

"That was stupid. This is ten thousand bucks, but we can't use it because it's burnt?" Kath slaps the money on the table. Little pieces of burnt money flake off and rise into the air. Kath crosses her arms and scoffs with disgust. Sam sips his beer and then leans back and crosses his arms too, mirroring her.

I'm being a bitch, she thinks to herself. The job is over and done, so she wants the night to be over too, and wishes he was gone. But they're stuck together.

"I wouldn't have burned them if I'd had the time I needed," Sam says.

"I had a little trouble with pushy Frederick, thank you very much," Kath spits back.

"I know, you left me on that balcony for twenty minutes."

"I saved your ass tonight," Kath says.

Sam downs his beer, gets up and throws the dead soldier in the trash. "And I saved your ass on the last job, but I don't rub your face in it," he says. He pops open the Lazzaroni tin and unwraps a cookie. "Just once I'd like to hear you admit that I'm not so bad."

He pops the cookie in his mouth and chews it slowly, staring at her. Then, out of habit and without thinking, he folds the cookie wrapper and slides it into his breast pocket. Kath wonders what his next wish will be, which softens her heart.

Kath gets up and walks over to him. "I admit it. You did a good job. And you were fun to watch," Kath says.

"So were you," Sam says, raising his eyebrows. "But I did get jealous of Fredrick."

"Jealous? I almost killed him," she says, and they both laugh, breaking the tension in the room. Sam takes a step forward. They are inches apart. Sam looks down at her and smiles. He touches her forearm and runs his fingernail along the inside of her arm, and she feels a shiver shoot up her spine to the back of her neck.

"Why are we fighting this so much?" Sam asks.

"Because I still don't trust you," Kath says.

"And I don't trust you either. But maybe a decrease in trust creates an increase in lust," Sam says, and cracks his titled sideways grin.

"You are so lame," she laughs. Sam moves close and pulls her tight to him. She leans her head back and closes her eyes, giving him permission to kiss her. He does.

After a long kiss with just the right amount of moisture and pressure, he pulls away. "There's a bottle of champagne in the fridge," he whispers.

"We don't need champagne," she whispers back, and they crab walk sideways toward the open bedroom door, kissing and pulling at each other's clothes as they go.

Sam falls onto the bed and fumbles out of his pants, kicking his shoes and socks off his feet at the same time. Kath exhales and pulls the dress down past her feet and then drapes it over the back of a chair. Sam rips his tie off, and Kath falls on top of him and yanks his shirt open, sending the buttons flying everywhere. She runs her hands across his muscular chest and inhales with pleasure.

Last time, things went bad for them right at this point, Kath thinks. She's got to keep the party moving. She falls back into his arms and gives him another long kiss. He rolls on top of her, and she feels the hardness between his legs, but she also sees the growing fear in his eyes. She rolls back on top, and almost bangs her head on a metal box attached to the headboard. She stares at the printing on the side.

"Magic Massage? What's that?" she asks.

"I got the same thing in my room in the Tenderloin. It never works."

Kath touches the top, sees the coin drop and reads the side. "Come on, let's try it, it might be fun," she says and kisses him.

He rolls his eyes, but he's smiling. He rips off the rest of his shirt and tosses it aside. He and Kath are in just their underwear now. He scurries to the edge of the bed and finds his pants with his left hand while Kath bear hugs him from behind and nibbles his ear.

"Hold up, I need to find some quarters," Sam says as he digs through his pants pockets. Kath sticks her tongue in his ear and rubs his chest while giggling, and now he's suddenly giggling too, as he turns his pockets inside out.

"Four quarters! Victory!" he says, and they dive back onto the center of the bed. Kath lays herself down in the middle of the mattress, ready to receive the full effect of the Magic Massage. He drops two quarters in and the bed, headboard, and pillows vibrate to life. Kath's eyes widen.

"My God. This is fantastic," Kath whispers, and pulls Sam on top of her. Their bodies slide and slap against each other like two colliding tectonic plates jiggling across the mattress. They yank each other's underwear off while trying to kiss, but their lips are moving targets. He positions himself above her and is about to enter the sacred zone – and the bed stops vibrating.

"Quick! More quarters, don't stop!"

Sam rolls off her, tumbles off the mattress and finds the last two quarters on the floor. He slams them into the coin slot and then dives back onto the bed. The mattress roars back to life, vibrating them like astronauts on a rocket ship who forgot to belt in before blast-off. They collide and slam their lips together. Kath grabs on, wraps her legs around his waist, clamps her hands on his torso, and helps guide his vibrating manhood inside her. She moans as her eyes roll back – and the bed stops vibrating. "That was a less than a minute!" Kath screams.

Sam jumps out of bed and dashes out of the bedroom and into the kitchenette, his erection flopping like a flagpole that broke loose in a windstorm. He finds a knife in the drawer, grabs his shoe and runs back into the bedroom, his unit swinging side to side.

"I love your look!" Kath howls and pointing. Now she can't stop laughing.

Sam glares at the Magic Massage unit and wipes the sweat out of his eyes. He's more intense right now than he ever was during the robbery. He jams the knife into a metal seam on the Magic Massage unit, slams the heel of his shoe against the blunt edge of the knife, and pops the unit open. He stares inside the guts of the machine, which look a lot like the starter unit on a Ford Fiesta. He wraps his hand in a sheet and yanks out the wires. He touches one exposed wire to the metal and then twists the other two together, and the bed roars back to life.

Sam dives back onto the vibrating bed. They reach for each other, like two falling skydivers who find each other while falling in a hurricane. They're getting better at it now, however, and Kath wraps her thighs around Sam's velvet ribs and straps her hands across his engines.

Their lovemaking is wild, deep, and moving. Literally moving, since they start at the top of the mattress and vibrate to the bottom. If they were a painting, it'd be a cubist abstract called *Nudes Vibrating on a Mattress*. They both climax…and laugh.

Sam reaches inside the wall unit and pulls the wires apart. The bed stops, ending the blur. Their shaken eyeballs adjust as their faces come back into focus.

"My wish just came true," he says.

"So did mine," she answers.

She remembers what he said about wishes, and wonders if he's lying.

Sam also remembers what he said about wishes, and wonders if she's lying too.

CHAPTER TWENTY-SIX

Detective Stone stands in Marjorie's bedroom watching a young officer dust the back of the metal safe with a brush, trying to reveal a fingerprint. He brushes the back, the edges, the side, but nothing emerges.

Marjorie sits cross-legged on the side of her bed, dressed in a long caftan with bone clasps down the front, with a long silk ribbon in her hair. She lights a cigarette and tosses her head back and exhales smoky irritation, like a burdened Greta Garbo.

Stone glances at his watch. "It's 11 a.m. This happened twelve hours ago?" he asks.

"Give or take an hour. How are you going to catch them?" she asks.

"It would help if your friend Fredrick would agree to talk to us," he says.

"That's not going to happen," Marjorie says, rolling her eyes.

"Was it just cash in the safe?"

"Yes."

"How much?" he asks.

"That's hard to say," Marjorie says and shrugs.

"Do you remember their names?" Stone asks.

"He was Victor, and she was Barbara, I think. They were just bartenders."

Stone points to all of Sam's gear, still lying on the floor by the window. "They were professional thieves. Very good too."

Marjorie blinks as if realizing something for the first time.

"We've had reports of a man and a woman robbery team working in South San Francisco. They may be the same two people. If you can give our sketch artist a description, then look through a mugshot book, that would sure help."

"You want me to ride in your car and go to your office?" she says.

"Yes, ma'am. It'll take about an hour."

Marjorie looks at Detective Stone, sizing him up from head to toe. "You could interview me here if you like."

"No thank you, ma'am."

She spots the wedding ring on his finger. She shrugs. "Suit yourself. Let's go then."

CHAPTER TWENTY-SEVEN

S am and Kath lie in bed together, entwined in the soft, worn white cotton sheets. The sound of the waves on Ocean Beach and a few cars on the Great Highway drift in through the window, on a stream of Sunday morning sunshine. The smell of coffee fills the suite, along with burnt toast and bacon, Sam's favorite breakfast. Used napkins and dirty plates lay on the bed and the floor.

Sam finishes his last bite of burnt toast covered with blackberry jam, chewing that sweet charred goodness down his throat, followed by the last greasy slice of crisp bacon, and then chasing it with a final sip of black coffee from the mug on the nightstand. He sighs, filled with a bliss he hasn't felt in a long time.

"You know how the lid on a jam jar can be twisted on so tight it won't come off?" he asks. "That's how I felt inside. But not anymore."

"I'm glad I could help get the lid off your jam jar," Kath says. She leans over and rubs her finger on his canine tooth, getting rid of a black piece of charred toast stuck there. "Why do you like burnt toast so much?" she asks.

"I loved making it as a kid, with butter and dark jam. It just tastes good. I'd put it in the toaster three times, which is how long it takes to cook the bacon."

"You cooked it yourself?" she asks. "As a boy, I mean."

"I did. And I ate it myself."

She stares up at his handsome face, marred only by the long thin scar. "How did you get that?" Kath asks, touching his face.

"I fell off my bike when I was a kid. I landed on a broken bottle," Sam says. "My mom wasn't home, so I tried to fix it with Band-Aids. I waited too long to go the hospital, and by the time I got stitches, it was guaranteed that I'd have a scar."

She lays her head on his chest and caresses his right hand, noticing for the first time that he's completely missing three fingernails. Only his pinkie fingernail and thumbnail are intact.

"You're messed up all over. How did that happen?" Kath asks.

"My first safe cracking job. My dad was teaching me on an old York Cannonball. I got it open without any help, then got so excited I let it slam on my fingers."

"My God. How did your dad react?"

"He laughed at me," Sam says, forcing a little laugh himself.

"Your dad taught you how to crack safes?"

"He taught me everything I know. He and my mom were divorced, and she hated him. She didn't want me to know that he even existed. But people in the neighborhood told me he was around, and when I turned seventeen, I went and found him. He was working at a garage down in the Mission District with a bunch of pals. But they weren't working on cars, they were stealing. They were all smart guys who didn't like to work much. They just hung around and planned different ways to get rich. And they planned robberies. I'd lie to mom when she asked where I was going, and whenever I went over there, he had a new trick to show me."

She runs her fingers along the tips of his, where the nails should be. "A father teaching a son how to steal? There's something wrong there."

Sam nods. "He could've been a brain surgeon, but he preferred being a thief. And he was hilarious. A real charmer. He was great to be around," Sam says.

And he was an asshole who didn't care about you, Kath thinks, but she doesn't say that out loud. That's too much for her to bring up this early in the game, whatever game it is that they're playing. "Do you blame him for making you this way?" she asks. That's a fair question.

"No. I could've walked away, but I liked it. Then I got caught up in it. Then I tried to get out of it, but it was too late. Prison seemed to be the only way to start fresh," he says.

"To get away from Paul?" Kath asks.

"And myself," he says, staring out the window. He narrows his eyes, thinking about Rose, and Carl, and Mrs. Wilkenson, and all his ideas about fancy coffee shops, and people driving their cars as taxis, and pagers that can write messages but also be phones, and all the ideas he has. He wonders if Hal is right, that he is smart enough to make something of himself if he just tried.

Kath clears her throat, and he glances back down at her, remembering the bliss of the now instead of the regrets of the past. He spots a tiny scar underneath her chin, which he touches. He wonders how many other hidden marks and secrets he'll find on her body.

"How'd you get the scar?' Sam asks.

"I don't remember. My mom says I fell getting out of the tub," she answers, looking away, which makes Sam suspect she's lying.

"What about you? Do you have an excuse for this life you lead?" Sam asks, stroking her arms. She has a lot of sun freckles on the tops of her shoulders, probably from too many sunburns as a kid.

"I blame my mom. She had no clue how to deal with life, or me."

"Is she still around?"

Kath rolls off his chest and lays down next to him, staring at the ceiling. "I haven't seen her in fourteen years. We were in Arizona, in the desert just outside Tucson. She was screaming at me to get in the car, this ugly cream-colored Buick that her fat, loser boyfriend drove. He was trying to fix a flat tire on the side of the road and couldn't get the lug nuts off. He got so pissed that he took the crowbar and was just beating the tire and the wheel, like that was going to make a difference. Then the crowbar bounced off the rubber, and he hit himself in the face," she says.

This is becoming a big enough story that Sam sits up against the headboard and looks down at Kath's face as she speaks, watching her beautiful face with the scar on the chin from upside down, with her brown hair spilling to one side on the pillow.

"Wow," Sam says.

"He whacked himself hard, too. Moron Boy had a huge gash on his forehead, and the blood was streaming down his face. Mom pushed him into the passenger seat, got behind the wheel, ready to drive the last ten miles into Tucson with a flat tire. And that's when I knew I didn't have to stay with her anymore. I grabbed my one suitcase out of the back seat and stood there, watching her scream at me, like she was a TV episode I'd already seen way too many times. Then she gave up and drove away. I was sixteen," Kath says.

She turns over onto her stomach and hugs her perfect breasts into a pillow, with the rest her smooth naked body rising and falling in curves down to her heels at the bottom of the bed. She looks up at him and smiles, her face more honest and open than he's ever seen.

"That's a hell of a story," Sam says. And it explains a lot, he thinks, but he doesn't say that out loud, either. That's too much for him to bring up this early in the game, whatever game it is that they're playing.

"Let's walk on the beach," she says, looking out the window at the sunshine.

They get out of bed, throw the dishes in the sink and get dressed. Sam gives Kath a pair of sweatpants and a big t-shirt and a sweater to wear, so she doesn't have to put her perfect purple dress back on. Sam puts on jeans, a t-shirt, and his leather jacket. They avoid eye contact with everyone as they leave, avoid the office, and walk a block and a half down to the beach.

It's June the first now, Sam thinks, only sixty-one days since he walked out of prison, and he's back in the same motel. Back then, however, he was so accustomed to being locked in tiny spaces that being this close to the beach made him feel untethered and helpless. Now he can stand in the sun and look out at the blue water that stretches all the way to Japan. He can stare at the clouds and the blue sky and breathe deep without his heart racing so fast that he needs to rush back inside and shut the blinds.

"It's nice out here," he says.

"I wish the water were warm enough that we could go swimming."

"Everyone in San Francisco says that," Sam says.

They kick off their shoes, pick them up and walk barefoot. She snuggles close, and he puts his arm around her. There are people on the beach, mostly joggers and isolated families bundled up with blankets.

"What happened between you and Rose?" Kath asks.

"Rose was my first real love," Sam says.

Kath snuggles closer. This is what she's been waiting to hear, and she must be ready for whatever he says, she thinks. It's also what Paul wants to hear too, and she must be ready for that as well.

"What about your son?" she finally asks.

"I don't have a son," Sam says.

"I went through your wallet the morning after you shot my bed. There's a photo of the three of you."

Sam exhales, appreciating her honesty. "I met Rose when Carl was two. He's a great kid, and he was part of my life for nine years, but he's not my son," Sam says. "Any chance of that is gone now, which is how I have to look at it."

Kath nods. Walking side-by-side is better for talking, Kath thinks. It's less of an interrogation. But there's more she wants to know. "When did you first meet?" Kath asks.

"When I was twenty-one. Carl's dad wasn't in the picture. We fell in love, and I married her. An instant family unit," Sam says.

To make up for the one you never had growing up, Kath thinks, and imagines Sam as a latchkey kid making burnt toast and bacon for himself while his mom was at work and his dad was busy stealing.

"But something went wrong?" Kath says.

"I earned my living as a thief. I was good at it, and I gave them a good life. I had a six-year run and never got caught. I decided I should try for bigger scores.

"So, you hooked up with Paul," Kath says.

"Bingo," Sam says, pointing at her for emphasis.

They trudge through the dry sand until their calf muscles hurt, then head down toward the water where the beach is hard. They let the incoming waves lap at the cuffs of their pants, then lift their feet high because the water is so cold.

"How many years were you with Paul?" Kath asks.

"Three years. And I made him a lot of money. But he kept pushing me into bigger and bigger jobs. I knew my winning streak wasn't going to last. And he'd make veiled threats about Rose and Carl," he says.

"That he'd hurt them?"

"That if I quit, he'd tell Rose. She didn't know about my stealing. She thought I was working for a private trash company. He said that he'd make things hard for them. So, I had to plan my escape."

Kath nods. He planned his escape routes well on their last two jobs, and considering he was escaping from Paul, the plan had to be perfect. "And what was your plan?"

A Frisbee flies close to them, and Sam catches it with one hand and flicks it back to the group of teenagers playing on the beach. The disc floats in a perfect arc back to them. He is graceful, Kath thinks, comfortable in his skin. But like her, he got caught in a terrible career.

"Paul kept harping on me about one job. An Asian Import Company that was a front for some Hong Kong criminals who had burned him. Paul found out that they always kept cash in their safe, especially over the weekends."

"Let me guess. $500,000 in cash, right?" Kath asks.

"At least. I made a deal with him – I'd do this one job, and he'd get everything. All the money, revenge against the Chinese guys, and I would walk away. I planned it for months. I even told Rose, and I promised I'd go straight when it was over. She promised to leave me if I got caught. Then the night came, I went in alone, I opened the safe, and it was empty. Thirty seconds later the police showed up, like they knew I was there. I went to prison for two years, and Rose left me, just like she said she would," Sam says.

Kath stops on the high side of the wet sand and tugs him to a stop. He turns to face her as the cold water rushes up and buries their feet deeper in the cold sand.

"Paul thinks you took it."

"I know."

"Paul will forgive my debt, and give me one hundred thousand, if I find out what you did with the cash and get it back to him," she says.

"I know that too," he says.

"You do?" she asks, confused.

"I figured there was some other reason he made us work together, besides wanting us to make him a lot of money," Sam says.

"And we have made him a lot of money, for very little work on his part," she says.

"That's for sure," Sam says.

Their feet are now ankle deep in the cold sand. Kath lifts her feet up to keep them warm, while Sam stands stock still, letting his feet turn into blocks of ice.

"Why did you agree to it?" Kath asks.

"Maybe I wanted to get to know you." He flashes her his grin.

She hits him. "Stop grinning like that! It's so fake!"

"I can't help it. I've been practicing it for too long."

"Then don't lie. Just be honest, to me at least. You're planning something."

"I'm not planning anything.'

She scoffs. "You're such a coward! Tell the truth! Be a man for once!"

"Do you want to know the truth? Why I'm not a man? Paul tracked me down the day after I got out! He strong-armed me and threatened to hurt Rose and Carl if he found them. He offered me a gun, and I took it. Two days out, and I'm stuck working for Paul all over again. And I can't get a real job anyway, I tried! My life was supposed to get better, not worse!" Spittle is flying, his face is red, and he's loud enough that all the Frisbees and laughter around them all stop.

"Your life is worse?" Kath asks.

Sam sighs. "You're not worse. You're the only thing about my life that's getting better," He pulls his frozen feet out of the thick sand and reaches for her hand. She lets him take it, and they turn back towards the motel.

"All done here, people! Thank you!" Kath yells at the watching crowd. Their laughter starts back up again.

They walk in silence. Sam bites his lip, embarrassed that he let himself go like that. He spent two years in prison keeping it all under wraps, staying cool, perfecting his wry persona, dodging conflict, and now that the lid is off his jam jar, he loses it. Still, he managed to dodge the question.

Kath bites her lip, wondering if Sam meant what he said. He sure looked like he did. If he didn't, then it was quite an act, and she fell for his performance.

"You could leave town," Kath says.

"It's not that easy. I can't just request a parole transfer," Sam says.

Kath knows that if someone were in a lot of trouble and had to leave town, there's always a way. Something is keeping him here. Or someone. But it's too early in the game to ask.

"You could leave too," Sam says. "It's a big country, and you've seen a fair amount of it. You could leave town and find a place to hide and be done with Paul forever," he says.

"I have my reasons," she says.

She could tell him about Bella, but she doesn't. It may not be worth sharing so much of herself with him yet. Or at all.

Is any of this worth it? she asks herself. If she knew what he did with the money, she could tell Paul and be done with both these men and be free. She'd be debt free and have money to take care of Bella, the only family she's got. Would she go through with it if she knew?

"Paul is going to push you to tell him what's happening with us," Sam says.

"What do I tell him?" Kath asks.

"Tell him the truth. It's easier that way."

"Are you setting up an exit?" Kath asks.

"I've been working on that since the day I got out of prison," Sam says.

"Am I part of that exit plan?" Kath asks, stopping in the sand.

"You weren't initially, but you are now."

"Paul expected me to snitch on you by now. We were never supposed to get to three jobs in this arrangement. He figured we'd have sex, and you would turn into mush and tell me the truth about everything."

"I have told you the truth. It's just not a truth he's going to believe."

"He picks the third and final job. And he's going to screw us. You know that."

"Let me work on it. I can handle Paul," Sam says.

He leans forward and kisses her, and she falls into his arms. He feels her naked curves under the sweatpants and sweater and brushes the goosebumps on her arms and legs. He senses her nipples stiffen through the sweater, and he stiffens too.

"Should we try some more Magic Massage?" Kath asks.

CHAPTER TWENTY-EIGHT

Detective Stone sits behind his brushed metal industrial desk and watches gallery owner Marjorie McKale slowly leaf through yet another three-ring binder of mug shots. There's a stack of five more binders on his desk, and two dozen more line the shelves along the walls of the crowded and noisy Detectives Pool. Marjorie has only gone through two binders so far.

"No luck?" Detective Alden Stone asks, ignoring his ringing phone.

Marjorie turns another page, shaking her head. "They're all dressed the same. And they all have such bad haircuts."

Stone stares at his watch, wanting to get back to his new word processor. He's almost figured out how to run the Wordstar program. Then again, what's the rush? All these mug shots, all the files in his desk, every report, is supposed to somehow end up on a computer? That's never going to happen, he thinks. Meanwhile, there are bad guys out there he wants to catch today.

"You said it was a man and woman," Stone says, and opens a side desk drawer. He pulls out a plastic baggie with Kath's brown calfskin glove inside and puts it on the table. "Was she wearing gloves like these?"

"Please, she was working at a cocktail party. That's not evening wear."

Stone sits up straight when he spots Captain Yee striding through the maze of desks, heading right for him. He's got a young officer in tow, a criminal sketch artist named Yancy Mendoza.

"Ms. Watkins, I'm Captain Yee, chief detective for the SFPD, and this is Officer Mendoza, our sketch artist. We'd like you to describe to him what this man and woman looked like who robbed you."

"Of course," Marjorie says.

Captain Yee and Detective Stone trade glances as Officer Mendoza pulls up a chair and sits down facing Marjorie. He flips open his sketch pad and smiles.

"Can you give me an overall description of the man first? Was he tall, short, skinny, heavy set?" Officer Mendoza asks.

"He was wearing a light wool blue suit, with a thin pinstripe, I remember that. And he's broad across the chest, but not fat. In good shape. He's got thick wavy brown hair and blue eyes, and he has a thin scar on his cheek. He's quite good-looking actually," Marjorie says.

Marjorie, Detective Stone, and Captain Yee watch Officer Mendoza sketch away. He bites the inside of his mouth in concentration as his charcoal pencil flies across the page. Mendoza turns the pad around and shows Marjorie a rough sketch.

"Thicker hair and the scar is thin and long," she says. "And he smirks when he smiles, with one corner of his mouth going up."

Mendoza nods, erases, sketches more, and turns the page over. It's a decent portrait of Sam. Marjorie smiles. "That's him," she says. "How long have you been doing this?"

"Three years, ma'am."

"I'd like to see more of your work. Have you ever thought about a gallery show? We could build a great backstory for you."

CHAPTER TWENTY-NINE

S am walks into the Fior d'Italia restaurant carrying a silver brushed metal briefcase. He spots Paul and Inge in the first circular booth, and slides in next to them. Paul and Inge both wear blue and white tracksuits with matching white and blue bandana headbands, like they're starring in an Olivia Newton-John workout video.

It's the same booth where Sam and Kath sat before Kath's first job, and Sam has a plan. He's going to have tortellini, a squid salad, some fresh sourdough bread, a glass of crisp white wine, and lots of tiny cups of black espresso. He also plans to irritate Paul to the point of fury.

"We've been waiting," Paul says.

"I said 12:30. It's 12:30 on the nose," Paul says.

"Inge is hungry," Paul says.

"You could have ordered. I'm sure the kitchen can dig up some skull for her to gnaw on."

Paul leans across the table and points his finger at Sam. "Inge is my girlfriend. Be nice to her, understand?"

"Last time we were all together, she attacked me with the Vulcan death grip, remember? She doesn't make a very good impression," Sam says.

The same young waiter with the curly hair arrives with a menu. He's wearing the same black bow tie, white shirt, and long white apron.

"I'd like a glass of white wine, the salad with squid, and a plate of cheese tortellini with pesto sauce," Sam says, and hands the menu back to the waiter.

Sam looks at Paul and Inge. "Are you going to order? I thought you were hungry."

"We ordered tuna salads," Paul says, contradicting everything he just said. "This restaurant doesn't have the healthy choices Inge wants for us. The health club is better."

"I prefer to not meet at your place of business anymore. Being in public gives me some safety from Vicky the Viking over there," Sam says.

Sam smiles at Inge, who growls like an angry house cat. Sam slides the silver case to Paul across the red leather tuck-and-roll cushion. Paul opens the large briefcase and inside is a smaller leather case.

"What are you, James Bond? Where's the money?" Paul asks.

"The satchel inside is yours," Sam says.

Paul takes the smaller leather satchel and opens it. Inside are a dozen thick stacks of hundred-dollar bills. "Nice little score. Congratulations," Paul says.

"That's twenty-eight thousand. The whole job earned us eighty-four. I am also willing to throw in my cut. You'd make fifty-six thousand, more than Kath pulled in on her entire job."

"Why?" Paul asks.

"Because we should stop now, while we're ahead. While you're ahead."

"You don't know how much my job will earn. You haven't heard it yet," Paul says as he zips up the leather satchel. "And you and Kath seem to be working together quite well. I think that's a good reason to keep going."

The waiter arrives with salads for Paul and Inge, and a squid salad and white wine for Sam, which is the perfect opportunity for Sam to poke at Paul.

"We do fine, considering she's calling me stupid every moment we're together. Which makes me have to ask – did you ever sleep with Kath?" Sam asks.

Inge's face turns beet red when she hears Kath's name. The young waiter takes his time placing the plates in front of each of them. Sam sips his wine and enjoys watching Paul twist his napkin like it's someone's throat, until the slow waiter nods, smiles, and leaves.

"We were together for a little while," Paul admits, stabbing at his tuna salad.

"That explains everything," Sam says, rolling a piece of squid in the salad dressing and then popping it into his mouth.

"Explains what?" Paul asks, rising to the bait.

"Why she hates you so much. I had to fight her about giving you your fair cut. The only time a woman wants to burn a man that bad is for love gone wrong. Hell hath no fury like a woman scorned,'" Sam says, chewing on his rubbery gastropod. He takes another big bite and talks with his mouth full. "You did a real number on her, because she's still not over you. You're all she talks about."

"You just said she wants to rip me off. Which is it?" Paul asks.

Sam pushes away his empty plate and takes his time to chew on the last piece of squid. "She hasn't said anything specific, but she's planning something. That's why I think you should take this money now, be happy with two jobs, and avoid the risk."

Paul smiles, and shakes his head. "We're doing the last job. That's the deal we made, and now it's my turn. Then we're done."

The waiter returns with Sam's tortellini, swapping plates as fast as he can, then dashing away. Sam takes a bite and enjoys the warm salty, tangy bite of pesto mixed in with the tiny pasta hats. He sighs, closing his eyes.

"I hate watching you eat," Paul says, which makes Sam love the food even more.

"You made me watch you slurp your protein smoothies. You and Cro-Magnon Mary can't share lunch with me?" Sam asks.

Inge grabs a steak knife and stabs at Sam with a lightning-fast lunge. Sam dodges it just in time, but she still jabs a hole in the arm of his jacket. He stares at the wounded leather, shocked. He's got two holes now, one in his breast pocket, and another in the sleeve.

"Like I said, don't make fun of Inge," Paul says.

"I have an idea how to fix your Kath problem," Sam says, digging back into his food. "Let me plan the last job with you. When she tries to burn you, I'll be able to tip you off that much sooner. Catch her in the act."

Paul stares at him chewing, then leans back. He smiles and pats Inge's arm. She leans back too, out of attack mode. "My job will make five times more than your Mickey Mouse haul," he says, patting the leather case on the cushion next to him.

"Suit yourself," Sam says, wiping his mouth with his napkin.

"You must miss Rose. Have you heard from her?"

"I haven't heard from her."

Paul and Sam stare at each other with blank poker faces.

"I'm looking for her, you know. I have some questions for her."

"Let me know if you find her because I have questions for her too," Sam says.

"I'll chat with her someday," Paul says.

Sam doesn't react. Paul smiles and stands up. "I'll be in touch with both you and Kath about the final job, and you'll come to the Health Club. No more meeting in restaurants crap. Come on, Inge, let's go." He grabs the leather satchel with the money, and he and Inge slide out of the booth.

"What about my offer?" Sam asks.

"What offer?" Paul asks, looking at the satchel.

"I offered you my cut to not do the last job. Kath is too much of a risk."

"I'll take my chances," Paul says. He and Inge adjust their blue and white bandanas, zip up their tracksuits and head out.

Sam slides the silver case back over to his side of the booth. He shuts the lid with the napkin and picks up the case like it were fragile.

"Sir?"

Sam looks up. It's the young waiter with the floppy hair. "Yes?" Sam asks.

"Those two big guys you asked me about? The football player and the Samoan guy in the 49er jerseys? They're parked across the street."

Sam hands him a fifty with some burned edges. "Keep the change. I'll go out the back."

CHAPTER THIRTY

Sam steps off the 22 Fillmore Muni bus on the busy part of Lombard Street, with four lanes of traffic flowing toward and away from the Golden Gate Bridge. This section of Lombard has two dozen motels for travelers, tourists, and couples who need a room for a few hours.

Sam walks next to the noisy flow of traffic, carrying his silver briefcase, lost in thought. He ordered squid, and they ordered tuna. Paul wanted a big pelagic predator fish that swims free, while Sam chose a fish that hides in the dark, changes color and shoots clouds of black ink to distract its enemies, so it can escape. Sam wishes he could be more like Paul, the tuna swimming free in the world, and not like the squid, lost in the dark with his strange thoughts.

The time window is narrowing. Hal, his parole agent, will want to see real pay stubs soon, not cash. And his alibi at the remediation company won't take his payoff money much longer. Kath is the best thing that has happened to him in a long time, but he can't tell her everything. He knows she's not telling him everything yet, either. They are both liars with pasts to protect, and if they get caught the less they know about each other, the better.

Paul's job is coming up fast. They will be committing another crime within a month. Until then, he must find Rose, meet with Hal, avoid Cliff and Dozer, handle Paul, and convince Kath to trust him. That's like shooting an arrow through five rings and hitting a bullseye, while the clock is ticking down.

Sam walks into the parking lot of the Vista Motor Lodge Motel on the corner of Scott Street and Lombard. He steers clear of the ground floor office and darts ups the wooden stairs without being seen by anyone. He paid in cash two days ago. He explained his house up in Napa caught fire, and he came down to San Francisco to hire some people to help him rebuild. He wore a cowboy hat and sunglasses and a three-day beard, so hopefully, the manager will remember his fire story and not his face.

He enters Room 23, locks the door behind him and goes straight to the bathroom, where he holds the silver case up to the light, careful to only hold it by the handle. There, on the metallic edges and on the metal clasps to open the case, are Paul's fingerprints.

"Gotcha," Sam whispers. His plan is taking shape. Sam wipes down the handle with a towel and slides the entire case into a large clear plastic bag he pulls from under the sink, and ties the top shut with a rubber band.

He exits the bathroom and goes into the darkened motel room and slides the plastic bag into yet another black duffel bag.

The bedside light clicks on. Sam spins around. Kath sits on the bed, leaning against the headboard. "Tough day at the office, honey?" she asks. She drops her hand and opens the belt on her long silk robe, revealing a matching negligee underneath.

"It was tough, but it's getting easier," Sam says.

Kath then pulls back the covers to reveal the Magic Massage box attached to the headboard, and a hammer and a screwdriver lying on the exposed sheets. Sam picks up his tools, jams the screwdriver into a metal seam, whacks the butt end of the screwdriver with the hammer and pops the metal box open. He pries the metal apart, twists the wires and the bed roars to life. Kath giggles with happy anticipation.

"Lucy, I'm home," Sam sings, in his best Ricky Ricardo imitation. He drops the tools onto the floor and falls into her arms.

CHAPTER THIRTY-ONE

Sam and Kath walk along the blustery path of Land's End, a strip of wildness that hugs the northwestern edge of San Francisco. The dirt path hugs a cliff that plummets down to the frothing ocean and sharp rocks below. On the other side are thick Monterey Pines that shield Sam and Kath from view, but the ocean wind whips them and they must pull their wool jackets tight to their bodies.

"Another summer in San Francisco," Sam says.

"I've never had a summer tan in my life," Kath says.

"If we can figure out how to get out of this, I'll take you to a place where that olive skin of yours can turn nice and brown," Sam says, pulling her close. The smell of salty wet wool drifts up into his nostrils.

"How much does Paul know about us?" Kath asks.

"Cliff and Dozer haven't spotted us. We've done a decent job of hiding in the right motels," Sam says.

"That by itself is a tip-off. He knows that we have something to hide," Kath says, and looks up at the hill with the steep trees as if half-expecting to see thick-necked Dozer and broad-chested Cliff in their red and white 49er jerseys, spying on them.

"We'll know a lot by what kind of job he presents to us tomorrow. He didn't think we'd ever get this far," Sam says.

"Can't we just leave town? We have enough money," Kath says.

"We could," Sam says, and then says nothing.

She says nothing back, which is proof to Sam that she has her own reasons to stay. They walk in silence, each with their thoughts.

Sam would leave town in a second, except he needs Rose. And leaving town means talking to Hal Weinstein, who is the only honest man who has ever seen through his layers of lies to the possibilities underneath. And if he jumps town too early and Rose returns, Paul could get to her, and bad things could happen.

Kath would leave town in a second, too. She must worry about Bella, however; that mean old woman is the only family Kath has, and the only person who has given Kath unconditional love. And if Kath leaves without explanation, she knows Paul would seek out Bella for answers.

"I'm not scared of Paul. One more job and we're done with him," Sam says.

"You really believe that?" Kath asks.

"We can always leave. Let's see how this plays out."

Kath pulls out from under his arm and steps in front of him. She walks backward as he walks, forcing him to look her in the eyes. "You're planning something, aren't you?"

"You still don't trust me? Even now?"

Kath stops, which forces him to stop. She lowers her chin and raises her eyes at him, doing her best Lauren Bacall glance. "You didn't answer my question."

A gust from the ocean whips at their hair. "I could just tell you something. But how would you know I wasn't lying?" Sam says.

"I'll trade you. An honest answer for an honest answer."

"How many honest answers will I get from you?" Sam asks, but inside he's more concerned with the number of honest answers he must give to her.

"Three each, and you can ask first," she says, then loops her hand through his arm and tugs him so they're walking on the path again. It's easier to talk when you're not face-to-face.

"How did you end up in San Francisco?" Sam asks.

"I came looking for my father's relatives, who I'd never met. I couldn't find any of them. I was homeless for seven years, huffing airplane glue on street corners to get high and forget. That's when Paul found me. I was twenty-three. He took me in, helped clean me up," Kath says. "And he taught me how to be a thief."

"And you were his girlfriend too?" Sam asks.

"Only because I was young and stupid and thought I had no other choice. It lasted a year, and then I ended it," Kath says, remembering her teased hair with the frosted tips, and hanging out in gay discos.

"So why do you still steal for him now, this many years later?" Sam asks.

"I borrowed a lot of money from him. I got clean, got clothes, got an apartment. I also needed it for a someone close to me who had medical bills."

"Last question –"

"Nope. That was three questions."

"This one is easy," Sam says, kicking at the rocks on the trail. They reach a bluff where the trees end, and Sam and Kath can see the Cliff House and the ruins of Sutro Baths, peeking through a thick blanket of fog. A foghorn on the Golden Gate Bridge behind them blasts two notes, low and long. "What is this love/hate thing you have with cars?"

"My mom was a loser who ended up with a string of losers. We were always on the road, either escaping someplace bad or hoping to find someplace better. From age six to sixteen, cars were home. Some bring back good memories, most bad."

"That sounds rough," Sam says and leads her off the bluff and up the wide path toward the noise and traffic of the Richmond District.

"It wasn't bad when I was young. I just thought we were always on a trip. But as I got older we'd pass schools and playgrounds, or some perfect house in the country and there'd be kids like me in the front yard. And I would miss something that I never had."

"We'll find you a nice place in the country," Sam says.

"Right, and you can raise turnips," Kath says. "Now it's my turn to ask questions."

"Let's get something to eat. The Seal Rock Inn has a nice diner," Sam says, and darts across Geary Street. Kath runs to keep up. He holds the diner door open for Kath.

"Don't think you can get out of answering," Kath says, stepping inside.

"Bring it on," Sam replies.

Five minutes later, Sam and Kath sit across from each other in a small booth, each of them warming their hands around a warm mug of black coffee.

"Do you have half a million dollars hidden somewhere?"

"No," Sam answers.

"Do you love me?" Kath asks.

"It was love at first sight when I saw you shoplifting at Macy's."

"Will you betray me?" Kath asks.

"Only if you betray me first," Sam says.

"What's that supposed to mean?" Kath asks, outraged.

Sam glances at his watch and swears. "Shit! My parole meeting starts in twenty minutes, and it's all the way downtown!" Sam says. He throws down a five-dollar bill and darts outside, looking for a nonexistent taxi. There are plenty of cars, however, and he knows most of their drivers would happily take him downtown to Bryant Street for less than ten dollars, if he just had a way he could communicate his need, and then have someone fill it.

Kath bangs out of the diner behind him. "You asked me four questions, I still get one more," she says, slugging his arm hard.

A Lincoln Town Car pulls up. The tinted passenger window lowers, and Cliff sticks his head out. "Sam! Kath! Glad we finally found you," Cliff says. "Get in, we'll drive you to your meeting with your parole officer. We have to make sure you stay on the straight and narrow."

CHAPTER THIRTY-TWO

Sam exits the elevators on the third floor of the Hall of Justice, and dashes into the Parole Department, waves at the receptionist on the phone before she can stop him, and weaves through the maze of metal desks toward the office in the back.

Hal Weinstein sits behind his desk, working his way through a tall stack of manila folders while listening to the Giants game on a transistor radio. Hal is still embracing the brown and white color scheme, and he pats his dome yet again to make sure his hair and yarmulke are still in place as he sips coffee from his white Styrofoam cup. Sam bursts in, but this time Hal pushes away from the desk fast enough that he only spills the coffee on his white shirt.

"You still can't knock?" Hal asks. "Or be on time? Or wait outside until I call you?"

"Sorry, Hal, I knew I was late," Sam says, sitting on the metal chair with the green industrial padding. "I work at night, so my body clock is way off."

Hal hands him a plastic cup with a snap-on lid. "I want a urine sample."

"You know I don't do drugs," Sam says.

"Just covering my bases."

"Can I at least use the bathroom?" Sam asks.

"Nope. You can pee right here in front of me," Hal says, and points at the wall. You haven't been staying at your residence hotel the last two weeks. Been working that hard?"

"You could say that," Sam says.

Sam stands, drops his pants, lowers his underwear and turns to the corner so Hal isn't staring at his unit. Sam concentrates. It's always been hard to pee in front of other people. It was especially hard at San Quentin, where he often had to pee on command. The urine starts to flow.

Sam finishes, caps the cup and zips up. Hal rips open a moist towelette packet and hands it to Sam so he can clean his hands. The smell of rubbing alcohol fills the room.

"You don't work twenty-four hours a day. What are you doing?"

"Okay, I'll come clean. I met a girl."

"Don't lie to me," Hal says, as he picks up the cup. "And if there is a trace of anything in your piss besides alcohol and bad cheeseburgers, I'm sending you back to prison."

"It's the truth. I met a girl."

Hal hands Sam a pen and a piece of paper. "Write down her name, address and phone number, as close as you can recollect. Do it now and do it fast. No talking, because talking is how you make up a story and you can't write a lie as easy as you can say one. Go!" Hal shouts, and Sam starts writing.

"Why? She's not the one on parole," Sam argues, holding the pen aloft.

"No, but you are. And that may be ending soon," Hal warns.

"Wait a second, I just remembered!" Sam yells and then reaches into the inside breast pocket of his pea coat and pulls out a handful of papers. "These are Xerox copies of the checks I got for working for the remediation company. He was paying me in cash, but I told him you wanted to see proof, so he started paying me with company checks. I get my first real paycheck this Thursday. I've been on the job less than a month, and he wanted to make sure I could do the job right before putting me on the payroll. See? I'm doing everything right!"

Sam hands them to Hal, who takes the copies of the checks and examines them, then stares over the top of his reading glasses at Sam. Hal Weinstein reduces Sam to quaking jelly with one long laser gaze. "How did you copy the checks?" Hal asks.

"At that new fancy copy store. What's it called? Kinko's. And then I put them in the bank at Wells Fargo. I have a checking account there."

Hal staples the photocopies of the checks into Sam's folder. "Or maybe you paid someone to write these checks and make copies, and then he tore the checks up, and you never cashed them. Maybe you're making money some other way, but you won't tell me. So, you put this elaborate con job together, trying to trick the only man who cares about you," he says.

Sam leans back against the thin green padding on his metal chair. "Come on, Hal. That's an elaborate con job, don't you think?" Sam asks.

Hal closes Sam's folder. "I want you to stay clean. I want you to have a real job. A real job puts you on a real payroll, where they take out taxes and contribute to unemployment insurance. That's a real job. I want you to find one of those," Hal says.

"Got it," Sam says, and gets up to go.

"Hang on, you still owe me her info," Hal says, tapping the piece of paper.

"She doesn't know I'm an ex-con. Let me tell her first. I'll bring her in myself for the next meeting. Please, Hal. I don't want to mess this up."

Hal snaps off the transistor radio and sighs. "You are incredible. I care more about you than anyone you deal with out on the street, even more than your new 'girlfriend,'" Hal says, making air quotes with his fingers. "Yet you throw up more obstacles to me helping you than my teenage daughter. Write down her name, now."

Sam writes down a name and hands it to Hal, who reads it aloud. "Katerina Trulli, 29th Street, San Francisco," Hal says.

"I don't know the number. It's a pink house."

"I need the number."

"I'll get it for you and call you tonight. She's meeting me outside right now," Sam says.

"Bring her up then, I want to meet her."

"Like I said, she doesn't know I'm an ex-con. She thinks I'm in here paying off traffic tickets. Let me break it to her first, please," Sam says.

"I want to meet her," Hal says, not giving in. "I've broken better liars than you, Sam Webb. And you will thank me for it someday."

"How about we wave at you from the bus stop?" Sam says, standing up again and looking out the window. I'm supposed to meet her there right now."

Hal looks out the window down at Bryant Street below. He shakes his head and sighs, which is his "tell" to Sam that he's giving in. "I'm standing at this window until I see you both. And bring her in next week with ID. And you must bring in a real pay stub," Hal says.

"You got it," Sam says.

Hal holds up the plastic cup with the blue lid full of Sam's urine. "And if your piss is any less than pure golden urea, I'm sending a squad car to pick you up. Now go find your girlfriend and start waving at this window."

Sam grins and heads for the door. "Thanks, Hal. See you next week."

Hal smiles as Sam rushes out. He turns the transistor radio back on and tunes in the Giants game. Vida Blue is trying to keep his fast ball low, but gusts are blowing the ball out of the strike zone. The Giants deserve a downtown stadium where the sun shines and there's no wind, Sam thinks.

Five pitches later he spots Sam at the corner bus stop, standing with an attractive brunette wearing her own blue pea coat and a red scarf. She and Sam lift their hands and wave, and then Sam plants a long kiss on her lips and flashes the thumbs up, proving she exists. Hal wonders what lies Sam is telling her, and he prays to God that she will stay with him once she learns the truth about him.

Two floors up, Detective Stone sits at his desk, entering data into his new computer console while listening to the Giants game on his own transistor radio, not realizing that in less than twenty years, both machines will merge into one, along with sixteen other machines.

He gets out of his chair and goes to the window so the natural light can fix his vision. He's been staring at a green cursor against a black screen for too long. Down at the bus stop, he sees a man and a woman waving at someone on another floor. The man has dark curly hair, the woman is a brunette, with short hair. The man is stocky but strong, and the woman is thin and attractive –

– and he runs to his desk and rifles through the pile of papers and finds the artist sketches of the criminals from the safe robbery at Marjorie McKale's art gallery. He grabs them and runs to the window –

–and the man and woman are gone.

But they know someone in this building. Maybe some office has a record of them. Maybe someone in this building knows them.

And his mind starts to spin.

Sam sits next to Kath in the back of a moving Muni bus. They managed to jump on and avoid Cliff and Dozer, but when Sam looks out the window he sees the Lincoln Town Car in the next lane, keeping pace with the bus. Cliff has the passenger window down. He glances up and sees Sam's face in the window and points at him with a look that says, "got you."

Sam gets up out of his seat and moves into the aisle.

"Where are you going?" she asks.

"I'm getting off the bus. We should spend the night apart tonight. Go alone to Paul's tomorrow. Get there on time. I'll make sure I'm ten minutes late. It will give you time to talk. He'll tell you things he won't say if I'm there. Stay relaxed and remember everything he says, and how he says it. Remember body language. He still doesn't know everything that we've been doing, and Cliff and Dozer only found us today."

"I feel our luck is running out."

Sam reaches into his pocket and hands her a piece of paper. It's a bus transfer.

"Thank you, but I can get a transfer from the driver myself."

"Add up the numbers. That will tell us whether our luck is running out or not.

Sam pulls the cord for a stop request. Kath grabs his arm and looks up at him, scared. He smiles and grabs the hand bar for balance as the bus lurches to a stop. He steps down, the back door opens, and Sam disappears into the street.

Kath adds up the numbers. 21.

CHAPTER THIRTY-THREE

C ome on, get the lead out!"
Paul screams at Cliff and Dozer as they struggle to do push-ups in the mirrored workout room. The big boys arch their backs and groan, creating strange yoga poses as sweat stains creep across their football jerseys. Inge and Paul lead the session, both cranking out push-ups like Marines, dressed in sleek white workout clothes without a mark.

Sam walks in and scoffs. He's wearing his once fancy black leather jacket with the bullet and knife holes, and he's got yet another all-purpose army surplus bag slung over his shoulder. Sam spent enough time working out in his prison cell that he doesn't abide indoor exercise. Sam prefers running up and down steep Nob Hill and doing push-ups and pull-ups in the tiny park next to the Union Pacific Club, alongside the kids in the playground.

"Planks!" Paul screams, as he and Inge drop into a plank push-up position. Their backs are straight, their arms bent, and their torsos are low to the ground as if frozen at the lowest point of a push-up. Dozer and Cliff groan and twist, not able to do them.

"They need an alignment," Paul hisses to Inge.

Inge throws herself on Dozer and pulls his arms back into a brutal stretch.

"Please, Inge, No Rolfing!" Dozer screams, as Inge twists his spine, ready to hogtie him.

Cliff darts away, but Paul blocks his exit and points at him to stay put. "Don't you leave, you need this too," he says to the huge Samoan cowering in the corner.

Paul then walks over to Sam, still leaning against the mirror. "You look like you could use some realignment yourself, Sam. That's Inge's specialty."

"I got third place in the San Quentin boxing competition. If she comes close to me I'll realign her."

Dozer whimpers as he tries to escape from under her, but she keeps pulling him back, like a rabid bear mauling an overweight Yosemite camper. His fear rises until his narcolepsy kicks in…and he passes out.

Inge drops his limp limbs, confused that her plaything suddenly seems dead.

"You're late," Paul says to Sam.

"I'm here, aren't I? And my offer to skip this last job still stands. You'll make more."

Paul snickers. "That's funny. Shall we go back to my office?"

Kath is already in Paul's office. She leans against his desk, dressed in jeans and a tight motorcycle jacket, and a red shirt underneath. Her hair is back in a bun, with a wisp that's fallen loose across her face. The whole image drives Sam nuts when he sees her, but he keeps quiet, aware that Paul is observing them.

"Hello again," Sam says to her.

"Hello," Kath says, backing away from the table. "You want to see the madness he wants us to attempt? This job is impossible."

"For experts like you? This is a cakewalk," Paul says.

Sam moves closer to the table. There are charts and architectural blueprints stretched out and held down with paperweights. Sam glances at the corner and sees the address – 404 Montgomery Street, in the heart of downtown.

"You want us to break into the Flood Building? If we don't get caught going up, we'll get caught going down. The entire building has got those new security cameras, and guards in the lobby," Sam says.

Kath has given up fighting and leans against the back wall, shaking her head.

Paul moves behind his desk, forcing Sam to step aside. "Hear me out. On the sixteenth floor is Kearne Securities, the largest brokerage house on the West Coast. Stock and bond sales are all electronic now, but sometimes, clients still want the actual papers, the real stock and bond certificates. They're either old and they don't trust computers, or they want to hand them out for gifts, wills, graduations. So Kearne gets them and vaults them." Paul pauses for emphasis, looking at each of them. "My sources say that there are two million dollars in unmarked certificates in their vault right now."

Sam examines the architectural designs. Paul has also arranged photos of the lobby and the sixteenth floor where Kearne Securities is. There's a stack of paperwork with phone numbers, plus a breakdown of the number of guards working, their shifts, their names, the loading elevators, the number of security cameras – it's all there.

Sam is impressed. Paul has done his research. That doesn't mean, however, that the plan is going to work. If he studies these papers, he will know everything about the Flood Building and Kearne Securities, but he still won't know how to break in.

"How do we get past this security team? And their cameras?" Sam asks.

"You can't. He knows it's an impossible job, that's why he gave it to us," Kath say, crossing her arms. She puts the back heel of her boot against the white wall, marking it.

"You just put a mark on my wall," Paul says.

"I know," Kath says, and drags her heel down, leaving a long black streak. "Are you going to blow up over a mark on the wall?"

Paul mumbles his fake laugh to keep from exploding. "You people act like it's Fort Knox! Their security is lax. I've been planning this for years, waiting for the right team, and you two are it. It's all there on paper. You will each have over seven hundred thousand dollars. You can retire forever."

Paul steps away from the desk and allows Sam to move close again. Sam leafs through the plans, examining the elevator shafts and the camera setups. He looks at the pages with the guards' schedules and the garbage pickups. He examines the electrical and fire systems. After ten minutes of close examination, he steps back again.

"Kath is right, it can't be done. You can't stand that we're almost out from under you, so you stick us with this."

Paul crosses his arms and stands by the door. As if by magic, Inge opens the door, enters and closes it behind her and leans against it, blocking any chance of an exit. "This is what we agreed on. Three jobs, and we pick one each. But if you all want to back out now, we can restructure your debt and we can make other arrangements."

"So you can string us out forever? You are the devil," Kath says.

Inge growls and moves toward her, and Paul puts his arm up to block the white she-bear from attacking. Kath stands her ground, even though the hair on her neck stands straight up.

Sam rolls up the papers and slides them into the cardboard tube. "I'm not backing out now. I'll find a way to do this job. I'll use what you've given me, and then come up with my own plan. That means it will be on my schedule. Then I'll never owe you a damn thing again." He opens the satchel and slides in the stack of composition books, legal pads and the book of photo prints.

"You can't take all that," Paul says. "You have to work on it here."

"You worried I'm going to go to the cops? Or do something stupid? Leave it on bus seat? That hasn't happened so far," Sam says, and heads for the door.

"Those stock certificates won't be in that safe forever."

"You said you've been planning this job for years. Now you want it done in two weeks? You can wait a couple of months."

"Wait a second, you don't speak for me, "Kath says.

"Then I'll do it alone. Have fun working for Shorty the rest of your life," Sam says. Inge lunges at Sam, who ducks her punch and then trips her with a sideswipe with his foot. Inge staggers three steps but regains her footing. Sam slams the door behind him.

Paul and Kath stare at each other for a full minute. Inge stares at them staring at each other. "Make her leave," Kath finally says.

Paul nods at Inge. "Darling, can you bring us two cups of iced coffee?" Inge makes her low cat growl noise and departs. She looks crushed as she walks out.

"You're such a lucky man," Kath says. "Cujo loves you."

"Say what you're going to say, or I'll have her punch your teeth down your throat."

"The job is too big."

"That's why I picked it," Paul says, and sits behind his desk, gesturing for Kath to sit opposite him. Kath obeys.

"What's that supposed to mean?" Kath asks.

"I know what's going on with you two."

Kath is glad she's sitting so Paul can't see how much her legs are shaking.

"Relax! I asked you to get close to him, and you did!" Paul says.

She crosses her legs and her arms, trying to look chic and in control, while she fights to keep from dry heaving.

Paul points at her, now serious. "Except you think you know him. You don't."

"But you do?" Kath asks.

"You want to know how much he bad-mouthed you the last time we met? He'll do anything and say anything to get that money he stole and get out from under me. Even if he has to roll over you to do it."

Kath exhales with disgust, but as she does her breath trembles, giving away her heartbreak. That's enough for Paul to know he has an opening and he flies into it.

"Poor Kath. Still have a soft heart? Trust me, he has other things planned."

Kath stiffens in her chair and narrows her eyes at the man she hates most in the world. "Yeah? What's he got planned instead?"

"He'll say he's doing this job. He may even plan it out, perfecting every detail. But what he'll do is find the half million he stiffed me for, and then skip town."

"How did I know it would circle back to this?" Kath asks, shaking her head.

Paul leans forward, putting his elbows on his desk. "I know this man. If he had the money, he'd have taken off a long time ago. This forces him to make it happen now."

"You're wrong; there's no money."

Paul laughs. "Don't be naïve, Kath. He's playing you. Sam is a smart man who likes to play dumb. But I'm smarter."

"I'm not breaking into the Flood Building. I'm done." Kath gets out of her chair.

Paul wags his finger at her. "You're not done. And you won't have to break in."

"What will I do instead?"

Paul gets up out of his chair and walks over to her. "Tell him you want in after all. He won't refuse. Then just keep your eyes open, and let me know when he makes a move," Paul says. He lowers his voice. "And anything he does could be a move, remember that."

"You two are like *Spy vs. Spy* in Mad Magazine, two idiots trying to outsmart each other," Kath says. She tries to open the door, but Inge is on the other side, blocking her exit.

Paul reaches out and gently shuts the door again. "He will betray you. Just make sure you do it to him first."

"I will. And then I'll be done with both of you, forever," Kath says, looking down at this ruthless man two inches shorter than she is.

Paul reaches up and strokes her face with the back of his hand. "Am I that bad? I'd hate to lose you from my life. We can always make new arrangements. We can all benefit."

Kath recoils from his touch, but Paul steps closer, leaning in to kiss her. Inge swings the door open. Kath ducks under her arm and darts down the hallway, past the exercise equipment and out the front door of the health club.

CHAPTER THIRTY-FOUR

Sam spends the day riding Muni, thinking about his options. He rides the 38 Geary bus out to the Ocean and then back downtown. Then at the Embarcadero Station, he jumps on the L-Taraval streetcar and rides it all the way to Wawona and 46th Avenue, out by the Zoo. He sits in the very back on the right-hand side, with the window open, the same seat he chose as a teenager when he rode buses everywhere in The City. Every few minutes he scribbles an idea down on a tiny pad that he pulls from the inside pocket of his jacket. Then he puts it away and looks at the traffic out the window.

He ends up on the sidewalk in front of the purple house where the mean old lady with the eye patch lives, Mrs.Wilkenson. He looks up at her window, starts to head up the stairs, then changes his mind, then goes up and almost rings the doorbell, but changes his mind, more nervous than he was on his last two heists.

He rubs his face, paces some more, then pulls out an envelope from inside his jacket. He makes sure Mrs. Wilkenson isn't ready to dump bleach on him from above, then dashes over and slips it into the mail slot next to the garage door. Mrs. Wilkenson appears in the upstairs window in her Hawaiian print housecoat and black eye patch, swearing and shaking her fist.

CHAPTER THIRTY-FIVE

Sam carries two heavy-duty plastic shopping bags and darts up the stairs of the Fog Cutter Motor Lodge on Lombard Street. No one sees him pull out a key and go inside Room 28.

Kath comes out of the bathroom and watches him stow the heavy bags by the bed. "Where have you been?" she asks.

"Thinking. And buying."

Sam pulls out his purchases and tosses them onto the bed. Hammers, rope, pliers, screwdrivers, headphones, dishwashing gloves, bolt cutters, electrical wires, batteries.

"You can't do this."

"We'll use our plan. Otherwise, it'll be a rerun of what happened to me two years ago."

"You're trying to beat him and he's trying to beat you. Both of you will lose."

The bed is covered with tools and electrical equipment. Sam stares at it, his leg shaking. He bites his fingernails, which Kath has never seen him do before.

"Did you hear what I said?" Kath asks.

Sam turns fast to face her. "You've got to trust me, Kath. Please."

"I'm trying."

Kath stares into his eyes, waiting for him to look away. That would be proof that he's lying. But he knows enough about how lying works to keep his pupils locked on hers.

Sam doesn't answer; instead, he winks at her and flashes that charming smile that he perfected staring into the brushed aluminum mirror in his prison cell.

Kath knows she's being played, but she's falling for the player and she so badly wants to believe him. He reaches for her and she walks into his arms.

They kiss, long and hard, while inching towards the bed. They're about to fall on a bedspread full of tools and gear but catch each other just in time. Sam gathers the edges of the bedspread up like a sack, lifts it off the mattress and lays it on the floor. He pulls out a hammer and screwdriver, jams the metal of the flathead into the seam of the Magic Massage box, and with one good whack, pops it open. Two twists on the wire and the mattress whirrs to life.

Sam pulls Kath down onto the bed. He smiles, and she giggles, as they hide their worries, both from themselves and each other, at least for one more night.

CHAPTER THIRTY-SIX

S am and Kath spend every night in a different motel in San Francisco, moving from neighborhood to neighborhood, always choosing a motel with Magic Massage units. They always pay in cash ahead of time, leave early, and leave a slightly charred fifty-dollar bill to pay for the damaged Magic Massage box they smash open. They have plenty of slightly charred Ben Franklins from the safe heist that they can't use otherwise, and leaving an anonymous payment for the damage done makes them feel like they are paying off a karmic debt.

Sam uses cash to buy a blue and white Volkswagen microbus, one of the few larger vehicles in which Kath is willing to ride. He takes out the backseats so it can hold all their gear, and it's anonymous enough that no one notices them parked in the same spot every day.

They always leave their current motel early, with the next one already prepaid. They are up and out the door by four a.m., and then they set up shop across the street from the downtown Flood Building where Kearne Securities has offices on the top floor. They park their microbus at five a.m. and watch everyone arriving for work. Since the Stock Market opens at nine in New York, traders in San Francisco must be at their desks ready to trade by six a.m., so there is a steady stream of Kearne employees coming in early. Sam and Kath watch everyone entering through the front and the back, cross-checking the schedules of every delivery truck, every postman, and every security guard who comes in and out of the building throughout the day.

The Flood Building was built in the 1950s, so it doesn't feel ancient in 1980, like some of the other downtown buildings that were built in the 1920s. It's sixteen stories, which makes it a difficult job, but it's not as impossible as doing a heist in the eight-year-old Transamerica Pyramid, just a few blocks away, which is impossible to penetrate.

For lunch, they move inside a small cafeteria restaurant called the Marlin Spike and watch more deliveries and exits. Eating tuna melt sandwiches and drinking black coffee, they note which delivery guys are friends with which guards. If they sit at the right table they can also see deep inside the loading dock to the service elevators, and how often they run.

After a week of constant observation, Sam and Kath start scouting the lobby.

One afternoon, Kath dresses in a crisp business suit, but snaps off a heel, scrapes holes in both knees of her pantyhose, musses up her hair and leaves a dirt streak on her cheek. Then she limps into the lobby of the Flood Building and holds up a broken strap to a purse.

"Purse snatcher! He came out of this building!" she shouts and points up the street toward some nameless thief who's not really there. Two guards run outside after the nonexistent perp, while two others help her sit down.

They call the police, give her water, and when she demands to see their monitors, they tolerate her coming behind the security desk to examine all the TVs they have, allowing her to see all the cameras broadcasting in the lobby, in the elevators and on the loading dock. Their cameras only record twelve hours at a time, and when they go back and examine the grainy electronic footage, they see no snatcher appear on any monitor.

"Maybe I was wrong about him coming out of your lobby," Kath says. "I'm sorry."

She disappears before the police arrive. However, she knows the number of cameras in the building, and the number of guards on duty.

The next week, Sam walks into the Flood Building wearing green overalls with an Otis patch on the chest pocket and a tool belt around his waist. He signs the building visitor ledger as an elevator maintenance worker named Otis Holbrook.

"I'm here for the safety check on your elevators," Sam says, as he signs the guest log.

"Safety check? The building manager never told us," the guard says.

"That's the point. I'm with the State Certification Board, so I do spot checks," he says.

I thought you worked for Otis Elevators," the guard says pointing at his patch.

"I do that, too. And my name is Otis, which is another reason I love elevators. Come see," he says and waves for a guard to follow him into an open elevator.

Sam points at the elevator safety certification mounted above the rows of buttons. "Your certification is five years old. Time for inspections."

"How long is this going to take?" the guard asks, not thinking that Sam's multi-tiered story invention makes no real sense.

"Not long, but I have to go up through these trapdoors," Sam says, and points up at the metal flap in the roof, common on older elevators, which grants you access to the elevator shafts. "I'll turn each elevator off for about half an hour. I'll do these two in front first. You have two service elevators on the loading dock too, right?" Sam asks, looking at his notepad.

The guard nods and then allows Sam to spend the rest of the morning creeping around inside the elevator shafts and examining the inner workings of the Flood Building. He learns everything about the electrical system, the garbage chutes, the mail drops, and the security system, and the layout for each floor of the building. In truth, he learns enough that he could become a decent maintenance worker for the Flood Building if he wanted, which the building management needs…but that's not how Sam thinks.

On another day, Sam poses as a bike messenger with a leather satchel across his back. He stops for a cigarette break in an alley across the street and lights a match for a young African-American man named Devon. Young Devon is a student at San Francisco State, with plans on becoming a doctor. But to earn cash, he pushes a food cart for the catering company that delivers meals to the different accounting, legal, and financial offices in the Flood Building.

Starting at seven a.m., men and women wearing black pants, white shirts with black bow ties and white aprons push metal trays on wheels through the halls, bringing fresh breakfast to all the mid-level young executives so busy they never leave their desks. In the morning, they can choose fruit salad, yogurt, orange juice, breakfast burritos, bacon and eggs, fresh bagels, dry cereal and even pancakes. At lunch, the servers return with carts with hardboiled eggs, salads, sandwiches and smoothies. There is no reason for the young workers to leave the building.

"Where do you get your uniform?" Sam asks Devon. He's the same size and shape as Sam. They lean against opposite brick walls in the alley, inhaling and exhaling their nicotine. Devon also wears a silver name pin on his breast pocket that says, "Apex Catering – Devon."

"Linden Lane Tailoring. It cost me twenty-five bucks. They have them on racks, ready to go. You just walk in and say you work for Apex Catering. They measure you, hand you one off the rack and you're an instant servant, ready to feed the worker bees," he says, stubbing out his cigarette butt. "Time to get back to the hive."

The kid's boredom with his job reassures Sam about his own career choices, forgetting the months of crushing boredom he endured in his prison cell not so long ago. It's all part of the necessary self-delusion he must create to make this job happen.

That afternoon Sam buys a uniform at Linden Lane Tailors and gets a fake silver Apex Catering pin that says "Bob – Trainee." Kath also gets her own uniform, and her pin says "Joanie – Trainee."

At five the next morning, Bob and Joanie join the gaggle of ten young cart pushers as they exit the BART station at Halliday Plaza and walk the downtown streets to the Flood Building. They all walk up the loading dock steps before anyone notices that "Bob and Joanie" are with them. When they do, Bob and Joanie give their new colleagues a wave.

"Hey," Sam and Kath both say.

"You two didn't punch in," the guard in his little wire-covered kiosk says to them. He points at the paper punch cards in racks lining the wall alongside the old metal punch time clock, where each employee must stick in a daily time card to get marked, once coming in, and then again going out.

"Yeah, I don't recognize you," Theresa, the young blonde senior caterer says.

Sam and Kath point to their trainee pins and shrug. "Haven't been officially hired yet," Sam says. "Probationary period."

The ten young cart pushers glance sideways at the newcomers. Devon is not one of them; Sam and Kath made sure to come to "work" on the day Devon has biology class at SF State. They all move to the large refrigerator on the loading dock, the one Sam and Kath can see from the Marlin Spike restaurant at lunchtime, when the sun lights up this cement cavern. The Apex delivery truck fills this refrigerator twice a day with food, so all the worker bees can eat.

For weeks, Sam and Kath have been watching these youngsters load cardboard boxes and plates of food onto rolling metal carts that they then push into the service elevators. Sam and Kath each grab a rolling cart and do the same.

Ten minutes later Sam and Kath exit the service elevators on the sixteenth floor, in the kitchen area of Kearne Securities. An older secretary with a bouffant hairdo waits for them.

"You're new," she says, eyeing Sam and then Kath.

"Apex trainees," Sam says, pointing at his pin. "Didn't they call?"

She scoffs and leads them to the newest technology in the office break room – the four-hundred-dollar microwave oven that Mr. Kearne bought himself. He is what the tech crowd will eventually call an "early adopter," and like the microwave oven that he bought to reheat food, Mr. Kearne always invests in the latest computers and monitor screens for his traders. He wants to create a "network" of computers that can directly trade with the traders on the floor of the Pacific Stock Exchange a few blocks away, and then use the phone lines to do the same with Wall Street. The floor traders at the Stock Exchange think Mr. Kearne is a fool to create such a network with the Exchange so close by, but Mr. Kearne will soon prove them all wrong.

The secretary shows Sam and Kath how to "reheat' the small cardboard boxes with the locking lids. The yellow ones have bacon and egg sandwiches and the red ones hold pancakes with sausages, the blue ones have breakfast burritos and the muffins and bagels are on small paper plates. The older secretary watches them load and unload the microwave oven, making sure that the catering staff does not damage this new and valuable machine.

"Don't reheat more than two boxes at a time, the machine can't take it," the woman says to Sam when he tries to fit in a third egg sandwich box. "And the bagels get too hot on the inside, no more than twenty seconds."

They load the warm food on the top shelf of the rolling cart. The cold fruit salad and yogurt cups and fresh orange juice sit in a long tray of ice on the second shelf. The bottom shelf has plenty of napkins and metal cutlery.

"Do we serve them coffee too?" Kath asks, gesturing at the large metal coffee maker in the corner, with the tall stack of Styrofoam cups.

"These boys don't need more caffeine," the secretary says. "And it tastes terrible."

"Got it," Sam says. He thinks for a moment about his coffee store idea, and how he could expand it to deliver great coffee to businesses like Kearne Securities, but the idea passes by fast.

"Make two passes on the trading floor, then go to the window offices and the front reception," the secretary says, and she leads them through a metal door and onto the trading floor.

The trading floor is loud. They push their rolling carts down rows of desks lined with men in suits, their jackets hanging on the back of their chairs, looking at black monitors with the green cursors, all of them talking on phones and yelling out their trades.

Sam and Kath wheel their carts behind the traders. There's an amazing view of the Bay Bridge and the San Francisco Bay out the window, but everyone faces the middle of the room so they can look at their trades and shout at each other over the partitions. A big electronic ticker tape hangs on the wall with rolling red LED lights zooming past with all the trades for the day.

"Breakfast, fruit, yogurt, orange juice," Sam says, and the men spin and grab food and plastic containers of fruit off the rolling cart. No orders, no bills, just food that rolls past and they can grab it, never saying *thank you* and never making eye contact. That lack of connection bothered young Devon when he told Sam about it on one of their smoke breaks, but for Sam it's perfect. Sam rolls his cart slowly and scans the room, learning everything. Kath does the same one row over.

Sam notices that the four security cameras are aimed only at the trading floor. The partners are more worried about employees stealing from within than from thieves coming in from outside.

Sam finishes feeding one row of traders, turns and makes his run past the offices with the windows. The sun is rising over the Oakland Hills to the East, and it fills the entire sixteenth floor with soft morning light.

Where on this 2,000-square-foot 16th floor would they hide a safe? From his day as an "elevator maintenance worker," Sam knows there's no point in searching the middle section, which houses the guts of the building: there's a square cement shaft that holds two elevators that face the lobby, and another two service elevators that open facing the back-loading dock. The central shaft also holds the pipes for the bathroom plumbing, the electrical wiring, and the air-conditioning ducts that branch off on each floor. Throw in the kitchen, and the bathrooms, and there's no space left in that middle section to put a vault, or even a closet.

The rest of the 16th trading floor surrounding that middle section is wide open. There are some walls around the reception area, but you wouldn't put a safe there. The safe that holds the actual stock certificates that Paul wants so badly must be in one of these window offices, where an executive works.

He goes slow, making sure to peek into every office, even making eye contact with some of the guys talking on their phones. They all ignore him except for the man in the corner office who gestures for him to stop.

"Bring me an egg sandwich and a muffin," he says in a thick Queens accent and snaps his red suspenders that hold up his black suit.

"Here you go, sir," Sam says, and lays the paper plate with the muffin and the carton with the egg sandwich down on his table.

That's when Sam spots it. Behind the executive is an oak end table that doesn't match the rest of the sleek, space-age furniture. It's a Honeywell Steel Security Safe, made to look like an oak end table. It's perfect for holding valuable papers, like stock and bond certificates.

Sam pauses for a second too long, because the trader speaks.

"You want a tip or something? Buy Walmart and don't stop buying. That's your fucking tip. Now leave," the trader says. He runs his hands through his thin grey hair and then grins at his sandwich before devouring half of it.

"Thank you, Mr. Kearne," Sam says, taking a chance.

"Don't call me that. That son of a bitch is in the corner office. My name is Smythe and I'm the CFO," the man says, and stuffs the rest of the sandwich in his mouth.

"Sorry, Mr. Smythe," Sam says and leaves.

The CFO hates the CEO. He has a motive to steal. The safe happens in his office. If it's an inside job, he may be the one who has communicated with Paul, letting him know about the safe full of certificates. Sam is learning a lot.

Sam and Kath wait until they are out of the building, back in their street clothes and driving away in the microbus before speaking.

"We're getting close," Sam says.

"Can you get into that safe?" Kath asks after she hears his story.

"I'll figure something out. I'm more worried about their office security."

On another day, Sam wears a wig, sunglasses and his bike messenger outfit, and he delivers a package addressed to Mr. Kearne himself. It's a package with nothing inside, but it has plenty of *rush* and *urgent* and *time-sensitive* stickers on the outside. He makes his fake delivery at six p.m. on a Thursday.

"We're closing," the young receptionist tells him as Sam exits the elevator. She's got teased-up brunette hair and a turquoise jacket with padded shoulders. She jingles the ring of keys in her hand.

"Urgent. For a Mr. Kearnes," Sam says, holding up the package.

"Leave it on the counter," she says.

"I need a signature," Sam says.

The receptionist sticks the elevator security key in the silver slot in the wall, leaving the keyring dangling in the lock. Sam stares at it as she walks back to the desk and grabs a pen.

"Aren't you a little old to be a bike messenger? You're at least thirty," she says, as she grabs Sam's clipboard and signs.

Sam points to the Grateful Dead t-shirt he's wearing. "If you follow the Dead, this the best part-time job you can get. I'm on the road with

Jerry a lot. When I'm not following the band, I stay in-shape doing deliveries."

She rolls her eyes and tosses Sam's package on her counter then points at the open elevator. "Let's go. I got places to be."

Sam gets on the elevator. He watches the receptionist twist her key in the lock and turn on the security system. She steps into the elevator and twists another key into the slot next to the "sixteen" button, sealing off access to the top floor. She pushes the lobby button and she and Sam ride down in silence.

Sam wishes he could ask if her security key automatically locked off the service elevators too, but that would be too obvious. Instead, he watches her put the keyring away in her large purse. It's a keyring with a Hello Kitty keychain, and the purse has no zipper, just a magnetic clasp. They ride the elevator down in awkward silence, and Sam disappears out the front glass doors.

The next day, Sam and Kath follow the receptionist after work. She walks through the maze of downtown buildings to the House of Shields bar and restaurant on New Montgomery Street, across from The Palace Hotel. At half past six, she eats bar snacks and drinks gin and tonics with her friends and colleagues. They are all well-dressed men and women, young urban professionals who work hard at corporate jobs in finance or accounting or advertising. All of them are smart. All of them have plans to make it big, and each is hoping to meet someone of the opposite sex who also has big plans. Sam and Kath watch the Kearnes Securities receptionist through the window. She laughs and flirts with her friends, pointing and talking, with her purse on the stool next to her. They'd stand out if they walked in right now, dressed in their funky bohemian jeans, scarves and leather jackets, so they linger outside in the fog.

"We need those keys," Sam says, staring at the purse through the window. "She's got two keys on a Hello Kitty keychain. One is for the elevator floor and the other is for the security system. They're stamped 'Do Not Duplicate.' We need one security key and two elevator keys. I'm just guessing, but I think I'm right."

"Are those keys the last thing we need?" Kath asks.

"Yep. But I'm no purse snatcher, and neither are you. And no following her home and breaking into her place. We're commercial burglars. Businesses only, never people."

"Maybe I can help."

"I'll figure something out," he says.

Kath doesn't talk anymore. Instead, she does some thinking of her own.

CHAPTER THIRTY-SEVEN

The next evening, Kath sips a cocktail in the House of Shields, dressed in a blue pencil skirt with a blue blouse. She glances at her watch every so often, to make it seem like she is waiting for someone who is late, but no one notices her. The receptionist arrives with her group of friends. Kath stares into her drink and listens to them talk about Stanford and Cal, Oracle and Apple, and their own plans to buy San Francisco real estate before the prices skyrocket. Kath wonders if she should have spent her twenties thinking about buying real estate too, and envies their youth and their plans.

She waits until the group of young men and women are loud and ordering their third round of drinks. Kath walks past them on the way to the bathroom, just as the bartender serves their drinks – and she knocks the receptionist's purse off her stool onto the floor. Kath picks it up and puts it back on the stool for her.

"Sorry about that," she says, and keeps walking with her own purse toward the bathroom.

She walks out the back of the bar and into Stevenson alley, then turns right into a two-story indoor garage, where a parked Vespa is waiting. She hops on and zooms down Stevenson Alley, turns right on 2nd Street, right on Mission, right on 4th Street and right up on the curb in front of Fox and Cole Hardware, the only real hardware store in downtown San Francisco. She walks inside, opens the purse, pulls out the keychain and hands them to the man behind the counter, along with an envelope.

The man checks the envelope, counts the cash inside, then pulls the keys labeled "Do Not Duplicate" off the keychain and twists the first one into the duplicating machine. Kath glances at her watch. She's been gone two minutes.

Five minutes later he finishes one copy of the security key and two copies of the elevator key and hands everything back to her. She pockets the copies and twists the originals back onto the Hello Kitty keychain.

"Will they work?" she asks.

"You won't know until you try. But don't come back."

Kath walks out, hops back onto the Vespa, zooms through traffic back to the parking lot, parks the Vespa, smooths her skirt and re-enters the House of Shields through the back. She glances at her watch. She's been gone exactly ten minutes.

The young urban professionals are right where she left them, now talking about Charles Schwab's new 24-hour stock price quotation service, and they're on their fourth round of drinks. As Kath passes the stool, she knocks the purse off it a second time.

"Sorry, I keep doing that," she says, sliding the keychain back into the receptionist's purse. She then puts the purse back on the stool and then walks down to her own.

The receptionist looks at her purse, checks the inside, and then her eyes follow Kath as she sits back down on her stool by the entrance. Kath watches the group out of the corner of her eye for a few minutes, then finishes her drink and leaves.

CHAPTER THIRTY-EIGHT

Sam and Kath vibrate across the shaking mattress, climaxing at the same time. There are no giggles, no laughing, no sweet talk. They disengage, roll away from each other like two opposing football players picking themselves up after a tough play.

Sam untwists the wires in the broken Magic Massage unit on the headboard. They are in the Buena Vista Motor Inn on Lombard Street, close to the Golden Gate Bridge.

"We're running out of motels on Lombard. We're going to have to move to Fisherman's Wharf next," Sam complains as he pulls out a charred fifty-dollar bill from a plastic bag and puts it on the bedside table.

They sit up against the headboard, side by side, and stare out the window at the lights of the cars heading down Lombard towards the Golden Gate Bridge.

"This is getting old," Kath says.

Sam shifts and Kath touches his leg.

"Not us. Just living in motels."

"You're avoiding Paul, I'm avoiding Hal Weinstein, and we're both avoiding Cliff and Dozer. It makes sense for a little while longer."

"How much longer?" Kath asks.

"I'm working on it," Sam says.

"I got you something today," she says, and pulls out a keyring from her bedside table. She tosses it on the bed sheets between them.

Sam inhales. "You got the keys. You got the damn keys."

"I guess that means we're ready."

Sam gets out of bed, grabs his clothes off the floor, goes into the bathroom and shuts the door. Kath stares at the closed door, listening to him pee and then running the shower. Kath puts the keys away. Feeling naked, she pulls on a t-shirt.

He comes out dressed. Kath stares at him as he sits down and puts on his shoes and socks, waiting for him to look up and make eye contact.

Look at me, she thinks. If he just looks at her when he talks, she could tell whether he's lying or not. He doesn't. "I thought getting the keys was a good thing," she says.

He stands up and puts on his jacket. "It is. And soon we're going to have everything we ever wanted. I promise. You want Chinese or Italian takeout tonight?"

"You're leaving because you don't want to talk to me, and the reason you don't want to talk is because you know I'll see through your bullshit story. You're a lousy liar, Sam Webb!"

The people in the adjoining room bang on the wall. Sam motions for her to stay quiet and then sits on the bed next to her. Kath crosses her arms. She now wishes she had gotten dressed first so that she could be the one leaving, and not him.

"When have I lied to you?" Sam asks.

"That's just like you. You won't say that you've never lied to me. Instead you ask me to prove it."

"Don't do this. Not now. You're too suspicious."

Kath scoots away on the bed, getting as far away from him as she can. "Fine. I trust you. Let's do the job. We're ready. Pick a day."

Sam puts his wallet in his pocket to avoid having to look at her. "I don't feel right yet."

"That's because there is no right day! There'll never be a right day!" Kath screams, and the people in the next room bang on the wall even louder.

Kath grabs her own clothes off the floor and pulls them on, not bothering to take a shower. She just wants out. She grabs her leather bag and stuffs in her loose clothes, her business outfit, her cosmetics, her socks, her *People* magazine, her toothbrush and toothpaste, just jamming it all inside.

"Where are you going?" Sam asks.

"I am going home. Paul knows we're together, so there's no point in hiding," she says, pulling on her jacket and beret. She grabs the leather bag, but he blocks her before she can get to the door.

"He wants us to fight like this. He's setting us up against each other. Can't you see that?"

She can't get past him. But he's trapped, too, because as long as he stands there blocking her, she can stare into his eyes, looking for the truth.

She thinks of her mother. She'd watched her confront many men just like Sam, in different motel rooms on different road trips around the country. The man would try to block her exit, just like Sam is blocking her now. As a young girl, she'd usually already be outside, ready to go, but looking back inside the open motel door, over the man's shoulder and into her mother's face. She'd stare at her mother, a blonde version of herself, willing her to find the strength to push past him so they could both escape, but her mother never could. She'd end up staring at her feet instead of at Kath, waiting outside the door. Her mother would cry, the man would make her put her bag down, and Kath would know they'd be trapped with him for another three months.

Kath swore she'd never let herself sink as low as her mother – yet here she is, in love with a liar she can't trust. She pushes past him. "Pick a day next week. I won't wait."

CHAPTER THIRTY-NINE

D etective Alden Stone sits behind his desk, still trying to figure out how to enter names into his new computer. He wishes he could just jump forward thirty years and speak into a microphone and have the computer create the file for him, but this is 1980, and working with a computer is like carving wood with a butter knife.

Tab. Write name. No. Just the first name. Then tab again. Then middle initial. Then tab again, and last name. Tab down. Description box. Is this how he must write up every case?

He needs the Giants game on for this. He turns on the transistor radio and leans it against the computer monitor – and sees something worse than data entry headed his way.

A heavy man dressed in loose polyester pants with a belt cinched tight in the middle strides toward him. He looks like a moving sack of potatoes as he weaves his way through the maze of metal desks. He's Mr. Hiram Valosek, the young, angry sales director for the Magic Massage Corporation. Detective Stone doesn't want to deal with him right now.

"I have it," Hiram says, waving a stack of cardboard punch cards in his hand.

"That looks like a stack of airline tickets," Stone says.

Hiram sits down in the chair in front of Stone's desk. "Detective, I am beginning to doubt that you take my case very seriously."

"I do take your case seriously. I just consider robberies and burglaries more important than vandalism."

"This is happening every *night,* Detective. You may think these are minor random occurrences, but this is a crime wave. It costs our company a fortune," Hiram says. He plops his stack of cards down on the desk. "But I have the data to catch them."

"Data?" Stone asks with a heavy sigh. He hates the word "data."

"I've collated all the information from each crime scene, and I've been able to identify a predictable pattern to these perpetrators. With the computer program I just wrote, we can predict, with a high degree of probability, the motels where they will strike next. All we must do is alert all the motels the computer gives us."

Stone stopped listening back when he heard the word "computer." Hiram's words turn his brain to mush, making Stone drift back to happier times when he was working the streets as a detective, instead of sitting behind a desk feeding an electronic brain.

"Excuse me," Stone says, and gets up and heads to the water cooler by the window. Maybe he'll phone Weinstein about sneaking away from their desks and going to a Giants game this afternoon. It'll be cold and windy as hell in Candlestick, but at least they'll be outside. Willie Mays would have beaten Hank Aaron's home run record if he hadn't been batting into the wind at Candlestick, he thinks to himself as he fills a paper cup with water.

"Alden, can we chat?"

Stone looks up. His boss, Captain Han, is standing a foot away.

"Where are we on that man and woman burglary team?"

"I've been busy, Cap, but I'm on it."

"The South San Francisco heist and the art heist may be linked. A man and woman burglary team? That's already odd, but two?" Han asks. "We have four witnesses. We can catch them."

"I put a list together of suspects from the mug books, but it's long," Stone says and crushes the paper cup in his hand.

Captain Han moves closer. "I know this computer stuff is bugging you. You want to be out on the street again. I get it."

Stone smiles. He knows Captain Han has his back.

Captain Han fills two more paper cups with water and hands one to Stone and mirrors him, acting like they're colleagues, and not boss and underling. "Find a computer expert to help you out, someone who you can work with. Just get your current files into the stupid machine and start using it. The Department will pay for it," he says. "If it pays off once, all this crap will be worth it."

Han slaps him on the back and heads out of the Detective Pool. As Stone walks back to his desk, Hiram Valosek picks his stack of computer cardboard punch cards off the table and waves it at him and smiles, like it was a stack of hundred-dollar bills.

Stone ponders Hiram Valosek and his cardboard punch cards, and then his own stack of manila folders that he must get into the computer, data he must enter just right so it doesn't take up too many megabytes of computer memory. Stone sits back down across from Hiram.

"Stop waving those cards at me. What do you know about the Tandy 1000 computer?"

"I know a lot. I just installed three at the Magic Massage Corporation."

Stone pushes the stack of files towards Hiram. "You help me with this, and then we talk about your Magic Massage units. The City will pay you your rate."

"Let's program your keyboard with some shortcuts and get started," Hiram says, rubbing his hands together.

Meanwhile, at the Buena Vista Motor Inn, the maid cleaning Sam and Kath's room from last night runs over something with her vacuum cleaner. She turns off the motor and digs it out from the brushes. It's the right-hand calfskin glove that Kath shoplifted from Macy's. The left glove she left at the first robbery. The maid stares at it, then at the broken Magic Massage unit and the charred bill on the bed stand.

CHAPTER FORTY

K ath sits at Bella's kitchen table comparing Bella's paper bank statements to what Bella has written in her checkbook register. Bella sits across from her eating cinnamon toast while playing Solitaire. "I wouldn't need to cross-check your statements against your checkbook if you'd just let me pay your bills for you. I can save you money."

"I can write my own checks," Bella says.

"I'd prefer to come down here and just visit you, and not bust your chops about how you send too many charity checks to the Veterans of Foreign Wars."

"Your grandfather Vito fought the Nazis in the Battle of the Bulge. Never forget that," Bella says, and wags her finger at her. "Other Italian Americans supported Mussolini. We never did. We fought on the side of freedom."

Kath ignores the finger-wagging as she adds up the check totals. She wishes she'd bought that new Casio calculator for sixty bucks, the kind that you can fit in your purse. They'd be at the track by now, instead of adding and subtracting amounts with a pencil.

"You haven't mentioned my flowers from my secret admirer," Bella says. She points at a new bouquet of sunflowers in a large blue vase on the coffee table in the living room.

"I saw them when I came in, Bella. Don't rub it in."

"What's up with you and that man?" Bella says.

"Do you mind? I can't monitor your spending and talk about my love life at the same time, it's too depressing."

"In fifty years, you'll look back on all this as the best time of your life."

"Great, something to look forward to," Kath mutters. "You made a mistake. We need to go to the bank and transfer $300 from your savings to your checking or you'll be overdrawn."

"Can't we just phone them?"

"No, Auntie. Banks don't work that way. You have to go stand in line and wait for a teller and explain the situation, so they can then make the transfer for you."

Bella reaches out and grabs Kath's hand, getting cinnamon and sugar all over it. Kath stares at her great aunt, wishing she could reach out and adjust her bad black wig, which sits too far back on Bella's head.

"Do you love him?" Bella asks.

"How can I? I don't even trust him."

"But do you love him?"

Kath puts down her pencil and looks at the bouquet behind her on the table.

"Yes. I think I do."

Bella waves her hand at Kath. "Then tell him. Just because he's a coward doesn't mean you should be one too. Be the best version of yourself. That's all you can do. It will give him something to live up to."

Kath nods. This makes sense.

CHAPTER FORTY-ONE

M rs. Wilkenson, in her little stucco house on 28ᵗʰ Avenue, comes upstairs from the basement with her mail. She tosses it on her dining room table, adjusts her eyepatch and examines each piece.

"I kill my knees going up and down those stairs for what? Junk mail," she says to her white cat sitting by the floor heater. She comes across another letter addressed to Rose, from Sam Webb. She scoffs and tosses it on the growing pile of letters from Sam that's already on her rosewood dining room table.

Her hallway phone rings. She walks past the kitchen door to a phone built into the wall with a little chair that folds down, so you can sit down while you talk on the phone, a 1940s luxury feature built into all the homes in the Sunset district.

"Hello? No, there's no Rose here," Mrs. Wilkenson says into the phone.

"No, Mrs. Wilkenson, I'm Rose. It's me, Rose Armanini, your old neighbor."

"Rose! I'm so glad you called! That Sam character keeps sliding letters for you into my mailbox. One came just today!"

Mrs. Wilkenson flops down the wooden seat from its slot in the wall and sits down, so she and Rose can have a long talk and catch up on all that has happened since Rose moved away.

"How's your boy, Carl? Is he doing okay?" Mrs. Wilkenson asks.

An hour later, Sam walks down Turk Street toward the Taj Mahal hotel. It's the first time he's been back in the neighborhood in weeks. He smells the urine and the rot and notices again how every color is muted except for harsh black and white, and he realizes the streets no longer hold any film noir nostalgia for him.

And right in front of the Taj Mahal is the black Town Car, with Cliff and Dozer sitting inside, eating fast food hamburgers. Cliff lowers his window and waves as Sam walks up.

"Hey Sam, we knew you'd show up eventually! Paul wants to see you."

Sam makes a left into the Taj Mahal lobby instead of answering him. He almost gets to the stairs before Mr. Pavel stubs out a cigarette and shouts at him.

"Sam Webb! Wait!"

"I paid you through the end of the month," Sam says back.

"Someone's been calling for you," Pavel says, just as the payphone on the wall rings again. Pavel looks at his watch and points at it. "She calls every two hours. That's her again. Answer it and talk to her before I throw your stuff into the street."

Sam stares at the ringing phone like it's a ticking bomb. He picks it up and whispers into the phone. "This is Sam Webb."

"Hello, Sam. It's me, Rose."

Sam's face brightens, and his face seems to grow ten years younger. "I knew you'd call."

"Sorry I didn't call earlier. Mrs. Wilkenson was busy protecting me. How are you?"

"Much better, now that I'm talking to you," Sam says. He glances outside. Dozer sits in the front passenger seat and stares at him through the plate glass window. Dozer nudges Cliff, who is mid-bite on his hamburger. Both men stare at him until Sam turns and faces the wall.

"We have a lot to talk about," Rose says.

"We do. When can I see you?" Sam asks.

An hour after that, Sam walks into Hal Weinstein's office. Again, he catches Hal mid-sip from his white Styrofoam coffee cup, but this time Hal doesn't spill.

"I need an out-of-town pass to go to Sacramento."

Sam bounces from one foot to the other, like he's ready to run a sprint.

Hal stands slowly, puts his cup down, and adjusts his comb-over.

"Where have you been the past few weeks?" Hal asks.

"I haven't missed an appointment. I saw you last Friday."

"I went by the Taj Mahal this past weekend and Pavel says you're hardly ever there. You come by only to change your clothes," Hal says.

"I've been spending a lot of time with my girlfriend," Sam says.

"What's her name again?" Hal asks, eyeing him carefully.

Sam waits a moment, wracking his brain. Did he give him a name? Did he give the right name? "Katerina Trulli. She lives on 29th Street, the steep part, in a pink house below Diamond Street."

"So, you've been sleeping in her pink house on 29th Street?" Hal asks.

Sam feels the sweat pooling under his arms and his porkpie hat. For all he knows, Hal's gone to the house already and knocked on the door. He decides to lie by not lying and give just enough truth to keep his bigger lie going. "We've been spending a lot of time in motels. Her landlady gives her a discount because she lives alone. Kath doesn't want to mess that up."

"She goes by Kat?" Hal says, scribbling all this down on a legal yellow pad.

"Yes sir," Sam says. "Can I get a pass to go to Sacramento?"

"You said you'd bring your girl in the next time I saw you. Maybe you thought I'd forgotten, but I haven't. And now that you want something, I can insist."

Sam looks across the desk at this beanpole skinny man with bad posture, but with the steely eyes and confident swagger of a gunslinger from the 1880s.

"I can't make her appear out of thin air. And I need this pass, Hal. I could've gone without asking and been back before you even knew I was gone."

"What's it for?" Hal asks.

"A job interview. They're building new condos up along the Sacramento River and they need someone who knows construction and electrical wiring and security systems, and I know all three. They hire ex-cons, too, but I'd need a letter to give to them."

Hal bends over his desk and writes it all down as fast as he can, then looks up. "That's a hell of a story. Keep talking, you're good at this."

"I like this girl, Hal. The City isn't good for me. Sacramento might be the place for me."

Hal looks up from his scribbling and puts his pen back inside his pocket protector. "That's the first believable thing you've said since you walked in here." He pulls out a form from one of his manila folders. "I can push and get you a week's pass today. Call me the minute you get there so I can check it out. Is she going with you?"

"If she can get off work. I don't know yet," Sam says.

"Either way, I want you both of you to call me on my office phone, today. I have to at least hear her voice," Hal says while filling out a form in pen. He fills in every box, signs it, dates it and hands it to Sam. "Show your potential employers this letter when you get there."

Sam takes it and puts it in his breast pocket. "Thank you, Hal. You're a friend."

"Good luck with the job. But if I don't hear from you in two days, I'm having both of you arrested," Hal says. "And I'll find out whether to be proud or ashamed of you as I enter my retirement."

Sam flashes a "thumbs up," as he dashes out of the office. "Go Giants."

"Go Giants," Hal says back to him as he sits back down.

CHAPTER FORTY-TWO

K ath walks into the lobby of the Taj Mahal Residence Hotel carrying a canvas tote bag. The three retired Merchant Mariners in their pea coats look up and stare at her like she's an alien.

"Hey, boys. Is it Fleet Week?" Kath asks.

"We're Merchant Mariners, not Navy. And we're retired," the Irish one says.

"Which means it's always Fleet Week for us," the Filipino one says, and winks.

Kath laughs and walks over to the counter where Mr. Pavel sits, enveloped in his perpetual cloud of blue cigarette smoke. Kath coughs and waves her hand.

"Can I help you?" Pavel asks as he lights another cigarette.

"I'm here to tell Sam Webb that I love him," Kath says, and pulls out a small gift-wrapped box from her canvas tote bag. "Can you give this to him?"

"He's never here," Pavel says, and exhales smoke in her face.

Kath fights the urge to cough. "I'll wait. I'm being brave. This is new for me."

Pavel stares at her with dull eyes and sighs, as if she were a boring TV show that he can't be bothered to turn off. Kath gets the message and sits on a broken chair near the three Merchant Mariners. She nods at them and smiles, and they do the same in return.

The payphone on the wall rings and Pavel scoffs and walks from behind the counter and answers it. "Hello? No, he's not! Why does everyone want to talk to Sam Webb?"

Kath keeps looking straight ahead, but she focuses her hearing on Pavel's conversation.

"Yes, I can take a message, hang on a sec," Pavel says, and grabs a pad and a pen from the counter and returns to the phone. "Go ahead…It's all set, we meet in Truckee on Monday, the same spot. I did everything you asked. Love, Rose…Yes, I have it!"

Kath stares at the three Merchant Mariners and the shiny white wall behind them. Her chair rises in the air and the whole room seems to tilt, like the men might spill out of their chairs and out the window, with her following close behind. She jams her hands in her pockets, so no one can see her clenching her fists. She grits her teeth until her chair touches the floor again and the room returns to level.

Pavel slams down the phone. "I should charge your friend extra rent for being his secretary," he says, but the chair is empty. Kath is already gone.

CHAPTER FORTY-THREE

The early afternoon sun pours through the windows of the Hall of Justice Building, filling up the entire floor of metal desks with golden light. Detective Alden Stone breathes deep and stretches like a cat, feeling good. Then he spots something that makes him feel even better. His buddy from the Parole Department, Hal Weinstein, is weaving through the desks, wearing his Giants hat and jacket.

"You good to go, Stone? I want to get to Candlestick before the close parking runs out."

"The wind is up. It's going to be cold out there," Stone says, meeting him halfway.

"No home runs today. But I got us seats in the sun."

"Are you officers going out to do field work?" a woman detective asks as they walk past.

"You could call it that," Stone says.

They hit the down button on the elevator and smile at each other.

"How's business?" Hal asks.

"Wonderful. I conquered the Tandy 1000. I've got six hundred files entered in the database. Life is good. How about you?" Stone asks.

"I'm so close to retirement that I'm refusing all electronics. The job still gets done."

"Whatever works, right?"

"Whatever works," Hal confirms.

The elevator doors open and Hiram Valosek steps off. His mouth turns up in a gigantic grin just as Stone's face descends into a frown.

"I have a breakthrough!" Hiram cries.

"Not now," Stone says.

"But you promised," Hiram says, sounding like a disappointed child.

Stone closes his eyes and sighs. "Can it wait? It's Willie McCovey Day."

"I don't know who that is," Hiram says, blocking the elevator doors.

As the doors close, both Stone and Weinstein think the same thing —they'll be late for the game. They'll have to park in the faraway lot, maybe miss the first inning, but if they're lucky they'll still get bobblehead dolls.

Hiram digs into his leather bag. "But we found this," he says, and pulls out a plastic baggie. Inside is a woman's leather glove.

"That's the other glove!" Stone yells and grabs for it.

Hiram pulls it back before he can take it. "Will you talk to me now?"

"Where did you get that?" Stone asks.

"The Buena Vista motel on Lombard Street. It's another room with a destroyed Magic Massage unit, but this time they left something behind."

Stone turns on his heel and waves for Valosek to follow him. Hal falls into place behind them both. "What are we talking about here?" Hal asks.

"A burglary team. A man and a woman. They've done two big jobs in the last three months. Professionals. No prints. One was a safe job. They got a lot of money both times." Stone reaches his desk and starts leafing through his files trying to find the right folder.

"What are you doing? Use the computer," Hiram says, with a condescending enough tone to make Stone and the other cops in the room freeze. Hiram senses that all eyes are on him. "What I mean is that I entered all the files for you. Just plug in the information."

"Show me," Stone says and points at Hiram to sit down in front of the Tandy 1000. He and Hal trade looks as Hiram turns the computer on.

"After entering all your data for you, I also added my own data cells on your computer, and then plugged in my information on the criminals. The motel managers say the man is six feet tall, with black hair, and about two hundred pounds. They always pay in cash, and use the same three aliases every time," Hiram mutters to himself as he taps away at his keyboard. "I'm now accessing your data and compiling a list of anyone arrested for burglary in the last five years...you said that one of the jobs was breaking into a safe, so I'm entering that as well...and now I'm entering in all his aliases...and then I ask the computer to cross reference all the data and give me some names."

He hits return, and four names appear in green on the black screen.

"Dennis Sitze, Robert Newton, Glenn Morgan, and Sam Webb."

"Sam Webb? I just wrote a pass for him to go to Sacramento," Hal says.

"He's one of four people who could be on a crime spree damaging Magic Massage units in motels across San Francisco," Hiram says, sounding more like a 70s TV show cop than a real cop.

Stone looks at his friend from Parole, sees the crushed look on his face, and feels bad for him. Parole officers are a different breed. Detectives get excited when they're getting close to a bust. Parole officers feel regret when a criminal turns out to be one of their own.

"Magic Massage? You mean those boxes that make the mattress shake?" Hal asks.

"It's a therapeutic massage treatment," Hiram says, sounding offended.

Hal Weinstein leans over the desk and points his finger hard at Hiram, and the Magic Massage sales director feels Hal's deep inner power hit him. Hiram rolls back in the chair, stunned.

"You will now bear witness," Hal says. "Tell me everything you know."

"A man and woman check into a motel every night. They pay in cash ahead of time. He uses the name DeMartini, Smith, or Randazzo.

They always get a room with Magic Massage close to the ice machine. They destroy a Magic Massage unit every night and leave behind a fifty-dollar bill. Some of them have burn marks, like the money was in a fire."

Stone leans in, adding to the story. "On the safe job, they used a torch and burned a lot of the money. And on the South San Francisco job she left a brown calfskin glove," Stone says. He digs through the larger drawer and pulls out the right-hand glove that Kath left behind. He puts it on the table. Hiram lays his glove down next to it. It's a perfect match.

"It's not Sam. He's straight now," Hal says.

"How do you know?" Hiram asks.

"My gut."

"Your gut doesn't matter. The data tells us that it could be Sam Webb," Hiram says.

"Any chance your boy is getting hot?" Stone asks.

"He's staying at the Taj Mahal. Maybe we should head over there."

"The Taj Mahal! I met this man! He destroyed a unit in Room 222 on April second of this year!" Hiram says, then lowers his voice when he feels everyone's eyes on him again. "Sorry, I'm good with dates and numbers."

"That's Sam's room. And he was released from prison on April first of this year," Hal says, with growing defeat in his voice.

"Let's get over there and arrest him," Hiram says.

"He's not there. He's leaving town," Hal says.

"Where's he going?" Stone asks.

"He said Sacramento. But he could be going anywhere," Weinstein says, with true disgust and disappointment now.

Hiram leans back, crosses his arms and smiles. "We'll catch him. We just call every motel with Magic Massage within a five-hundred-mile radius of San Francisco. If anyone fitting their description checks into a motel and asks for a room with Magic Massage near the ice machine, I'll get a call."

Stone looks at the smug computer programmer and feels a wave of fear wash up his spine. Hiram, or someone like him, will take his job someday.

"We can start with Paul Barnes," Hal says. "If Sam has slipped, he may be involved."

"Really?" Stone asks. "We've been trying to nail that guy with something for years."

"I suggest we go with my plan," Hiram says, with a warning in his voice. You'll get faster results."

"Get out of my chair," Stone says with enough venom in his voice that Hiram jumps up. "We're not doing that yet. We're going to work the streets first, no matter what your computer list says."

CHAPTER FORTY-FOUR

It's five a.m. Sam sits behind the wheel of the Volkswagen parked across the street from the Flood Building. He watches the delivery men drive up to the loading dock and greet the guards in the same way they have done every weekday for the last month. He looks at the clipboard on his lap with the box chart that he's made, and he checks off boxes. The people coming and going is confusing at first, until you recognize the patterns in the chaos and you can predict what will happen next. At ten a.m., the Marlin Spike will open, and he'll have coffee and a tuna melt and check his boxes yet again as the postmen and garbage collectors arrive.

There's a tap on the passenger window. It's Kath. Sam lifts the lock and Kath opens the door and slides in.

"I didn't know if you were going to show," Sam says. "But I'm glad you did. We do the job tomorrow."

"Tomorrow?" Kath asks.

"Right here, at three in the morning. You said to name the day, and I'm naming the day. That's the answer you wanted, right?"

"It is. Thank you."

"We start a new life tomorrow. We give Paul his cut and then we can leave town and be free of him forever. I have it all figured out."

Kath stares ahead through the windshield. Sam wants her to look at him, but despite his willing it with all his might, she doesn't. "I was wrong to doubt you," Kath says.

"I'll be at the Bay View Motel in Fisherman's Wharf. They have Magic Massage."

"I think we should spend the night apart tonight," Kath says.

"Are you going to spend the night at home?" Sam asks.

"Down in San Mateo with a friend. I don't like to be at home the night before a job."

"Like a bride and groom spending the night apart before the wedding."

Kath laughs, then snorts, trying to swallow it. "That's funny."

"We've put as much planning into this as a wedding. More."

"But it's not a wedding. It's a robbery. Let's just get through that first, okay?" Kath says, and stares into his blue eyes. Her eyes soften, and her lip curls up in a tiny smile that tells him that she still loves him, no matter what he's about to do to her.

"Will you do a favor for me?" Sam asks.

"It depends," Kath answers.

"I need us to call my parole officer today. If he hears your voice, I can leave town without any hassle."

"You can leave town?"

"*We* can leave town. It's a week pass. Then we'll call him in a couple of days and tell him that I got a job in Sacramento and then I can apply for a total transfer. We'll never come back here again."

"We can call tomorrow after the job."

"I need to call him today," he says.

"I'm not talking to him until we're safe and out of town."

"You don't trust me," Sam says.

"I'll see you here tomorrow at three," she says, and gets out of the microbus.

Sam watches her walk away in her long coat, willing her to look back at him. That would be proof to him that his plan will work. So many pieces must fall into place, like tumblers inside a lock that must all match up, which then opens a window so that he can escape from the burning house and bust through to freedom. She gets to the corner and glances at him and smiles. It's not proof of anything really, but it makes him feel lucky enough that his crazy plan will work and maybe not hurt her too much.

He's taking a chance not calling Hal, though. He just hopes Hal will continue to assume the best about him and grant him one day of grace before calling the cops. Hal will be disappointed in him if he ever finds out the truth. Sam pushes the thought from his mind. He's too far gone to turn back now.

CHAPTER FORTY-FIVE

Four hours later, Kath walks into the Mission Bay Health Club. It's 9 a.m. on a Tuesday, and the place is packed, which makes Kath hate Paul that much more. Paul is successful, despite being a sociopath. Maybe *because* he's a sociopath. He was also right about Sam, which is the most infuriating fact of all.

Kath ignores the young woman dressed in white behind the counter asking for her membership card and walks past the weights and treadmills and Nautilus exercise machines and finds Paul in a back corner with Inge. The big Swedish gal is holding a heavy punching bag, so Paul can punch it without it swinging. They both wear thin boxing gloves, red velour tracksuits and orange terry cloth headbands. Inge growls when Kath walks up.

"Now is not a good time," Paul says, punching the bag hard.

"You were right about Sam. He's going to screw us both. Tomorrow."

Paul steps away from the bag. "Inge, I must talk to her, but to protect you we have to be alone. Understand?"

The towering, monosyllabic, lethal, beautiful, and devoted Swede steps away from the bag and looks down at Paul with hurt eyes. She loves him, Kath realizes, and Kath envies her love. Paul is a pig, but Inge doesn't care. And between Sam and Paul, the shorter guy is the better choice of man, it turns out.

Inge leaves. Paul gestures for Kath to approach. Paul's body smells of sour sweat and his breath is like a poop sandwich, but Kath obeys and moves close.

"Rose showed up," Paul says.

"Yes."

"Give me all the details."

CHAPTER FORTY-SIX

S am lies on his motel room bed, trying to enjoy Johnny Carson's monologue, but he's too distracted. There's a knock on the door.

Sam leaps off the bed and goes to the door. "Who is it?"

"It's me," Kath says. Sam swings the door open, and she steps inside.

"I thought you were spending the night somewhere else," he says.

"I was in church praying instead," she says. She takes off her long coat and throws it on the bed. Sam moves close and tries to kiss her, but she pushes him away.

"I want to go over the plan," she says.

"You're tense. We should try to get some sleep."

"I want to go over the plan!" she shouts, and he pulls out his clipboard with his grids and timetables and checked boxes. Kath takes it and sits down at the little writing table tucked into the corner, and grabs a Bay View Motel pen and a pad of paper out of the drawer.

There will be no Magic Massage tonight, Sam thinks to himself. He turns off the TV and lies down on the bed, hoping for some sleep.

Three hours later, Sam walks alone on a dark beach with huge waves crashing to his left. There is a thick fog and the sound of distant foghorns coming from across the water. A woman's figure appears in the fog, in a long green dress, with red hair. Sam walks faster, but she seems to stay the same distance away. He runs faster, yelling her name.

"Rose? Rose!"

An insistent beeping starts. Men appear out of the water with rifles and guns and dash up on the beach shooting at him. A battleship appears out of the dark waves, about to run aground.

Sam waves his arms hoping the ship will see him. A soldier aims a pistol at Sam's face, and Sam knocks it away with his fist. Someone catches his hand in mid-air.

"Sam!" Kath yells.

Sam is in the Bay View Motel, and Kath is holding his fist in her hands. He pulls his hand away and turns off the beeping alarm clock on the nightstand.

"You hit me in your sleep. What are you doing?"

"I was defending the beach," Sam says.

"Was Rose helping you? You were yelling her name."

"Sort of," Sam says, and gets off the bed. They are both still dressed in their street clothes. The sound of foghorns drifts across the neighborhood. A thin beam of light from a street lamp ekes through the window, lighting up one side of Kath's face.

Sam goes to the small desk where his plans are spread out from last night. "You have this memorized?" he asks.

Kath nods. Sam tears the pages in half, then rips them again, and again, until his months of work is just confetti. He tosses it all into the trash. He carries the can into the bathroom, dumps it all into the toilet, and flushes it away. Sam exits the bathroom and picks up his black canvas bag with all his supplies. Like an Eagle Scout gone bad, he's prepared.

Kath opens the door, and they walk out.

They climb into their blue and white Volkswagen bus. In the back is a large canvas rolling cart with a locking wooden top, the kind Sam used to push when he worked in the laundry in San Quentin. This one, however, is clean and new and full of gear. Sam tosses his black canvas bag in next to it.

"Am I going to fit in that cart with all our gear?" Kath asks.

"You'll have room to spare. I measured," Sam says, and they drive along the Embarcadero towards downtown. They park in the darkness underneath the Embarcadero Freeway off ramp that leads into the Transbay Bus Terminal. They exit the Volkswagen. Sam opens the back and pulls out his black bag, but they leave the canvas cart on wheels inside. Sam pulls out two pairs of yellow latex gloves and hands one to Kath. They pull them on.

"How much money did you put in your shoe?" Sam asks.

"Five hundred dollars. Just in case I have to run."

"Good. Me too. He'll be coming out in five minutes," Sam says.

The guard who works at the Flood Building loading dock during the day exits the Transbay Bus Terminal and walks up Mission Street towards work. As he passes Bluxome Alley, Kath steps out of the darkness.

"Good morning," she says in a voice with just enough allure that he stops – and Sam walks up behind him and puts a gun to his temple. "Get into the alley," Sam whispers in his ear.

The guard obeys, and Sam handcuffs him to a drain pipe in the very back of the alley and slaps a thick piece of duct tape across his mouth. "Someone will find you by ten a.m.," Sam whispers in his ear.

Ten minutes later, a green S.E. Reikoff Food Truck with the restaurant logo – "Enjoy Life – Eat Out More Often," written on the side comes to a stop on Second Street and Bryant. It's full of food for the caterers at the Flood Building. Kath steps in front of the truck and waves. The man leans on the horn –

– just as Sam same steps on the running rail, opens the driver's door and puts a gun to his head. Kath gets in on the passenger side and grabs the man's keys.

Ten minutes later, Sam handcuffs the driver to a drain pipe at the back end of Cosmo Alley while Kath puts duct tape across his mouth. Sam also takes the man's shirt, but covers him with an itchy wool army blanket that he bought at the surplus store, just for this occasion.

Sam climbs behind the wheel of the food truck. Kath is already in the passenger seat.

Sam isn't thinking; he's just doing. His plan is proceeding, and there's no reason to talk.

Kath is proceeding without speaking as well, but she *is* thinking, however. She is waiting for Sam to divert from his perfect plan that she studied last night. That's the moment he will betray her, she realizes, and that's when she must put her own plan into place. All emotion must be pushed down. She will follow Plan A until he forces her to proceed with Plan B, and she will make her own plan happen, without emotion, like someone flipping a light switch.

Ten minutes later, Sam backs the truck up against the back of the VW bus. He and Kath hop down from the cab, and Kath opens the back hatch of the Volkswagen while Sam opens the back door of the food truck.

Inside the truck are tall metal racks full of food for the caterers, but there is space near the door for Sam's laundry cart. Sam slides out two long pieces of wood from inside the Volkswagen, and lines them up with the interior of the truck, making two little wood bridges between the backs of the two vehicles. He and Kath roll the cart along the pieces of wood from inside the Volkswagen right into the truck.

He slides the gun inside his front pocket, takes off his jacket and shirt and puts on the truck driver's official green shirt, zips his clothes up inside his black bag and tosses it in the laundry cart. He gestures for Kath to climb in next. She climbs in the truck.

"Once you lock me in here, there's no turning back," she says.

"We have to be on that loading dock in five minutes," he says, and slides the door shut.

Kath mutters a prayer to herself in the dark. She lifts the wooden top off the laundry cart, adjusts Sam's bag inside and climbs in. She gets the wooden top closed, sealing her in, just as Sam drives away.

Five minutes later, Sam backs the green food truck up to the loading dock of the Flood building. A guard steps out of the metal cage and punches out his time card as Sam climbs down from the cab of the truck.

"You're a little early, aren't you?" the guard asks.

"Tell me about it. Last minute order for a catered lunch for the bigwigs at Kearnes. It throws my whole schedule out of whack."

"I'm punched out, and you can't unload until Tom gets here. Sorry," the guard says. "I have to close the doors."

Sam puts his hands together like he's praying. "This job is a nightmare. Do me a solid and just let me unload my truck into the fridge or I'll miss my next drop off. Tom Jenkins is a friend of mine, we go to Raiders games all the time."

The guard looks at his watch, then waves at Sam. "Pick up the main phone and let the guards at the front desk decide what to do. Say that Tom's late and I'm already gone," the guard says as he steps off the loading dock and disappears into the grey predawn light.

Sam opens the back of the truck and wheels out the covered canvas cart on wheels. He wheels out the metal racks with all the food, but instead of loading them into the large refrigerator on the loading dock, he positions them in front of the elevator – creating a barrier that no one can see past, including the camera, mounted high on the wall.

In the front of the building, the one guard on duty walks back and forth along the marble floor by the front doors, waiting for the day to start. If he were behind the desk, he wouldn't be able to see the service elevator on his monitor, only the tall metal racks from the food truck blocking his view, but Sam watched his habits long enough to know he always paces in the early hours before the building opens.

In one hour, the caterers will arrive and want to load food onto their own smaller rolling trays. The first employees for Kearnes Securities will then arrive at five-thirty in the morning and prep the office for the traders, who will drive their luxury sedans and sports cars into the underground parking below. They'll ride up the elevators at five-fifty in the morning and be ready at their trading consoles at exactly six in the morning, ready for the stock market opening in New York.

On the loading dock, Sam lifts the wooden lid off the laundry cart and helps Kath step out, safe from view in their hidden area framed by the tall metal food racks. They push the button for the elevator.

The doors open and Kath and Sam step on. Sam pulls the stop button, freezing the elevator in place. He pulls out a walkie-talkie from his pocket. Kath pulls out hers.

"Channel one, copy," Sam says.

His voice crackles on her walkie-talkie. She pushes her button and replies. "Copy," she says, and her voice crackles back on his walkie-talkie.

"Keys," Sam says, and pulls out the elevator key and the alarm key she copied for him.

"And I have my key too," Kath says with a barb of sarcasm, and holds up her copy of the copy of the elevator key. "Let's hope they work, right?"

"Hope is my middle name, baby," Sam says. Kath rolls her eyes.

Sam jumps up and pushes the trap door in the ceiling, knocking it open. He had left it unlocked when he "serviced" the elevator. Sam jumps, grabs the lip, puts his feet against the elevator wall and pulls himself up into the shaft.

He leans his face back through the hole and motions for Kath to toss him his black bag from inside the laundry cart. She pulls it out and lifts it up, and he grabs the handle and pulls it through the trap door.

"I'll walkie you when the alarm system is off, and you can come up. If you don't hear from me in ten minutes, open the elevator doors and walk away," he says – and his face disappears into the darkness.

Kath sighs and looks at her watch. It's ten minutes past four. She must give him credit; his plan is right on schedule. No reason for Plan B yet.

Sam is inside the elevator shaft – a huge open square column in the middle of the building. It has four elevators – two service elevators that face the back of the building, and two more that face the front of the building, completing the four portions of the square. Sam steps from one elevator roof to the next.

Sam kneels on the roof of the front facing elevator and opens the trapdoor roof without making a sound. He listens for the guard. The lights are on inside, including the lights for the floors. He pulls up a section of duct tape that's taped to the roof of the elevator that he's on, and exposes wires – wires he stripped and prepped for this moment. He untwists one set of wires, and twists together another set of wires, and he peeks back down inside the interior of the elevator cabin. The interior lights go off, including the round lights above the door that illuminate the floor numbers.

Sam puts the duffel bag on like a backpack, sits down on the lip, and eases down into the elevator cabin. His feet make a noise when he lands. He listens for a second but does not hear the guard. He pulls out his flashlight and lights up the button panel.

"I hope these work," Sam says to himself. He sticks the elevator key in the slot next to the button for the sixteenth floor and twists it. The elevator rises, but all its lights stay out. Sam's rewiring trick worked. He swallows and wipes away sweat from his forehead.

Out in the lobby, the guard pacing the lobby's marble floor hears the elevator move, but when he glances over, he doesn't see the numbers light up. He goes back to staring out the front windows. He's more concerned with the Lincoln Town Car parked across the street and wonders how many people are inside.

Cliff and Dozer are in the front and Paul is in the back, but no one can see through the tinted windows Paul installed. "One hour doesn't leave him much time," Paul says, looking at his watch. "I'd like to see how he pulls this off."

"Are you *sure* Kath said he'd be doing it between four and five?" Dozer asks.

"I'm not even going to answer that," Paul says. He pulls out a walkie-talkie from his pocket, sets it to channel one and turns it on.

The elevator reaches the sixteenth floor. The doors open, and beeping begins. Sam steps off the elevator, sticks the alarm key in the alarm pad on the wall and twists – and the beeping stops. Sam carries his black bag past the trading area and the offices. The rising sun is just a red line over the distant Oakland hills.

He reaches the kitchen area. He tries the doorknob. It's locked. He puts down his bag and unzips it and takes out a screwdriver and a rubber mallet. He puts the screwdriver into the lock and smashes the rubber mallet hard against it, busting the mechanism open. He flashes the light inside the hole, flicks a latch and opens the locked doors to the service area.

He clicks his walkie-talkie. "Come up," he whispers.

"On my way," her voice crackles back.

The elevator reaches the sixteenth floor. The doors open. Kath pushes the laundry cart off the elevator. Sam looks at his watch.

"We have ten minutes," he says.

He helps her push the laundry cart out of the service area while avoiding the one security camera, past the trading area, ending at Mr. Smythe's office. His door is also locked, but with another two whacks with the rubber mallet against the butt end of the flathead screwdriver, the office door opens. Out the window, the sun is now a tiny yellow dot on the horizon, but it's growing.

They push the laundry cart inside and move all the chairs out of the way, until the laundry cart is butted up against the oak end table which hides the Honeywell Steel Security Safe. Sam opens the wooden lid of the laundry cart and lifts out a crowbar. He reaches inside the laundry basket and unclasps a dozen snap ties from around each corner post, and lifts off the canvas, leaving just a wood board nailed into a square of two-by-fours attached to wheels. He puts the cart's canvas skin aside, picks up the crowbar, jams it under the base of the safe, and lifts.

As the safe tilts, Sam drops the crowbar and grabs the safe before it falls over, and keeps it teetering on edge. He motions to Kath. "Push that thing against it hard," he whispers, and Kath pushes the wooden cart up against the safe that Sam holds at an angle. Sam lowers the safe down as Kath pushes, and the safe lays down on its side, right on the exposed wooden base of the cart. Sam pushes and teeters and shimmies the entire two-hundred-pound safe until he gets it onto the wood base of the tilted laundry cart...and then he eases the cart back down onto its wheels.

"Done," he says, and reaches over and grabs the canvas and wood top and he and Kath ease it back down over the four corner poles, covering up the heavy safe as if it were just dirty laundry. They snap all the metal clasps back into place.

Sam pulls out the final few items from inside his amazing black bag. The Apex Catering shirts they wore a few weeks back, with the Joanie and Bob name tags still pinned on. Sam takes the gun out of his pocket and tosses it in the cart – the gun is empty anyway – and he and Kath take off their hats and shirts and put on their uniforms. Last of all, Sam pulls out the metal briefcase with Paul's fingerprints on it and leaves it on the floor, right where the safe used to be. He then puts the wooden lid back onto the laundry cart and locks it with a padlock.

"It's a quarter to five, let's go," Sam says.

He and Kath push the cart as hard as they can, and it moves an inch. They push again, and once the wheels are moving, pushing it is easier.

The plan is working, Kath thinks. They'll ride the service elevator back down to the loading dock, push the cart back onto to the food truck, and drive it away just before the real caterers arrive. Then they'll go back to the Volkswagen bus, bring the two ends close, roll the cart back into the Volkswagen, and drive it to the garage she rents of Shotwell. Sam will crack the safe there, and leave Paul his cut in the garage. They will call Hal, Sam's parole officer, so the man can hear that Kath exists. They may even drop by his office and say "hello." Then they will escape The City and drive to Sacramento or wherever Sam wants to go. Wherever he chooses is fine by her, just as long as it's far away from here.

Kath realizes that she made a mistake. She was wrong about Rose. She shouldn't have called Paul, she thinks. She should have trusted Sam, and now she may have ruined it.

They push the cart hard and bang through the metal doors and into the service area and Sam pushes the button, calling the elevator back up.

"What if the catering staff is already there?" Kath asks. "Some of them get here early."

"Those are the gung-ho ones. They'll be unloading the racks of food we left out and putting them on the metal carts or putting them in the refrigerator. I'll just push the cart onto the truck and tell them it's an emergency and drive away."

"You mean 'we' drive away," Kath says.

The elevator doors open with a ding. Sam and Kath push the cart onto the elevator.

"No, I drive away. I want you to ride down one more floor to the parking garage and get off there first," Sam says, and instead of hitting "L" for the loading dock, Sam punches "P1" for the first floor of the parking garage. The elevator starts down. "We have five minutes before the first traders show up. I have a surprise for you."

Sam flashes his crooked smile, the same one she first saw in Macy's months ago. He's a liar after all, and she's a fool to have trusted him. Most of all, Kath wishes she'd never stolen those gloves in the first place. Then she would never have met him, and none of this would be happening.

Kath clicks her walkie-talkie "Plan B," she says, and hits the "L" button on the elevator.

"What are you doing?" Sam yells. "Your surprise is on P1!"

The elevator doors open on the loading dock. Paul and Cliff stand there, with guns pointed right at Sam. Cliff jams his foot against the closing door so it stays open.

"Let's go, Sam. We're taking a drive to your 'usual' spot in Truckee," Paul says. "Rose is waiting."

"What did you do? I had it all worked out," Sam says to Kath.

"I'm sure you did," Kath says.

"Shut up and get off the elevator," Paul says.

"What about the safe? There's a hundred thousand in certificates in there," Sam says.

"When Kath told me about your plan, I called Smythe and told him. That safe is empty," Paul says, and waves for Paul to step off the elevator. "I told you, always do it my way."

Sam doesn't move. Paul lowers his gun, reaches into the elevator, grabs Kath by the forearm and drags her out onto the loading dock. "Come on, Joanie from Apex Catering," Paul snarls. "We'll go visit the old lady with the eye patch and get her to tell us where Rose is hiding. Cliff, shoot him."

Sam jumps up on the laundry cart top, kicks Cliff's gun out of his hand and leaps up through the open trapdoor in the ceiling of the elevator. Like a circus gymnast, he lifts his upper body through and pulls his legs up next, before Cliff or Dozer can even react.

"Shit! Get him out of there!" Paul yells.

Paul shoots up at the ceiling and the bullet zings around the inside of the elevator. Sam's feet disappear up into the elevator shaft.

"You said no shooting!" Kath screams.

Inside the elevator shaft, Sam steps from the top of one elevator to the next and jumps back down inside the front elevator. Its doors open, and the brunette receptionist with the purple jacket with the padded shoulders steps on the elevator. Sam glances at his watch. It's quarter to six, time for her to open Kearne Securities, and she's got her Hello Kitty keychain in hand.

She looks at his name tag, then at him. "Aren't you supposed to be on the loading dock?" she asks, then stares longer at him. "Hey, you're the messenger who follows the Grateful Dead!"

She then looks at his dirty uniform, his messy hair, and then glances up and sees the open trap door into the ceiling. Her eyes widen in complete understanding.

"Guard!" she yells as she steps off the elevator.

Sam hits all the buttons. The doors close and the elevator rises. The elevator passes the first, second, and third floor, skipping every floor that Sam pushed. The guard is sending all the elevators to the top floor and locking them in place. He keeps punching the buttons, but the elevator doesn't stop, and the doors don't open.

At the back of the building, Paul and Cliff drag Kath down the steps and off the loading dock. Dozer darts ahead and opens the back door of the Lincoln.

"Let me go!" Kath yells.

"Cops are coming. We can find Rose in Truckee without him."

"I've got to see downstairs," she yells, and yanks herself free.

She runs down the ramp into the underground garage, weaving between the arriving brokers in their BMWs and Porsches. They honk at her, as she darts in and out of their car headlights. It's ten minutes to six and they are arriving right on time.

She makes it around the cement curve at the bottom of the ramp and sees it – a 1964 blue convertible Porsche Roadster, with the driver's side open. She falls to her knees.

"You bought me my car," she whispers to the sky.

The Town Car pulls up. Paul and Cliff jump out, grab her by each arm and toss her in the back. The Town Car tears back up the exit ramp and turns into the street, twenty seconds before the squad cars arrive.

CHAPTER FORTY-SEVEN

Detective Stone feels a rush as he walks into the lobby of the Flood Building. The breakthrough in the burglary team case was a jolt of excitement yesterday, and now they may be getting something on the hard-to-catch lowlife Paul Barnes. Then this morning he gets called for his first live burglary case in months. His work slump, magnified by all that computer hassle, may finally be over.

He weaves through a dozen street cops in the lobby, all of them dressed in blue with their hands resting on their Sam Browne gun belts, and reaches the marble reception stand and guard station.

All three of the Flood building guards are under thirty, muscular, with pencil-thin mustaches and curly brown hair, like they're trying to be the "Meet the Turk" guy in the cigarette ads. They're all shaking, however. This is the only action any of them has ever seen on the job. He looks at the oldest one, who seems to be shaking the least.

"What happened?" Stone asks him.

"We heard shooting coming from the loading dock. The receptionist from Kearnes Securities thinks there was a break-in. We sent all the elevators to the top floor."

"Anyone leave the building?" Stone asks.

"Not that we can tell," the guard says. "We don't have great cameras on the loading dock or in the garage, though."

"Call the building owner and ask him to come down here," Stone says, then turns to the Lead Sergeant on duty. "Hey, Hank. Is a perimeter set up?"

"All exits are covered," the Sergeant says. He's fifty, but with the physique of a super fit thirty-year-old.

Stone steps behind the guard station and looks at the grainy black and white security monitors. He sees no movement. There are four lines of vertical red LED lights that indicate where the four elevators are – all on the top floor. This is cutting-edge security technology, but it reveals nothing.

"Let's bring them down, one by one," Stone says. "Start with the front left."

Officers line up in front of the elevator, crouch, draw their weapons and wait for the elevator to descend. The doors open – and the elevator is empty. So is the next one.

They move to the loading dock. It turns out the morning guard still hasn't shown up, which is a bad sign. Either he's been hurt, or it's an inside job.

They bring down the first loading dock elevator, and it's empty as well – but the last one has a laundry cart. They put on gloves and pull the cart off the elevator and use bolt cutters to cut the lock. They lift the wooden lid, and inside the cart they find a Honeywell Steel Security Safe, a black canvas bag, and clothes for a man and woman.

Stone's back stiffens as a jolt of electric clarity runs up his spine. Sam Webb did this job. He didn't leave town like Hal thought. He and his female partner could be in this building right now.

He turns to the Sergeant. "I need to get a message to Hal Weinstein in Parole."

"We'll find a phone. Is he at Bryant Street right now?"

"He may be rolling," Stone says. "Try dispatch too."

Sergeant Hank nods and walks away. Stone knows it still may be an hour before they track Hal Weinstein down. In the meantime, if Webb is in this building, he'll find him.

Sam climbs down a ladder high in the elevator shaft; its rungs are made of bent rebar and it's set into the interior wall of concrete. He made sure to close and lock each trapdoor on each elevator before it began to move, which bought him some time.

He stops descending at the fourth floor. This is the floor with all the accounting offices, and since it's six months before tax season, they won't be coming in until ten. He reaches out with one hand and tries to pry open the elevator doors with his fingers, with no luck. Sam feels a vacuum suck at him. The duct that pushes cool air out of the elevator shaft and pumps it into the hallways is right in front of him. A wire mesh screen covers the outside edge of the duct as it curves and enters the fourth floor. Sam pulls his "Bob" pin off his shirt and slides the edge into one of the flathead screws that secures the square mesh screen in place.

It fits. If he pushes hard and twists, the metal name tag is a tolerable screwdriver. It takes him three minutes to remove one screw. It takes him three minutes to remove another screw.

He hears voices on the floor above him. The police have gone to the top and are going down floor by floor. If they think to open an elevator door and look down into the open shaft, they'll spot him.

He twists the nametag into the third screw – and it breaks.

The voices are close.

Sam pushes with his hand on the metal screen. It's made of aluminum and tin, and it folds inward when he pushes hard enough. He leans out from the ladder and presses hard against the mesh, dangling over the four-floor drop — and the bottom breaks and bends in, opening a six-inch crack.

He saves himself from falling and catches his breath. Rats can shrink their bodies down to the size of a quarter to fit through a hole, and this is what Sam must do. He crawls into the duct head first, pushing hard against the screen until it bends in and up even more, giving way against his body.

As he crawls through it rips the shirt off his back, the pants off his legs, and leaves long bloody scratches on his shoulders where the edges of sharp metal sliced through his skin.

He moves forward until he is over another metal grate that looks down into the fourth-floor hallway. He rests, breathing slowly, letting the pain flow through him. When he got his butt kicked in prison boxing matches, he would breathe slowly and try to meditate. His whole body would be screaming in pain, but if he cried out it would betray weakness, so he would lie on his bunk and just breathe, sometimes not moving for days. He can do the same thing here if he must. His legs and arms are bare, his clothes are in tatters, his back is bleeding, but he stays quiet. The police officers move below him, going from office to office.

It's still early. The garbage trucks come at 9 a.m. That might be his best chance.

CHAPTER FORTY-EIGHT

Kath is in Paul's office at the Mission Bay Health Club, watching Paul, Dozer, and Cliff stare at a map of California spread open on his desk.

"Truckee is south of here, I know it," Cliff says.

Kath knows exactly where it is, but she's not saying anything.

She hates Paul more than ever right now, but she hates herself even more for not trusting Sam like he asked, and mad at Sam for not telling her everything. They could be in her blue Porsche Roadster right now, zooming up to Truckee. And that briefcase Sam left in the office…what was it? Something that would incriminate Paul? She should have asked him, instead of going to Plan B so fast and radioing these jerks. But why didn't Sam just tell her? Only Sam knows that answer, and he's trapped in the Flood Building, the stupid fool…

The door opens and Inge steps in with a stack of towels and massage lotion.

"Not now Inge!" Paul yells.

Kath watches Inge's face shift from radiant love to black sadness. Inge then locks eyes with her, and the two women stare at each other, each shocked in her own way.

You actually love him? Kath asks Inge with her bitter look.

He's picking you over me? Inge asks Kath her icy stare.

"Found it!" Cliff says. "Truckee is by Lake Tahoe! The town is right off Highway 80!"

"Kath, you ride with me. You losers follow me and try to keep up," Paul says.

"I have to go somewhere first," Kath says.

"We don't have time, the police are coming," Paul says.

"I have to see Aunt Bella in San Mateo before we go," Kath says and crosses her arms.

"Why are you still dealing with her?!" he screams.

"Half the money you ever fronted me went to her and you know it. We're seeing her. Otherwise, I run away from you the first chance I get and tell the police everything."

Paul shakes his fists in her face and grits his teeth like he wants to punch her...but doesn't. Kath sees Inge out of the corner of her eye, standing in the corner still holding her stack of towels. With one micro-glance she can see that Inge is smiling.

Hal arrives at work. He's the first one there at seven-thirty in the morning, and he turns on all the lights for the entire floor. He hears a phone ringing, and as he gets close to his office, he realizes it's his phone. He runs in and answers it, knocking it off the desk and onto the floor.

"Weinstein," he says, catching his breath.

"Hal, it's me, Alden. Get a squad car and get to the Mission Bay Health Club now. There's been another robbery with Webb, and Barnes is involved," Stone says.

At eight-thirty a.m., Sam uses the top of the copper zipper from his ruined pants to twist the last of the screws off the screen mesh covering the duct opening to the fourth floor. He moves the screen to the side, and drops down feet first through the hole, catching the lip with his hands and hanging for a moment before letting himself drop.

He's naked except for torn underwear, half a torn t-shirt and his shoes and socks. The back of his thighs and his back are scraped and bloody. The floor is quiet. They haven't let anyone upstairs yet.

Sam darts down to the end of the hallway and finds a building benefit from when the building was constructed in the 1950s: a trash chute. He opens the lid and puts his left foot inside. Keeping his foot in place so the chute stays open, he twists his body and falls to the floor with his arms extended. His foot stays inside. He then does a push-up and gets his other foot inside the open lid of the chute as well. He then walks his hands backward in push-up position and eases himself backward through the opening.

It's like crawling inside a slime-covered mail slot. He props his feet against the inside of the chute, then gets his hands inside. The chute door closes, sealing him in darkness, except for the light coming up from the chute opening four floors below. He must push with both arms and legs against the opposite sides of the garbage chute to keep from tumbling down.

The chute also stinks, but no worse than San Quentin did, and the fear of going back doubles his strength. His years of weight-lifting in prison is paying off right now, as he locks his feet and hands into place. If he pushes hard enough, he can move one hand, then one foot, then the other hand, and the other foot, inching down slowly, like a mountain climber descending a chimney. The burn from the lactic acid building up in his muscles makes his legs and arms tremble. He inches his way down, getting closer to the trash bins at the bottom.

At eight-thirty in the morning, Hal Weinstein enters the Mission Bay Health Club and looks at all the fit young people in their track suits and bandana headbands, jumping around to music. Hal can't believe how dumb it all looks.

"Interested in a membership sir?" the petite brunette woman in white behind the counter asks him. "We have aerobics, free weights, and the latest Nautilus machines if you'd like a tour."

Hal opens his jacket and points to the police badge on his belt. "San Francisco Police. I'm here to see Paul Barnes."

"You're a police officer?" she asks, as if she doesn't quite believe him.

Two uniformed officers walk in behind him. "Believe me now?" Hal asks, jerking his thumb over his shoulder at them. "Again, where is Barnes?"

"He just left with his two assistants, Mr. Cliff and Mr. Dozer."

"Where did they go?"

"I don't know. They said they were taking the rest of the week off."

"Was this man with them?" Hal asks her, and shows her a photo of Sam.

"No. But there was a woman with them. Pretty, with curly brown hair. She and Mr. Barnes had a big fight in his office before they left."

"Is she Mr. Barnes's girlfriend?"

"No, that would be Inge."

"Which one is Inge?" Hal asks.

"She's a tall blonde Viking. But she drove away in her own car right after Mr. Barnes did. She drives a grey Datsun 610. Barely fits in it," the woman says.

Hal Weinstein writes it all down in his notepad, wondering if any of it is useful.

Back at the Flood Building, the police finish searching every floor, with no luck. The building tenants are outside, making noise, banging on the doors, demanding to be let inside.

Sergeant Stone brings over balding Mr. Smythe in his blue suit with the red tie and red suspenders. "This is the CFO of Kearne Securities, Mr. Ed Smythe. He says there is nothing of value in the safe," Hank says.

"In fact, it's empty. The only thing we lost this morning is two hours of trading. Will you please let my people go to work?" he asks Stone. "We're losing money."

"Let them in," he tells Hank, who motions to the guard across the lobby that they can open the doors. A stampede of young urban professionals rushes through the glass doors and crowds around the elevators. They stamp their feet and sway from side to side, moaning and complaining about being late, ready to get to work buying and selling.

Still in the trash chute, Sam hears the echo of people walking above him and the roar of an engine below. It's the garbage truck backing up to the loading dock, ready to dump the contents of the debris box into its belly.

Sam hears a creak above him and a shaft of light cuts through the dark chute – and a pile of wet garbage hits Sam on the head. His hands are slipping on the greasy walls…and he falls two floors down, out of the chute and into the metal debris box, right as the metal tusks of the front-loading garbage truck lift it into the sky and flip out its contents. The trash for the week tumbles into the open back of the garbage truck, Sam included.

At nine in the morning, the truck drives up Columbus Avenue and stops at a red light in front of Washington Square Park. The playground is full of moms and kids, enjoying a sunny morning, along with older Chinese men and women doing tai-chi.

Sam crawls out of the top of the garbage truck and climbs down the metal rungs on the side. He reaches the asphalt just as the truck pulls away, then dodges traffic until he gets to the park.

Everyone in the playground freezes as the almost naked man limps past, wearing only torn underwear, a ripped t-shirt, and shoes. The green slime covering his skin can't hide his bloody scrapes and bruises.

He limps to a line of sprinklers running over a section of the grass. He falls on the ground and lets the jets of cold water run over his body, washing away his putrid outer coating. Everyone returns to their tai-chi and their playing.

CHAPTER FORTY-NINE

In the Parole Department at the Hall of Justice, Hal stands behind his desk, Stone paces, and Hiram Valosek won't stop talking.

"The program will work. We notify every motel with Magic Massage within one day's drive of San Francisco to be on the lookout for a man and a woman who ask for a room with Magic Massage near the ice machine, and then pay in cash," Valosek says.

His desk phone rings. Hal answers. "Hello?"

"Hey Hal, it's me, Sam."

Hal gestures for quiet, waving his arms. Everyone turns to him. "Sam, you're in a lot of trouble. Where are you?"

"I can't tell you that. But I do want to tell you a long story about Paul Barnes, so get a pen," Sam says.

CHAPTER FIFTY

The parking lot for Bay Meadows Race Track is empty except for a Lincoln Town Car and Paul's blue Cadillac. Dozer and Cliff sit in the Lincoln, wearing their dark glasses and their 49er football jerseys. Paul paces in front of his car, stopping every twenty steps to look at the retirement home across the street.

"How long is this going to take?' he says.

"Relax, boss. We're about to take a long drive. It'll be nice," Dozer says.

Paul stares at the two huge men. "Do you guys ever move? Or do you sit all day?"

They look at each other and shrug. "We sit, mostly," Dozer says.

"It's what you pay us to do. We sit in the car and wait," Cliff says.

Kath runs across the empty parking lot toward them. She's still wearing her black pants and Apex catering shirt with the "Joanie" pin.

"Get in the back, let's go!" Paul yells.

"I can't! She won't let me in!" She holds up her hand to shield her eyes from the sun.

Paul points at the building. "Go say your goodbyes. We leave in ten minutes or you don't get to keep any of the money so far."

"I don't want the money," Kath says. "Not anymore."

"You're going to need it. The police will be looking for us and we have to disappear." Paul says. "And we have to buy you new clothes. That outfit looks so stupid on you."

Kath blinks and turns away, fighting back the tears. Once again, history repeats itself. Kath will soon be trapped in a moving car with yet another abusive man, worse than any man her mother endured during childhood, and so much worse than Sam ever could be.

"Blow me, are you crying?" Paul asks her. "Say goodbye! Now!"

Kath turns away so he can't see her crying, and runs back across the parking lot to the Meadow Song Retirement Community.

Kath exits the elevator on Bella's floor and pauses to catch her breath. The woman can be mean and demanding, but she's the only family that Kath's got. She knocks on her door.

"It's open, come on in!"

Bella is at her tiny kitchen table playing cards with an older gentleman who looks like a skinny and pale Omar Sharif, and he's dressed in just underwear and a dress shirt.

"What is going on here?"

"Strip poker," Bella says. "And I'm winning."

The old man looks at her and grins. He doesn't mind being a loser.

"Is this your secret admirer?" Kath asks.

"Yevgeni? God no. He doesn't even speak English. Our relationship is strictly physical. My secret admirer is in the kitchen."

Kath steps around the corner into the kitchen. Sam stands by the sink zipping up the pants that Bella just won from Yevgeni.

"You! How did you get here!" she screams.

Sam motions for Kath to be quiet. "The five hundred dollars in my shoe. I took a taxi. You still have your five hundred, don't you? Because we need it."

Kath grabs her temples. "Back up. How do you and Bella even know each other?"

"I followed you here. I wanted to know more about you."

"That makes you a creepy and weird stalker."

"Not a guy falling in love with you?" Sam asks.

"You're a liar. You've lied to me from the beginning."

"He's a nice boy!" Bella shouts from the other room. "He bought me the flowers!"

"*You* bought the flowers? That makes you an even bigger lying creep!"

"I had to win Bella over somehow!"

"Here comes his shirt!" Bella yells, and tosses Yevgeni's shirt into the kitchen. Sam grabs it before it hits the floor, and as he's bending over, Kath sees the horrible long gashes on his shoulders and back. She gasps. "Oh my God, what happened?"

"Getting out of the Flood Building was a little rough. Do I need stitches?" Sam asks, and turns his back to her.

Kath stares at the long deep gashes and covers her mouth to keep from crying out. Sam turns back to her and smiles to hide his pain. Kath's fear turns on a dime to anger. She grits her teeth and punches him in the chest. "I wish I'd never met you!'

"Stop it! We have to get out of here!"

"I'm not going anywhere with you!"

Sam buttons up Yevgeni's long dress shirt. "I have a 1980 red Camaro parked out back. Brand new."

"Really? Where did you get a red Camaro?" That car is on her "good" list.

"It's mine. I'm letting him borrow it!" Bella shouts from the other room.

Kath shakes her head and walks back into the living room.

"You bought a Camaro? You don't even drive. And you're on a fixed income!" Kath shouts at her aunt, trying to ignore the naked old man sitting across from her. Yevgeni grins. He seems to be thrilled that he's exposing himself.

"I won the money at the track, and I can do whatever I want with it."

"You won that much?" Kath asks, sounding jealous. "How?"

"Sam took me. He showed me how to win big."

"You took her to the track?" Kath says, sounding both jealous and sad.

"I have a system," Sam explains.

"And it's better than yours. He wins! Let the man borrow my car!"

Kath wipes away a tear and looks at Sam, softening. "I can't believe you took her to the track without me. I might have liked to have gone too, you know."

Sam takes Kath's hands and looks her in the eye.

"Let me show you the rest of my plan. We still have a chance."

Kath stares at him and nods. He kisses her lightly on the lips. She closes her eyes, letting it linger for five seconds…

He breaks away and grabs the car keys off the TV stand. "Thanks, Bella, you're a lifesaver! And thanks for the threads, Yevgeni!" Sam says, and he pulls Kath towards the door.

"Give us a call once you're settled!" Bella waves.

Once the door closes, Bella lays down her cards. "I have a full house," she says.

A naked grinning Yevgeni stands up, showing Bella his old man erection.

"Me too," he says with a thick accent, and Bella laughs out loud.

Paul looks at his watch, then punches and kicks the air like a toddler having a meltdown. He then freezes…and stares at Cliff in the front passenger seat of the Town Car.

"Why am I freaking out over half a million dollars? Are you wondering that?

"No, sir. It's your money, you can freak out however you want," Cliff says.

"Because Sam tricked me somehow. And I've spent the past two years thinking about it. It's driving me nuts, to the point that I want to cut him open, rip out his guts and read them like tea leaves to figure out how he did it."

"Yes, sir," Cliff says.

"Here's a deal for you. I want to hire you, and I'll pay you two million dollars. You want that job?" Paul asks.

"Yes, sir, that would be a good job."

"Great. To make your two million dollars, you must work eighty hours a week, all year long, making things for me. But there's one catch. I could end up making fifty million dollars, if I'm lucky, because I sell what you make. You still make your two million, guaranteed, while I make fifty million. Still think it's fair?" Paul asks.

"Yes, sir. I do."

"That's because you understand capitalism, Cliff! Sam doesn't! That's why he tried to take advantage of me, because he doesn't understand our relationship!"

Sam drives the Camaro out of the underground parking and makes a right towards the Bayshore Freeway. Kath leans back in the passenger seat and rolls down the window. A hundred yards away she sees Paul standing by the two cars in the parking lot – and he sees her too.

"Honk," Kath says. Sam leans on the horn as Kath waves at Paul.

"Son of a bitch," Paul mutters as he sees the Camaro head for the freeway.

He jumps inside his car, revs the engine and tears after them, but the Camaro gets on the freeway onramp before Paul even gets out of the parking lot.

CHAPTER FIFTY-ONE

Fifty members of the Mission Bay Health Club, all dressed in colorful spandex, mill outside the entrance. They want to get back in and finish their workouts, but they can't because the police are busy raiding the place.

Inside, police officers stack boxes of stolen VCRs, computers, TV sets, heart monitors and medical supplies. Two detectives question the six employees lined up against the counter.

Detective Stone and Hal Weinstein stand side-by-side watching it all.

"At least your boy was right about Barnes," Stone says to Hal.

"I wish he wasn't right. He was my last "bleeding heart" project before retirement."

Hiram Valosek sits in a metal folding chair next to them. He keeps trying to get up, but Stone keeps patting him on the shoulder to hold him down. "Stay still, Hiram," Stone says.

A patrol officer walks up. "Detective Stone? We found the two men in the Lincoln Town Car you were looking for. They're parked outside in front."

Stone and Weinstein walk out the glass doors and Hiram Valosek sneaks into step behind them. The Lincoln is parked in the red zone, and two huge men sit in the front seat. One looks like he's from Fiji or Samoa, while the other looks like a fullback from Nebraska. Both are wearing dark glasses and 49er football jerseys. Four patrol officers surround the car.

Stone motions for the Pacific Islander in the passenger seat to roll down his window. After the glass drops, Stone places both hands on the passenger door.

"Take off your glasses, boys, before I knock them off your faces."

Dozer and Cliff obey.

You boys work for Paul Barnes?" Stone asks.

They both shrug but say nothing.

"Put your hands on the dash and look at me," Stone says.

Cliff obeys, but the pale fullback with the rolls of fat on the back of his neck freezes. He grips the wheel so hard that his knuckles turn white.

"Yo, Cornhusker. Did you hear what I said?" Stone asks him.

The big Islander shakes his head "You can't talk to him that way."

"I'll talk to you however I like. I'm the law."

"No, you can't talk to him that way because it freaks him out."

The big white guy moans, his eyes roll back, and he passes out. His face hits the horn on the steering wheel, sending out a long honk.

"Narcolepsy," the guy in the passenger seat says. He reaches over and pushes his partner's drooling face off the horn, ending the noise.

Stone stands up and turns to Hal. "We're getting nowhere."

Hiram steps between them. "I'm telling you, the data doesn't lie. We should be focusing our attention on the motels. We need to make two hundred phone calls, now."

Stone and Hal look at each other and shrug. "What do we have to lose?" Hal asks.

CHAPTER FIFTY-TWO

Sam downshifts as he descends from Donner Pass towards Truckee, California. They're in the Sierra Nevada Mountains in the summertime, and the sky is a brilliant blue with fluffy white clouds. Deep green pine trees run in a thick carpet down the grey stone mountains. There's still a smattering of snow on some of their peaks.

Sam arches his back, trying to get comfortable. His wounds make him wince.

Kath lowers her passenger window and looks out at the passing alpine beauty. There are only a few cars on the road in mid-week in the summer. She spots a mountain cabin near Donner Lake. Even from half a mile away, she can see smoke coming out of the chimney and kids playing on a swing set on a green lawn. Kath feels like she's twelve again, and she gazes at the house with envy, wishing it was her childhood.

She faces Sam. "I was the one who told Paul about Truckee. I overhead a phone message when Rose called you at the Taj Mahal."

Sam shrugs. "It's my own fault. I should have told you everything. But I didn't know if any of it was going to happen."

"Tell me now."

They pass a sign: *Truckee, CA, population 2,350.* "We're almost there anyway," he says.

Sam takes the exit, but doesn't go into town; instead, he makes a left and heads up a rural road. They climb, passing through pine trees. They keep going higher and higher, until the trees thin out. It's mostly grey rock up here, but the views are tremendous, with crystal clear vistas down to Donner Lake, the Truckee River and Lake Tahoe in the distance.

They reach a flat part of the mountain that's hidden by a ring of trees. It's an alpine meadow with a tiny stream running through the tall green grass. Sam stops the car next to a "For Sale" sign. A classic Ford pickup is already parked alongside.

A woman steps out of the truck. She's dressed in a flannel shirt and jeans, and she has thick red hair that cascades down her back. She smiles and waves at them with a genuine warmth that makes her even more beautiful. Kath dislikes her immediately.

"That's her," Sam says, and gets out.

Kath exhales…and gets out too.

"Hello, Sam," the woman says.

"Hello, Rose," he says, with a smile. "This is my girlfriend, Kath."

"Sam told me a lot about you," Rose says. The women trade weak smiles.

'How's Carl doing?" Sam asks.

"He's the best pitcher in Little League. He wants to be an Army Ranger," Rose says.

"Would he remember me if I said 'hi?'" Sam asks.

"Yes. He doesn't want to use my name, Armanini. He wants to use yours. He says Webb is a better last name for a guy," Rose says. "You left a good impression on him."

Rose and Sam smile and shake their heads, remembering and regretting at the same time.

Rose pulls out a rolled piece of paper and tries to hand it to Kath, but Kath steps back and puts up her hands, not wanting anything from her. Rose hands it to Sam instead.

"Goodbye, Sam," she says, then turns to Kath. "I hope you get his good years."

Kath gives her an awkward smirk. Rose gets into her truck and drives away.

"Why don't you go with her? That's why you came, isn't it?" Kath asks.

Sam shakes his head. "That's not how it works."

Kath crosses her arms. The wind blows, sending strands of hair across her face. It's hard to focus on Sam with this gorgeous green meadow behind him. "Then explain it," Kath says.

"Paul was right. When I broke into that safe two years ago, there was a half-million dollars inside. More in fact. Almost seven hundred thousand. But I managed to get it to Rose just before the police arrived."

"And you went to prison for two years?"

"She ran, because she had to. I knew it was an inside job, and that Paul would have to pay the import company back, which is why he's had a hard-on to punish me for everything I did," Sam says. "But I knew she'd come back."

"That's so touching," Kath says, shaking her head. "You are such a liar."

"It was over between us the minute I got caught, Kath. That was the agreement. And that half the money in the safe would be mine someday." Sam holds out the piece of paper.

She opens it. It's a land deed with her name on it. "Land? What land?" she asks.

"You're standing on it," Sam says.

Kath looks around at the mountain, the stream, the meadow and the trees. "You bought me *land?*" she asks.

"You said you wanted to live in the country, in a house like the ones you would pass on your mom's road trips," said Sam. "That's what I told Rose to do with my three hundred and fifty thousand. Buy you this."

Kath stands frozen, until Sam gestures with his arms. "Look, it's perfect for us. It's the right choice with the money too. Harder to trace this way."

Kath stares at the meadow. It's so perfect it looks like a movie of a mountain meadow, with tall green grass and splashes of red and yellow flowers. "I don't know how to live here. It was just a dream from when I was a kid."

"Then sell it. It's yours; you can do whatever you want with it. I promised I would make something come true for you, and I did. See Kath? I never lied to you."

"Yes, you did. I asked you if you had money hidden somewhere and you said no."

"I had *land* hidden somewhere. Technically, that's not a lie. Politicians pass that off as the truth all the time."

Kath feels a lifetime of distrust lift from her shoulders. She breaks down, sobbing so hard her nose runs.

Sam touches her shoulders. "See how nice it is? We could build a cabin right in the bend of the creek," he says, pointing.

That makes Kath sob even louder.

"I can see it myself. How quaint," Paul says.

Kath and Sam turn. Paul points a very large gun at them. His Cadillac with the Dead Head sticker is parked a hundred yards down the hill.

"Thank you for driving a red Camaro. You were easy to find on the freeway. But you shouldn't have done that with my money. I hate the mountains."

"It was never your money! It belonged to some Hong Kong gangsters! And they got all their money back!" Sam yells.

Paul shoots his gun into the dirt. Sam and Kath jump back and put their hands up.

"Sorry, Sam, this is one time when I'm going to win for a change."

"What? You *always* win. I went to prison! You're rich!"

Paul shoots the gun in the dirt again, then aims it at Sam's chest. "Wrong. I've never had it like you. You're tall, you're handsome, and you're funny, without even trying. People like you. Me, not so much.

You think I could get a girl like Rose if I didn't have money? Or Kath? But you can, because life is easy for you."

Sam keeps his hands up. "Lots of women like you, Paul. You have a lot of fine qualities."

"Don't interrupt me." Paul shoots the ground again. Sam jumps back. Paul grabs Kath by the wrist and yanks her to his side. "This time I'm the one who gets the girl."

Paul raises his gun to shoot Sam in the chest – but a hand reaches from behind and pinches his shoulder so hard he drops the gun. The hand doesn't let go. Kath breaks free from Paul and turns –

It's Inge, and she's mad. Her little grey Datsun is parked behind Paul's Cadillac. Inge doesn't release Paul's shoulder from her Vulcan death grip. He drops to his knees, moaning.

"Inge, honey, it's just business," Paul says.

Inge kicks him to the ground and leaps on him, raising a cloud of dust. Kath and Sam step back and give her room, like you'd give room to a snarling badger.

Paul screams. Inge grabs his shoulders and stretches him back. She grabs the tendons of his forearm and pinches hard.

"Inge, not the Rolfing! Please! No!"

Inge flops him over, unbuckles his belt and yanks it through the loops. Paul weeps like a prison bitch who's ready to bite a pillow. Inge slaps his face, then uses the belt to tie his wrists and knees together like a rodeo calf. She rips his shirt and tears off a big strip of fabric and ties it in across his mouth to deaden his whimpering.

While she's knotting the gag in place, Paul stares at Sam and then at Kath, begging them with his eyes for help. They don't move.

Inge stands up. Her white jeans and white shirt are covered in brown dust. She brushes herself off, then reaches down and pulls Paul by the belt and heaves him over her shoulder, like he's a bale of hay to load on a truck. She turns and walks back down the hill to his car.

"I think they could be very happy together, if he gives it a chance," Sam says.

"And the police don't stop them," Kath adds.

Inge tosses Paul in the back of the Cadillac, gets in the driver's seat and heads back down the hill, leaving her Datsun behind.

"I hate Datsuns. I don't want that piece of junk on my land," Kath says.

"Now you're talking," Sam says, and he reaches for her. She walks into his arms and they kiss long and hard, like they used to kiss in the beginning.

Kath breaks away and looks at him. "How much money do you have on you?"

"I have the five hundred I took out of my shoe, minus fifty I used for the taxi."

"I still have my five hundred. How's your back?"

"I'll survive," Sam shrugs.

"Let's go somewhere and celebrate."

CHAPTER FIFTY-THREE

Sam and Kath park the Camaro on the road outside the Deep Water Motor Motel in rustic Incline Village, Nevada, a small town at the top of Lake Tahoe, right on the California Nevada border.

The Deep Water Motor Motel is built to look like a Swiss chalet with two rows of rooms running off each side of the main building, like a "V." The rooms are small, but each has a colorful carved wooden arch above each door, adding to the Swiss kitsch. Sam and Kath hug each other as they tumble into the motel lobby. The motel owner steps out from inside his Swiss chalet office. He's a young man, tall and with dark hair. He looks more Italian than Swiss.

"We'd like a room with a Magic Massage please," Sam says.

"We saw the sign out front," Kath says. "And color TV."

The manager looks them up and down, and then hands them a register and a pencil. "Fill out this form. It'll be forty-eight dollars a night, including tax. How many nights are you staying?" he asks.

"Just one. Can we get a room close to the ice machine?"

"That'll be room three at the end," the manager says. "Do you have a car?"

"We parked on the street," Sam says, dodging the question. He hands the man three twenty-dollar bills. "Keep the change."

He takes Sam's money and hands Sam his key "Enjoy," he says.

Kath and Sam smile and walk out arm in arm.

Once they are out of sight, the owner picks up the phone.

Five minutes later, Sam and Kath are in Room 3 with all their clothes off. Kath wraps her arms around him, forgetting the wounds on his back. He winces, and she pulls away. "Sorry my love," she says, and pulls him down onto the bed.

She rolls under him and they kiss, gently at first, and then with more passion.

Sam breaks away and reaches for a shoe at the foot of the bed. He aims and smashes the Magic Massage box. He so good at it by now, he can reach in and rip apart the wires and twist them back together, all with one hand while still kissing Kath.

The bed roars to life and Sam and Kath vibrate across the mattress. He gets between her legs and slides into her and she pulls him deeper into her. At last she can be with the man she loves without any worry or fear. Neither of them has any reason to lie anymore, and it makes her feel happy and free for the first time in her life.

CHAPTER FIFTY-FOUR

Hal Weinstein answers his phone on the first ring. He grabs a pencil and starts scribbling while Hiram and Detective Alden Stone rise out of their chairs and hover so close to him that Hal must push them both away so he can write.

Hal hangs up and looks at Hiram. "You were right. A couple fitting their description just checked into a motel in Incline Village, Nevada. They asked for Magic Massage and a room near the ice machine, and they paid in cash."

"I know that motel! We can be there in six hours!" Hiram says.

Stone calls for help from the Highway Patrol and within fifteen minutes he, Weinstein and Hiram Valosek crowd into the back of a Highway Patrol cruiser and zoom across the Bay Bridge towards Donner Pass and Truckee.

Six hours later, Sam wakes up. It's nine p.m. and dark outside. Kath is asleep, a look of bliss on her face. Sam eases out from under her. The Magic Massage box is ruined, and the white sheets have streaks of red on them from the cuts on his back, but he smiles with happiness. Sam is content, for the first time in years. He pulls on his pants and shirt and eases out the door with the ice bucket.

Sam stands behind a wooden lattice at the end of a long row of rooms and loads up his ice bucket with scoops of ice from the ice machine. Tomorrow they'll drive into town and get a First Aid kit so that Kath can bandage him up. He hears a car engine and peeks out from the corner of the building and sees a line of police cars hidden in the trees by the highway.

Then he spots Hal Weinstein and Detective Stone walking into the main office.

Sam darts back inside Room 3 and shakes Kath awake.

"What's wrong, my love?"

"I just saw my parole officer with a cop. They went in the main office."

Kath leaps out of bed and pulls on her clothes. She's still only got her Apex uniform from the heist, so it doesn't take her long to dress. "How did they find us?" Kath asks, running her hands through her hair.

"Does it matter? We've got to split up. You take the Camaro. Inge's Datsun is still on that mountain. I'll get to that somehow."

"I don't want that."

"You're not safe with me. I'm the one they're looking for."

"I said I don't want that."

"Let's get out of here first," Sam whispers. He lifts the edge of the curtain and sees two cop cars drive past on the road out front. "Shit."

"Can we go out the back window?" Kath asks.

"No. They're watching this room," Sam says.

He paces like a caged animal, but he's thinking. He stops and focuses on the closet, then throws open the flimsy folding doors.

"Sam, we can't hide in there!"

Sam grabs a chair, leans against it and kicks the inside of the closet with a hard mule kick with the heel of his boot. His foot goes through. He kicks again, making the hole larger. Three more kicks and the wall cracks. He backs up, lowers his shoulder and runs at the wall, and busts through into the next room. It's empty. Kath steps through the hole, then reaches back through the hole and closes the closet door behind her. She helps a dazed Sam to his feet.

Outside, three Nevada State Trooper patrol cars line up outside Room 3. The troopers exit the vehicles with their rifles and take position behind their open car doors.

In the next room, Sam yanks open the flimsy closet doors, leans against a chair and mules kicks the second wall. He puts a hole through the thin drywall and plywood, then makes it bigger. He backs up, lowers his shoulder and runs at it again, busting through. Sam lands in a pile of drywall dust on the purple shag rug. An elderly man and woman scream and run from the room, leaving their bags behind.

Detective Stone watches the older man and woman run out of their room and down towards the road. "What are they doing? We called them and told them to wait!" he yells.

Inside, Sam grabs his knees and gasps for air as Kath reaches back through the hole and again closes the closet door behind her. Sam gets air back in his lungs and staggers to his feet.

"Two more, honey. You can do it," Kath whisper to him as she slides him a chair to lean against. She opens the closet door behind him. Sam hauls back and mule kicks the thin closet wall and smashes his foot through once, then smashes through again. Kath and Sam can hear yelling on the other side.

Kath pulls the chair away and steadies Sam before he falls over like a drunken redwood tree. She turns him and aims him where he should run. "Go, big boy! Bust on through!"

Sam lowers his shoulder and runs low and hard – and smashes through in a shower of splinters. This time he lands in a cloud of drywall dust on an orange shag carpet. A younger couple stops packing their bags and runs screaming from the room.

Outside, Stone sees them exiting and motions for two cops to grab them. "These people are ruining everything!" he says.

Hiram Valosek rushes forward, waving his arms. "Move in, men! Attack!"

Hal throws Hiram against the car. "No! Stop!"

It's too late. Two cops run up with a battering ram and smash open the door to Room 3. Another four cops rush inside with pistols drawn. They look around and find nothing.

Kath opens another closet door, puts a chair in place and helps Sam to his feet. "You can do this, honey! You're doing great!"

Sam grins and flashes her a "thumbs up." He kicks hard, but the heel doesn't go through. He kicks again and again, and finally there's a crack.

Back in Room 3, the police surround the sliding closet door and slide it open, and they see the hole. One cop yells. "They're moving through the walls!"

A line of officers runs through the hole, then kneel and aim at the next closet door. Another cop gingerly slides the closet door open and reveals the next hole.

"Let's move, move, move!" one cop screams, and the officers run through.

In the last room, Sam runs into the closet hard enough to make a small hole – but bounces back. Kath darts inside the closet and looks through the hole. It leads to the outside.

"I can see the outside through the hole, we're almost there!" she yells.

Sam nods. He backs up and runs at the wall hard...

...and his upper body busts through to the outside. He crawls the rest of the way out of the hole and lays on a soft bed of pine needles until Kath crawls through hole and lands on him.

"Leave me. Go."

"Come on; it's right there." She digs through his pocket and finds his keys and pulls him to his feet.

It's pitch black. They stumble through the trees behind the motel and loop back around to the road and the parked Camaro. Kath unlocks the car, opens the back door and pushes Sam inside. Kath closes the back door with a quiet click, then dashes around and gets in the driver's side. She's glad it's dark.

Through the windshield, she can see a line of cars and people in the street, gawkers who have come to see the biggest news in Incline Village in years. Kath puts the car into reverse and lets it drift backward down the hill. When she's one hundred yards away, she starts the engine, does a reverse U-turn and drives away. She leaves the headlights off.

Back at the motel, the line of police burst through the hole into the last room, and then find the hole to the outside. They exit through the door and point at the road.

"They went north!" the loud cop screams.

Hal Weinstein and Alden Stone run to the street, with Hiram running close behind. They push through the crowd of onlookers and see the road rising and twisting into the distance. They all stop and listen. They hear the distant roar of a Camaro but see no lights.

"Where does this road go?" Stone asks the first cop who runs up.

"Highway 431 is the Mt. Rose Scenic Highway. It takes you to Reno," the cop answers.

CHAPTER FIFTY-FIVE

The Mt. Rose Scenic Highway is one of the steepest roads in the United States. The road rises from Incline Village to the Mt. Rose meadow, which is where the Ponderosa Ranch from the TV show *Bonanza!* was supposed to be. It then sneaks through a pass just below the 8,900-foot-high summit of Mt. Rose, and descends the other side of the mountain in steep hairpin turns to the desert floor, all in less than twenty-five miles.

Kath slides the muscle car into every turn, downshifts, and then accelerates into the next turn. Many times, her back tires slide into the gravel by the side of the road and they almost go over, but she knows how to accelerate out of the skid, and then adds even more gas.

Sam gets tossed like a cracked egg in the back seat, rolling from one side to the other.

"Sit up and put a seatbelt on! Right-hand side! You're throwing off my balance!" Kath yells at him.

Sam sits up and buckles in then rolls down the window a crack and sucks at the air.

"Inge's car is the other way," Sam mutters.

"I went where the cops weren't. We'll ditch the car at a casino. We have to get a ride on a truck going somewhere, maybe back up the mountain to Inge's Datsun."

"My shoulder's broken. My back is bleeding again. I'm hurt bad."

Kath downshifts again and throws the car into another sliding curve that bangs Sam against the side door. He grunts in pain. Kath looks over her shoulder at him and they lock eyes. He's in pain, and she feels it as bad as he does. "I'm sorry, baby," she says.

"Don't be sorry. Just keep hauling ass. You're a better driver than me."

Still, Kath slows the car. "Do you think they'll catch us?"

Sam doesn't answer. He looks out the window instead.

"Pull over at the next vista stop," Sam says.

The Mt. Rose Scenic Highway has vista stops every ten miles. Four minutes later, they reach the next vista spot. Kath slides the muscle car into the first parking spot, right next to the curved rock wall that runs along the perimeter of the parking lot. They limp out of the car. They are still up high enough that they can look down the steep mountain to Washoe Lake far below and see South Reno in the distance. The moon is reflected in the lake and the lights of the city sparkle in the distance.

"Pretty."

"Yeah."

They look up at the mountain. They don't see any lights from any cars chasing them yet, but they both know they're coming.

"Pop the trunk, babe," Sam asks.

Kath opens the trunk and Sam rifles through the back. "Bella only drove this once. We brought a picnic," Sam says.

"You had a picnic? I never had a picnic with Bella."

Sam takes out a blanket and a small coffee thermos. "You have the deed?" Sam asks.

Kath hands him the crumpled roll of papers from her back pocket. Sam opens the thermos, stuffs the papers inside, and then wraps the thermos in the blanket.

"Look at the road markers. Think you can remember this place?" Sam asks.

Kath looks around. The moonlight bounces off the thirteen-mile marker on Highway 431. She nods at him. They walk around to the other side of the rock wall and creep down on the steep side of the mountain. Sam feels for a loose rock in the wall. Kath does too.

"Found one," Kath says, and tugs.

Sam puts the rolled-up blanket between his knees and helps her pull. The small boulder comes out and falls to the ground in front of them. Sam and Kath dig the hole deeper with their hands, digging into the hole in the rock wall until their fingers bleed.

"See if it fits," Sam says, and hands her the blanket.

Kath slides the blanket into the hole, and it disappears inside. Sam picks the rock off the ground and puts it back into the hole, locking the thermos and blanket into place.

"Think you can remember this rock?" Sam asks.

"I'll never forget it," she answers.

They grip the wall and climb back up to the parking level. Far above them, they see the lights from a line of cars descending the mountain.

"What do we do now?" Kath asks.

"Let's use the money we have left to do something special."

"Like what?"

"We're twelve miles from Reno. Let's get married."

CHAPTER FIFTY-SIX

Reno calls itself "The Biggest Little City in the World," which is the perfect name for it. It has half as much excitement as Las Vegas but is twice as friendly. Highway trucks filled with California produce flow through Reno and across the country. Vital rail lines cross here. But Reno fights to keep its small-town feel. Gamblers like Bella often prefer Reno to Vegas, because Reno makes the old ladies feel welcome. There's also snow in the winter, so Christmas is nice in Reno.

It's got plenty of wedding chapels too, like Arch of Reno Chapel, Chapel of the Bells, and The Silver Bells Chapel. But first, Sam and Kath visit The Gem Gallery on Virginia Street. It's a small jewelry store with thick bars on the windows and doors. They ring the bell.

The owner, Frank Jefferson, eyes Sam and Kath carefully on his closed-circuit monitor. He's careful about who he lets in. He notices that the man is limping and wincing in pain, and that the woman is wearing a torn waitress shirt, but Frank has seen brides and grooms in much worse shape. They also got out of a handsome new Camaro, so they must have money. And how dangerous can they be at eight in the morning? He hits the buzzer that unlocks the gate and lets them in.

Sam and Kath stare at the rings in the glass case for just a few seconds.

"Those two look real nice," Kath says, pointing at two rings on the first shelf.

Frank opens the case and pulls out the two rings; one for a man, another for a woman. "Each band has three interlocking loops of gold. Very nice. They're one hundred fifty each," he says, then watches Sam and Kath very closely as they each try on their rings.

Sam and Kath don't see him staring because they're both too overwhelmed with giggling joy to focus on anything else but each other. Sam finally looks up.

"We'll take them," Sam says.

Sam and Kath each pull out their money and stack fifty-dollar bills until they reach three hundred dollars. They push the pile towards him and pocket the rest.

"Know a good place to get married?" Sam asks.

"The Chapel of the Bells is good. Go to the end of this block, make a right, and then go two more blocks. You can't miss it," Frank says.

Sam and Kath pick up their rings, but Frank stops them. "You should take his ring, and he should take yours," he says to Kath. "Remember, you're putting rings on each other's fingers."

"Oh, that's right!" Kath says, and she and Sam laugh and pocket each other's rings.

"Thanks!" Sam says, and he and Kath limp out.

Frank notices the spots of blood coming through the back of the man's shirt. He dashes to the back office and finds the front page of the Reno Gazette-Journal. The headline reads –

Massive Manhunt Underway. Underneath the headline is a photo of Sam and Kath.

CHAPTER FIFTY-SEVEN

The Chapel of the Bells is a white brick single-family home with a church spire, blue trim awnings, stained glass windows, and a neon sign that is twice as high as the house. In winter, this chapel is covered in snow, and if you squint real hard, it looks like it might fit in New England.

Sam and Kath stand by the front desk in the tiny entranceway. Todd, the minister, stands behind the cash register as his wife Becky comes around the counter to show Sam and Kath the big wedding book with photos.

"Is it too early to get married?" Sam asks.

"It's never too early. The chapel is open 24/7," Todd says.

"Would you like the Royal Rose or the Starlight Romance Wedding?" Becky asks.

"What's the difference?" Sam asks.

"Royal Rose comes with bouquets of roses and wedding photographs in our Chapel of the Bells. Starlight romance comes with an organ processional and a special wooden plaque carved with your names and the poem, *Ode to Love*. I wrote it," Becky says.

"It's a real tear-jerker," Todd says. "Gets me every time."

"We'll take both," Sam says.

"That will be five hundred and ninety-eight dollars," Todd the minister says.

Sam and Kath hand over the rest of their money – six hundred dollars – and they each get a dollar back. Sam and Kath each look at their dollar and laugh. "We each have a dollar to our name," Kath says.

"But you are rich in love. God bless you both. Let's get started," Todd says.

The chapel is a long room decorated with white chandeliers and long white curtains framing the stained-glass windows. Todd stands at the end of the chapel on a small wooden riser that acts as the altar. Sam stands next to him in a borrowed jacket and tie, waiting for his bride to appear. He's also wearing a sling that Becky made for him out of a ripped-up pillow case. Now he can rest his right hand, so its weight doesn't pull down on his broken shoulder.

Becky plays *Here Comes the Bride*, nice and slow on the stand-up Hammond organ at the front of the chapel. On cue, Kath turns the corner, dressed in a borrowed white wedding gown with huge puffy shoulders and lots of taffeta spreading out from under her dress. She walks with slow deliberation down the aisle, carrying her bouquet of red roses. She looks beautiful.

Sam grins. Todd slaps Sam on the shoulder, and Sam's smile turns to a wince of pain.

"Sorry, brother," Todd says.

Outside, a line of Reno police cars and Nevada Highway Patrol cars zoom up to the entrance and surround the chapel. Stone and Weinstein jump out of the lead car.

Kath reaches the altar, and Sam puts out his good left hand and helps her as she steps up onto the altar.

"We are gathered here today to join these two people in holy matrimony," Todd says.

The doors burst open and a dozen police rush in with assault rifles drawn. They rush down either side of the chapel and aim at the altar. Stone and Hal and Hiram Valosek rush in last.

"I'll pay the taxes!" Todd yells.

"You're under arrest! Everyone on the floor, now!" Stone yells.

Becky stands up from her organ and points at Stone. "How dare you! You are in a house of God and these two people have come here to be joined as man and wife in his holy eyes!"

Sam and Kath face each other and smile. The two lines of police lower their rifles.

"I say we shoot them!" Hiram screams from the back, and all rifles go back up again.

"Shut up Hiram! Or I will shoot you myself!" Stone screams, aiming his own gun at Hiram. The Magic Massage sales director retreats to the corner with his hands up.

Sam looks back at the crowd of law enforcement officers and spots Hal in back next to Detective Stone. "Can we finish this? Please, Hal? You said you wanted to see me settle down. This is me trying to repent."

Hal sighs, and looks at Stone. "What do you say?"

"What the hell. We've caught them," Stone says. "It can't hurt."

Becky rips into a Bach organ solo. A terrified Todd drops his Bible as the music rips through the chapel.

"Hurry it up!" Stone says.

Todd picks his Bible up off the ground, opens it and starts reading. "In the beginning, God created the heavens and the earth…"

"We better do the shorter version, Pastor," Sam whispers.

Todd leafs through his Bible. Drops of sweat land on the open pages, making it hard for him to turn them. He finds his spot again. "Who gives this woman?" he shouts at the crowd of officers. The two lines of cops all look at each other.

"Hey! Someone give us a hand here!" Kath yells at the room.

"All right! I will! I give this woman!" Stone yells from the back of the chapel.

Todd smiles as his confidence returns. "See, everybody? This can be easy if we all work together," he says to the room. He turns to Kath. "Now, do you –

"Katerina Georgette Battaglia,"

Todd picks it back up. "Katerina Georgette Battaglia, take this man to be your lawfully wedded husband, for better or worse, for richer or poorer, in sickness and health, until death do you part?"

"I most certainly do," Kath says, staring with adoring eyes at Sam.

"And do you –

"Samuel Carlos Webb," Sam says.

Todd keeps going. "Samuel Carlos Webb, take this woman to be your lawfully wedded wife, for better or worse, for richer or poorer, in sickness and in health, until death do you part?"

"Till the end of time. I do."

"If anyone objects to these two people being joined in holy matrimony, speak now or forever hold your peace," Todd says to the assembled crowd of officers with weapons drawn.

Hiram steps forward, but Stone pushes him back into his corner.

"I now pronounce you husband and wife," Todd says. He slams his Bible shut and leaves the altar fast, just as Becky blasts out Mendelssohn's Wedding March. Sam and Kath both turn and step off the altar into police custody.

Sam and Kath march out into the parking lot, led by five police officers with rifles in front and followed by five officers with rifles in back. Hal and Stone take up the rear. Becky runs up and forces a piece of paper into Hal's hand.

"Quick! Sign this, we need a witness!" she says, and Hal signs it fast and hands it back.

Becky dashes out to the front counter, finds her State of Nevada stamp, slams it on the document and then dashes out the front door and into the parking lot. She ignores the rifles and sticks her arm through the circle of officers surrounding the newlyweds and hands Kath the papers. Kath blows her a kiss.

A crowd of onlookers gathers just outside the chapel on the street, past the police line. They cheer when they see Sam and Kath.

Becky dashes over to the cheering crowd and hands people bags of rice, which they toss in big handfuls, until rice is raining down everywhere.

"Toss the bouquet!" someone yells, and Kath heaves it over her shoulder and it lands in Hiram's hands. He's surprised that he caught it, and then embarrassed. Hal nudges him as his face turns red.

Kath and Sam wave to the crowd, then hold hands so Stone can handcuff their wrists together. He then guides their heads so they don't bump their skulls as they get into the backseat of the squad car. Becky runs up and waves at them through the window.

"Enjoy your honeymoon!" Beck yells as the wedding party speeds away, with lights flashing. Someone has spray painted *Just Married* on the very last car.

In the backseat of the police cruiser, Sam and Kath cuddle up next to each other. Stone sits in the front passenger seat but twists himself around to face them.

"You are under arrest. You have the right to remain silent. Anything you say, can and will be used against you in a court of law. You have the right to an attorney. If you cannot afford one, you will be appointed one by the court. Do you understand these rights guaranteed to you by the Constitution?"

Sam and Kath look at each and then at him. "We do," they both say, then reach into their pockets and pull out their rings – and slide them on each other's fingers.

They gaze with deep love into each other's eyes, all lying gone. They smile and kiss, finally free.

CHAPTER FIFTY-EIGHT

San Quentin has not changed much in the months since Sam was released. It's still yellow and brown outside and lime green and white inside, with rusting iron bars and the smell of sewage mixed with damp salt water.

Sam, dressed again in blue denim, marches along with all the other prisoners in San Quentin. His arm and shoulder are in a large white cast. Corrections officer Mark Garrett, the skinny, tall African American guard with the pot belly shaped like a football, waits in front of Sam's cell. Sam turns and walks into his cell along with his new cellmate, Juan Pedro. The bars clang shut and lock into place.

"Welcome home, Webb. I knew you'd come back," Garrett whispers through the bars.

Sam sits down on his bunk and hangs his head…and then smiles.

Five counties away, Kath Battaglia Webb is dressed in an orange jumpsuit and marches in another line of prisoners, all of them women. She turns left and walks into her cell and the door closes shut. A female guard looks through the window at her.

"I'm watching you, convict," the guard says.

Kath sits down on her bunk. On a small shelf is a wooden plaque from the Chapel of the Bells, carved with the poem *Ode to Love.* Kath smiles.

EPILOGUE

It's five years later. Kath steers the Camaro into the Vista Point at the thirteen-mile marker on the Mt. Rose Scenic Highway. Aunt Bella still owns the muscle car. In fact, she's in the front passenger seat. Kath climbs out of the car into the sunshine. Blue Lake Washoe is far below.

"I'll be just a minute, Bella," Kath says.

"Hurry up, I want to get to the CalNeva casino before the buffet ends, and I want some time at the blackjack tables," Bella says. She's slower and older, but still tough.

"We've got things to do first, Auntie," Kath says.

"The hotel swimming pool is right on the California Nevada border. The line goes right through the middle. I want to see that," Bella says.

"I promise you'll see it," Kath says.

Kath closes the car door, goes to the rock wall and finds the path that leads down behind it, next to the steep drop off. She touches the wall, feeling the rocks and searching...

She finds a loose rock. She brushes the dirt away, then yanks the boulder out of the wall, sending it tumbling down the steep hillside, barely missing the hairpin turn below. She reaches into the hole and pulls out the old blanket. She unwraps it and finds the thermos still inside. She opens the thermos and the land deed is still inside. Kath pulls it out very slowly. It's wrinkled, but it's dry and clean.

Half an hour later, Kath drives the Camaro to the top of the mountain above Truckee and finds her alpine meadow. The "For Sale" sign is gone, and so is Inge's Datsun 610.

But Sam is in the middle of the meadow, waiting.

Kath gets out of the car and runs to him. They embrace in a long kiss. Kath breaks away and they both gasp for air and then laugh.

"Bella won five hundred thousand dollars at the track," Kath says. "She's giving it all to us to build the house. She just wants to live with us."

"I'll drive her to the casino every day. How about if the house faces this way?" Sam asks, pointing down towards Lake Tahoe in the distance.

"Great. Can the master bedroom have a Magic Massage?"

THE END

Here I lay me down to sleep
To wait the coming morrow,
Perhaps success, perhaps defeat,
And everlasting sorrow.
Let come what will, I'll try it on,
My condition can't be worse;
And if there's money in that box
'Tis munny in my purse.
— Black Bart

Special Thanks to:
Douglas Gorney, Joe Weiss, Robin Berlin, Pat McCall,
Deni Siedschlag, and Toni Gallagher

Ian Bull is the pen name of Donald Ian Bull. He has also written *Facing Reality (A Love Story),* and is the author of *The Quintana Adventures*, a series of thriller novels which includes *The Picture Kills,* and *Six Passengers, Five Parachutes.* The third book in the trilogy, *The Danger Game,,* will be out soon.

You can also find his nonfiction and downloads at:

Ianbullauthor.com

Please write a review of this book! If I can get 100 reviews, I can promote my writing and reach more readers.

Email me and I'll show you how:

Ianbullauthor@gmail.com

Made in the USA
Middletown, DE
29 January 2021